BEENIE AT FOURTEEN

MARGARET BUCKHANON

Running Wild

RIZE

The teenage narrator of this fresh, engaging story navigates the world with a fierce voice and uncompromising vision. In *Beenie at Fourteen*, Buckhanon gives us a colorful, complicated family experiencing trouble and love in equal measure. These memorable characters lingered long after reading.

~ Doris W. Cheng, Associate Fiction Editor, *Bellevue Literary Review,* and author of *Earthling*

Margaret Buckhanon has a rich and vibrant cross-genre writing style. Her essays and short stories are eagerly received and especially lauded by the readers of my publications when they appear there.

~ Nadia Giordana, Publisher, Mississippi Crow and WINK: Writers IN the Know magazines

Beenie's unabashed clarity guides her through an often unstable and intolerant world as she implores those around her to do better. Redemptive and ultimately heroic, *Beenie At Fourteen* announces the arrival of this indelible protagonist in a richly unapologetic voice. Wholly engaging.

~ Rita Williams Garcia, Newbery Honor Book Winner, Coretta Scott King Author Award Winner and author of *One Crazy Summer, A Sitting in St. James,* and *Gone Crazy in Alabama*

To the victims of abuse and trafficking, domestic and aboard—you are not alone, we hear you, we see you.

www.nokidhungry.org
www.amestyinternational
www.humantraffickinghotline.org

CHAPTER ONE

"Oh God, he's back!" He's at it again—sneaky Old Fart with his ratty gray hair begging for a comb, skin too white for a black man, with a big gold tooth you can check your reflection in. Treading carefully, snake-like, I approach the door and hear him on the other side, cheap splintered floors creaking. He walks heavy for a skinny man.

Through the peephole, I see him raise a hand. Then the other comes up too. I skedaddle, sock feet aiming a precise slide back to the window. "Sounds like a two-fist pound this time."

"Beenie, you need to get up from the window *now*." Ma takes a step toward me.

My little brother Jamal, wiping his dry eyes and chest heaving, releasing a volcanic eruption of snot. "I'm scared, Mama."

"Ma, he's got the cops on you now?"

Her eyes shoot poison darts at me. "I'm not telling you again." Her attempt to whisper fails, prompting machine-gun knocking on the door. Her eyes are locked on the door as she moistens her lipsticked lips. "He can't be seeing us. You gonna get us in trouble." Ma twists into knots when she gets heated. She can't stay still, wringing her hands, moving side to side like she gotta pee. One minute, she big and badass; next minute, she a wimp.

Ma deserves an eyeroll when she talking stupid. "Whatcha mean us? We're not in trouble, *you are.*"

Now she's flailing her arms to get my attention again as I turn away, blowing air on the window, drawing a smiley face for Jamal. The chill through the glass forces me to quickly put my gloves back on, which do nothing to protect me from the cold despite sweat sticking to my back like glue. Ma finally gets some courage, moving slowly over to the window, tugging at my jacket with a finger against her lips.

"Stop playing with me," she growls, then jumps at the knocking. Old Fart back to banging again. I put a firm hand up to Ma's face to keep her quiet as she about to part her lips. Old Fart from some Caribbean Island 'cause he got an accent that says I wasn't born here. Mal's eyes grow beyond the size of his head, teeth pulling his bottom lip so hard he'll stop breathing. His asthma gonna flare up. His eyes move from the door to me to Ma and then back to me, real tears flooding, his whimpering increasing by decibels.

Ma narrows her eyes to dark slits as she lowers her head to look at Jamal, lips pressed tight. "Where my soldier, Mally Mal?" She caresses his face as her thumbs wipe away tears.

The landlord switches from banging to incessant knocking. He must have fists of steel, pounding so hard the door gonna break, yelling at Ma to let him in. He wants his rent. He's sick of her ducking and dodging. His shouting draws our neighbors out of their apartments, asking what the hell is going on. He's telling them what a deadbeat Ma is. She owes him six months back rent. He wants his money. He got bills to pay. He says this five times. Ma can spend his money ordering junk, but she can't pay his rent. He says he's seen several packages delivered to her door every week. Why can't she stop shopping and pay her rent? He calls her a worthless scammer. If the city of New York wasn't so hard on landlords, she would be out on the streets.

The Badass part of Ma is back. She tries not to laugh, but it happens against her will. The landlord's accent so thick, he is hard to listen to without cracking up. My gut busts with hilarity, too, 'cause hard not to between the landlord's ranting in Caribbean patois and Ma's hound dog laughter. The rare times we laugh together is when I like her. I tell her I understand him completely.

"You must be well versed in West Indian." The volume of her laughter goes up a notch, but she quickly muffles it with a firm, manicured hand over her mouth.

"Imma stab him if he don't stop," Jamal says, covering his ears.

"You'll go to prison if you do."

"So I'll be with my daddy!"

"They don't send kids to prison," Ma says in his defense.

"In Texas, they do."

She rolls her eyes, shakes her head, signals to ignore me, a habit that pisses me off. She is focusing on the landlord's movement outside our apartment door as if she has X-ray eyes and can see his every move. Her ears are her eyes right now.

Jamal knows about prison. Penguin currently incarcerated for credit card fraud. The ringleader, the news said. He and his crew of two men and a woman installed skimmers at a couple of banks. Depositors withdrew their money; information stolen. Grandma suspected Ma was involved, and if she knew for certain, she'd dropped a dime on her. Penguin and his homies never snitched.

He was born with one leg shorter than the other and walks shifting left to right like a penguin. Ma says it is a medical condition, hip dysplasia. She says dogs are not the only ones who get it. Humans do, too. She regrets messing with Penguin for the bird brain he is. She stayed because he paid the rent. When she was ready to get rid of him, Jamal came along. Ma tells that lie to anyone who don't know the truth—Penguin took off screaming. He can't deal with her anymore. Ma, the dumpee, was in the dark a long time.

Penguin's mad cool. He makes me laugh with his tired ass jokes, always buying us nice things and clothes before he locked up. He'd take Jamal and me to the department store to pick out whatever we wanted. Grandma wondered aloud whose credit card Penguin stole to buy us things.

He filed a complaint for the judge to force Ma to bring Jamal to see him. She cursed up and down the highway during the six-hour bus ride to prison—really cold—somewhere near the Canadian border. Jamal keeps track on his calendar when Penguin's coming home, a red circle on his parole date; Ma added a smiley face to it, excited like a seal on Ritalin. His parole date is less than two months away.

The landlord's hand must hurt. He stopped banging on the door.

"Baby, go to the window. See if his car is out there."

Jamal takes his assignment like a soldier. He crawls on his belly and then stops, his arm and leg suspended in air, looking back at Ma for approval. She nods, smiling to gas him up. He rises slowly like he is dodging enemy fire and, with a little finger, gently pulls back a vertical blind for surveillance. "He leaning on his car."

"Is he by himself?" I ask.

"His car is black with gold rims, tacky ass foreigner." Ma slaps her palms, cracking up.

"He getting in his car, Ma!" Jamal's hyperactivity is up full volume. "He gone."

"Nah, he gone for now," I say, locking eyes with Ma. "You better check yourself. Old Fart might jack the Amazon dude if a package delivery got your name on it."

CHAPTER TWO

Ma waves me into her room, makeup smeared on her face like a baby licking a cake bowl. We're not cool.

She closes one eye with an unsteady hand holding her mascara, fixing an uneven cat's eye, unbothered by my staring. One eye focuses on the mirror while the other checks me, smiling at my unsmiling face. Less than a second is given to me, then her attention goes back to her favorite item of furniture in our apartment—an overpriced floor-to-ceiling vanity that scrapes the ceiling, exposing drywall, giving the old fart another reason to bang on our door for eviction.

Ma gives her time to everybody except me.

She is in love—*again*.

Her new lace front arrived in time for the new boyfriend. Earlier, she pawed over me with sloppy, unwanted kisses, petting me out of bed to do her a favor. Ma has the softest hands for it. "Beenie, my package is here—go get it for Mama, okay?"

I rubbed the sleep out of my eyes. "Get it yourself."

Her hands abandoned my face as she slowly lifted herself, towering, nose down, asking again using a higher decibel meaning business. "Come on, go get it for me." She softened the command with a smile.

"*You* getting on my nerves." I retrieved the package, running into Mr. Cortez, the undervalued super of the building. He looked at the package, then at me, shaking his head, saying in Spanish how beautiful and foolish Ma is. He does not know I understand.

Inside, I slapped her hand away, not caring that it smudged freshly painted nails, helping her open the package that contains the source of Ma's morning good mood. Her face lights up like Christmas whenever the Amazon guy delivers her packages.

Every time she gets a new boo, she says being in love is a better drug than any doctor could give her. The current bae will make his debut on her Instagram, replacing the ex's pics, deleted immediately like they never existed. Grandma will be furious when I tell her what Ma's been up to. She better stop making me mad.

Her eyes lock on the wig, concentrating, plucking the hairline, making sure there are enough baby hairs on the lace front. She shoots up, taking in air for a moment, then up at the dim lighting in our apartment. "Damn slumlord," she mumbles for the eye strain.

Ma says wig makers charge a fortune, and you got to do more work, so the wig don't look fake. She refuses to wear her glasses, squinting hard as she tweezes away excess hair, humming a song from her generation. I immediately recognize it; it's one she always sings when a new man comes along—Mary J. Blige's "Real Love." She's happy, moving her shoulders and hips, pulling away at wig hairs.

Ain't no use holding the face frown 'cause she ain't pressed about what's bothering me. My concern transfers to the welfare of the wig that cost two of Dad's child support payments, wondering if she gonna pluck all the hair off 'cause she ain't focusing, just dancing.

Three even lines form across her forehead as she rests an index finger under her nose, supported by a thumb under her chin.

"What's wrong?" I ask.

"I hope I didn't mess up the hairline. Hand me my phone, baby."

The Queen of YouTube needs help. She watches YouTube more than cable, which is suspended for non-payment most of the time anyway. The only bill Ma pays on time is her cell. If she must choose between buying groceries for the week and her cell bill, she will cut back on stuff we need from the supermarket. At our bodega, she'll buy stuff, put it on credit, and then take forever to pay Mr. Ali. He's a nice man with stale food and jacked-up prices, letting people buy on credit. Some of our neighbors are so foul, Ma being one of them—they accuse him of stealing from the neighborhood, so they steal right back. When she don't keep her promise to pay, she'll make us cross the street to avoid him and his store.

She got so many channels on how-tos, on lace front wigs, how to care for, how to dye, how to pluck hair properly, and so on. A relieved smile appears again. "Whew, I thought I jacked up my lace front, girl."

When she don't piss me off, I'm down for her, though it won't last long. If happiness slapped Ma in the face, she'd be ready to cuss and fight.

She don't care for herself when she breaks up, or worse, if the dude dumps her. She says it's way better to be the dumper than the dumpee; you in control. When you do the dumping, it don't hurt as much.

But it is not a good place to be when Ma's the dumpee. She don't talk, just lay on the couch, staring at the television, waiting for someone to jump out the TV to save her. If she does speak, it's to yell at us or something. Jamal loves when she is the dumpee because we can do whatever we want, eat all the fast food, soda, and sweets, and go to bed when we feel like it.

Jamal appears like a mole coming up for light with a full-on smile. He yanks me, spraying me with: "I hope she gets dumped soon." He says this while Ma's focus is her makeup, ignoring us, as he adds, "Then we can have Micky D, pizza, soda, cupcakes for a long time!" He can't stay still, dancing at the excitement of junk food, watching her finally done with her wig. Not satisfied with her beat face, she wipes it clear off and starts reapplying.

I slap him upside his head, reminding him of other things that happen. "Yeah, boy, you get yelled at too. Ma don't care about nothing but her feelings."

His return was a hard arm punch for a seven-year-old. "Don't care."

Jamal's good as long as he gets his junk food. When Ma is balanced—Grandma's word—we have to do homework and go to bed at a decent hour—Ma's words—for a teen and seven-year-old. When she's in love, she don't know how old we are—she's too happy to care.

Grandma worries about Ma when she's walking in the clouds. She yells at Ma the same way Ma yells at us. She gets on Ma's case to take her pills to keep her steady. Old people use codes when they think we're too young or dumb to know better. Grandma is dumb sometimes, but she's smart about some things, too. But she can't remember I have a phone and internet access; she got an outdated flip phone, those old ones companies donate to senior citizens. The agency gave her one for free. I know what she means by Ma must keep steady taking her medication.

Jamal calls her the polar bear. He does not understand, but that was the best way to explain without confusing him. I'll warn him: "Jamal, the bear's coming!"

He gets on my nerves sometimes, like most little brothers. I'll talk down to him like he's stupid, telling him, like Grandma does, that he's too young to understand. He'll get mad, ready to punch me, stomping his feet, screaming he's smart like me.

Jamal's sensitive like Ma. He takes medication for hyperactivity and attention deficit. Grandma says he has the attention span of an ant. He gets on her nerves with "all that electricity." Says she's too old for this. Ma sometimes takes him to a plant doctor, but when she's in her love state, she stops.

Ma has wigs, full frontals and lace fronts, that tell a boyfriend story behind each one. The cornrow was Harold, a mad-cool dude with stinky breath. The Diana Ross one was Karl, a German guy Jamal and I called The Terminator. He was hard to understand and tried to teach us his language. Rahim was a born-again Muslim. Ma couldn't grow her natural hair fast enough, so she bought an Afro wig. He was into plant medicine. He'd cook up herbs and roots, saying it would cure Ma of her polar bear and Jamal's attention deficit and hyperactivity. Grandma cussed and threw it in the garbage when Ma gave it to her with instructions when we spent the night. "I'm a servant of God; I ain't fooling with no voodoo mess in my house."

She shaved her head bald with Penguin. Grandma and Uncle Marsh tried to put her away. I cried blindness, eyes shut, closed tight at the thought of Ma leaving me with Grandma or, worse, with Uncle Marsh and Aunt Nelle. They couldn't give her no medication because she was pregnant with Jamal. Penguin tried his best to stay, but the polar bear drove him away.

I don't know the name of the boyfriend behind the latest wig. He won't last long. Once the polar bear comes out, he'll run away like the rest of them, including my father.

I don't know what kind of wig she had when she met him.

Ma looks pretty. Her wig is long, Beyoncé-blond with curls, but it looks too small for her head. Black people look funny with blond hair, but Ma's color is caramel, and, for real, the blond looks good with her skin. She makes it fit. Her nails are blood red. She is wearing jeans, spanking her big booty, and a silk tee without a bra and a jacket Jamal calls sparkly. "I look good."

Jamal, squealing like a pig, says, "You shiny, Mama. Can I have some pizza?" He takes off to the kitchen before her answer.

"What you think, Beenie, ready for the gram?"

Ma has two social pages; the one I'm not supposed to know about is MzDoll100. It's so basic and thirsty. She's got about 10,000 followers, dirty old men commenting they'd like to "tap that ass" bootylicious or lick her caramel skin. She gets a lot of DMs from those perverts. Disgusting. I heard her talking to one guy more than once; I'm tempted to remind her of the *stranger danger* talk she gave me when I was little.

Hypocrite. Ma is showing them what she got and what they want.

Her second Instagram page is rated G. DollFam has lots of photos of Jamal, me, and sometimes Grandma, but if Ma is upset at her, Grandma gets deleted. DollFam followers are less than half of MzDoll100.

She does not wait for an answer, whipping out her phone for the perfect selfie. This pic will be for MzDoll100, too stupid to worry about Old Fart watching her walk out the crib, seeing her new clothes. Maybe the DM perv will DM rent money to her.

I hate it when she calls me by my childhood nickname. I'm an adult now. I will start my freshman year in the fall.

I *prefer* Rubena.

CHAPTER THREE

She did not come home last night. Her bedroom door was left unlocked. The anticipation of the new boyfriend made her forget. Bed unmade from yesterday, rolling paper for weed on the nightstand next to a Statue of Liberty lighter, the carton from the wig on her bed, clothes tossed out of the closet in a frenzy for picking the perfect outfit strewn all over the floor, many of them still with price tags on.

So far, no signs of the landlord. Jamal stood sentry for Old Fart's shining gold tooth alert 'till he couldn't hold his pee. If he returns, we will be quiet, wait until his fists hurt, his voice goes hoarse, and then he'll leave. If he returns with police, we're in trouble. I'm hoping the neighbors who can't stand him will curse him, threaten to beat his ass if he don't leave. The tenants hate him; Ma instigates every chance, bad-mouthing him. She lied, "He has a girlfriend." She gonna tell his wife if he don't stop pestering her about rent. He tried to get fresh with her and she slammed him hard. That's why he's mad. He's the worst in the world, a real slumlord, asks for so much but gives very little in return; that's what Ma says about him.

I order Jamal not to open the door for no one. "Not even Ma?" he asks between mouthfuls of sugar-coated cereal I knew better than to give him. He will be electric until the sugar wears down.

"No." Phone in hand, a spiteful finger on speed dial to Grandma to snitch. But she will be yelling, fussing, and getting on my nerves, and I'll regret calling her. She will carry on, threatening to call child protective services. I put the phone away. I don't need Grandma stressing me this morning. She's nothing but talk about that, but the words frighten Jamal.

Ma's probably out with her new boo at her best friend Miss Tamara's place. With her new man in tow, Ma bragging to her friend and anyone with an ear how wonderful he is, showing him off, telling everyone he is the real deal.

They will start off the evening playing cards, drinking beer, smoking weed past dawn, ending with Ma on Miss Tamara's sofa. Miss Tamara seen this theater with Ma and men over and over. She will help Ma when the polar bear comes out. Ma draws everybody into her drama, real, mostly make believe, it's getting old.

It can't be easy being Ma's friend. Miss Tamara has red eyes and edema ankles from high blood pressure. She burdens herself, being in Ma's mess.

"Tamara Dixon, you a plain ole fool, carrying her nonsense like God gave it to you to hold," Grandma sniffed at Miss Tamara, greeting her when she visited her mother at the senior complex.

"Oh Miss Eudora, we been friends too long, I gotta be there for her," Miss Tamara brushed off, smiling.

"You ain't gotta do nothing," Grandma cut her off. "I wouldn't waste my time fooling with no friends like that." She leaned back, folded her arms across her belly, inspecting Miss Tamara from head to toe. "You put on a little more weight girl. Leave fatty foods and my daughter alone."

Ma can't make up her mind; I'm too young for one thing but old enough to watch Jamal when she's not home, then I'm treated like an adult.

I have some paper and a few coins Ma left for me to buy dinner. Jamal promised to do guard watch for the landlord, and when the coast is clear, I will order Chinese food for us.

Wish I could tell my father what's going on, but he'll take it too far, ruin it for Jamal. The sand in the hourglass starts now. Ma better come home before the money runs out. There is no food in the house. She will turn into pumpkin mash when Grandma comes.

Grandma will give Ma a tongue whipping—*that* is a million times worse than a whupping.

CHAPTER FOUR

Grandma is beating Jamal again. It's the third one he's gotten this week since the social worker brought us here in the middle of the night. Really, it was ten o'clock at night, but to Grandma after eight is the middle of the night.

She greeted us in hair curlers—no bra—in her favorite house-dress with a scowl on her face at the smiling white woman delivering us. Grandma is mean to white people. She swears on God she loves all people of all colors, but she rude to anyone who don't look like her.

"She back on that mess again." Grandma's lips twisted after the word *mess*.

She was not sleeping when we knocked on her door but watching her favorite station, TV Land. Those '70s shows when television had morals, characters had dignity; never a dirty word uttered, no flesh exposed, always a moral lesson and a happy ending, all in thirty minutes. Life lessons from episodic television.

I developed a love for *Happy Days, Sanford and Son, The Jeffersons, Barnaby Jones, Hawaii Five-o,* and, really, two favorites, *The Brady Bunch* and *The Partridge Family.*

But Jamal does not share our fondness for nostalgia TV. He always into something else. The social worker told Grandma he was diagnosed with ADD/HD. Grandma cut her off, dismissed it, saying Jamal is simply hard-headed and stubborn. He won't listen, spoiled, ruined by Ma giving in instead of whipping him. Grandma says it is Ma's fault because she is always on a mission instead of caring for her children.

The last time I saw Ma, she and her Beyoncé-blond wig were off to a dreamland date. She left money to buy a couple meals and, poof, she was gone.

I snitched.

"Grandma, she left the house like a happy puppy."

"She'll come home like a beat-up hound, once she is unbalanced," Grandma snapped back. "Did she take her meds?"

"Yeah, I saw her take it." I slapped my hand firmly over Jamal's mouth before he gave me away when Grandma turned her back.

Ma once had a good job that paid really well. We lived in a rented condo. Jamal and I had our own room, and there was a pool. We had everything until Ma lost her job for misappropriation of funds. Grandma said she's lucky she didn't go to jail for stealing those white folks' money. We got evicted a year later when the condo owner took Ma to court and won. A repeat offender, the owner called her a professional squatter.

I do not tell Grandma about the back rent with the West Indian landlord. Ma will yell at me for telling her business, and Grandma's sugar will shoot up—she might pass out, fearful that Ma, Jamal, and I will move in with her.

I wanna live with my father, but I can't leave Jamal with Ma; he cannot depend on her.

Jamal has an ear for mimicking people: Grandma, Ma, me, anyone. He imitated Ma smoking weed. She stupidly left her lighter on the nightstand and bedroom door unlocked.

I could have stopped him. I could have snatched it out of his hands, pushed him out of Ma's room, and locked the door. I am my brother's keeper, and sometimes I have to discipline him with words, but I don't hit him like Grandma. I feel bad after doing it. I hold him, give him a kiss, and make him a sandwich.

But I did nothing. I sat on Ma's bed, watching my brother rolling a piece of paper in his capable little hands, sucking hard and running the lighter back and forth. He looked up at me smiling, fueled by my giggling. I was not laughing inside.

Our crappy six-floor building is owned by Old Fart, the landlord, who gets section eight money for us. The state pays a larger portion of the rent, and Ma's supposed to pay the difference, which she refused to do. He's a thief and don't deserve one penny from the state, 'cause he don't fix nothing. We better off living in state housing, the projects, which is better than that dump. Ma said the waiting list for public housing was too long, and her patience too short.

So, I thought if the building burned down, I'd be free of the roaches and the smell of boric acid that's killing us instead of them. Old Fart freezes us during the winter and suffocates us during the summer. The ceiling leaks like a storm in the living room, causing mold, aggravating Jamal's asthma.

We wouldn't have to put up with decayed drywall in the hallway about to collapse and crush my little brother to death or be fearful he'll eat a paint chip and suffer brain damage like the cute little Dominican girl who lives next door to us did. The super, Mr. Cortez, does his best to care for the building, but it is not enough. He cares more about the building and the tenants than Old Fart Gold Tooth does.

The hallway smells of urine, dog shit. The intercom don't work. I'm scared to take the elevator but more scared to use the stairwell alone even during the day. LaShonda Biggs, a bookish girl of sixteen, lives a floor below me, escaped an attack recently.

"I gotta scholarship, gonna go to prep school in the country—

prolly be around lotta of white people, but it's all good." LaShonda rubbed her bruised bandaged arm when I visited her after the attack. "It gonna be lit. I get to stay on campus, away from here, far away from the city."

I gently yanked her multi-color beaded box braid. "Just don't come back to the hood talkin' like one. I'm glad you gonna escape."

"Your pops live Upstate?"

"Yeah, but I don't wanna stress him."

LaShonda tapped my arm with her good hand. "You will, you always on the honors list. My French teacher," she laughed, "*fille francophone sur le hood*—French-speaking girl in da hood." She looked down, reflecting. "I'm worried leaving my mom and Keshawn. She works so hard, two jobs, still ain't making enough paper."

The main building security lock been broken since we moved in, allowing drunken bums and dope fiends into the lobby, offering stuff to sell that they stole from the neighbors; drug gangs conducting customer transactions, Ma being a regular to purchase her weed from them. Old Fart don't care about his property or the tenants, building just like him, so if only the house burned down, I could save so many people, including LaShonda's mom, her brother Keshawn, and Jamal from the gangs roaming like wolves on the prowl.

Jamal lit the paper. I decided to do nothing, not caring about what would happen next.

Grandma's apartment building is a palace compared to our home. The senior citizen complex is neat, smells clean, and it quiet. She says her generation better raised than Ma, Jamal, and me.

But she is tired of us: tired of my mother's antics, tired of being a safety net when Ma screws up. She is tired of beating Jamal. I know she loves us, but she wants her life back, what little she has left.

Jamal has cried himself to sleep. Grandma will get a break until he wakes up tomorrow. But we can't stay here; it is housing for seniors only. She is sad and relieved by it.

She motions me to sit next to her, placing her flaccid arm around me while we watch *Barnaby Jones*. As I lay against her soft, sagging belly, I smell Ivory soap and Dax hair grease. Grandma may not realize what she is doing, but I hear a faint humming of a hymnal she sang so many times during service when she forced us to go to church.

"You all right, baby?"

Her soft voice is making my eyelids ready for sleep.

"The policeman called, told me what you did..."

I snap out of my slumber, freeze, preparing for the ass-whipping of my life. The truth about the fire—I was the accomplice who did nothing while Jamal played with Ma's lighter and threw the burning paper in the garbage. We nursed the fire until it was time to make our escape.

I want to tell the truth.

I want to tell her why I did it, but my tongue is dry, locked behind my lips.

"I'm proud of you." Grandma rubs my forearm back and forth in praise. "He said you got Jamal outta the house, ran back in screaming, banging on the neighbor's door." Grandma side-hugs me tightly. "If it wasn't for you, folks could have died."

Silence protects me from the truth. I'm afraid I'll slip on it like ice and fall. She thinks her lecture about humility has not gone to waste on me.

"You did a blessing, girl. Grandma proud of you. But you should've dialed 911 after you and Jamal ran out, but I give praise to the Lord for helping you to be brave, Beenie." Grandma draws me in closer, her lips press gently against my ear. "How did that fire start?"

"I don't know."

CHAPTER FIVE

We are in the emergency room, Grandma, Jamal, and me. Jamal won't stop crying. Snot keeps running out his nose. He jumps up, bolts out the room.

"Rubena!" Grandma says to me. "Get him back here."

"His nose still runny, Grandma."

I can't find enough tissues; Grandma yelling at me not to bother the nurses. Her sugar is high again. Jamal crying 'cause he thinks his electricity caused "Grandma's sugar to run out" before. I tell him to stop crying, but he won't. I tell him Grandma's old and old people get diabetes. He does not believe me even though he knows when I'm lying or telling the truth.

The people in Grandma's building say Jamal is psychic. Grandma's friends always bothering Jamal to pencil in winning numbers, give them the first six numbers that pop in his head. Those old people so happy a seven-year-old won them thirty, forty dollars. Grandma stopped him 'cause it's a sin to gamble; she stingy, wants Jamal's powers for herself. Jamal says Grandma pulls him close to her, whispering, "Baby, what's your favorite numbers today?"

But this morning, Jamal's magical power is not working. He still crying despite Grandma telling him to hush. The doctor, an African with every letter of the alphabet in his last name, cannot control Grandma's blood sugar. He tries to cheer Jamal up, placing the stethoscope around Jamal's neck, letting him hear Grandma's heart is working. This works better than Grandma telling him to hush as his crying has whittled down to a whimper.

The doctor says unless Grandma's blood sugar comes down, she may be admitted. Jamal's eyes are as large as saucers. Grandma dismisses the doctor, sniffs, saying she ain't staying unless her real doctor says so, ordering the African to contact her doctor, but either he does not hear her or he ignores her. Grandma shouts she has private insurance as the doctor closes the door behind him.

We still don't know where Ma is. Grandma real pissed about it. *That's* the reason her sugar is up. Ma promised to take Grandma to her doctor's appointment. She called, reminding Ma, but she neglected to tell Grandma the repo man took the car a couple of months ago. She had a ready-made lie every time Grandma asked about the car she and Uncle Marsh gave Ma the down payment for. When her latest wig arrived, Ma blew her off, forgot about Grandma, who depended on Ma driving her because her legs were bothering her. After a day or more waiting, missing her doctor's appointment, she cursed herself for believing Ma could just once be dependable for her. The pain finally forced Grandma to catch a cab with Jamal and me in tow to the Emergency Room.

Grandma proudly hands her insurance card to the ER clerk now in our cubicle using a computer on wheels. She then gave the supplemental insurance card to the lifeless girl banging away at keys not bothering to acknowledge Grandma talking about her primary, secondary, private insurance. She says her insurance is for working people, not charity insurance. It is shade, a diss, Ma and Jamal, they have state insurance. I'm on my dad's private coverage, but Jamal has welfare insurance, Grandma calls it. She says Ma better get a job 'cause the government getting tired of taking care of sorry people like her daughter. She knows Jamal and I would not repeat her words.

Grandma still gushing about her coverage to the uninterested girl, who forces a fake smile, returns the card, and leaves without saying the customary thank you, no goodbye, or feel better. Grandma growled at the non-responsive clerk, commenting on young folks' lack of respect, not possessing an ounce of manners, purposely loud, prompting the clerk to turn to Grandma with a nervous smile of contrition and then quickly turn away from her menacing glare.

Like a ghost without consequence, Ma waltzes in with a smile. She is the sole owner of the stench now choking the room. She has not been visited by clean clothes, soap, or water in days. Crocodile tears in place, her voice cracking, she says, "The neighbor told me to go to the ER. How you feeling, Ma?"

Grandma's face tightens into a big knot; her eyes, her nose gone like a car disappearing into a black hole. Slowly, Ma approaches Grandma, rubbing her hands, walking cautiously, like an attempt to gain confidence while facing a rabid dog. But Grandma's face is completely gone. Gone are her happy brown eyes twinkling when she is talking to God, making a joyful noise in church, or smothering Jamal and me with hugs. Jamal moves side to side searching for Grandma's face.

Ma looks over to me for rescue as I tuck in my arms without saying a single word. Beads of sweat march down the side of her face. She shifts her weight and cracks her knuckles, another Grandma irritant.

Grandma barks at Jamal and me to get out and then roars like a wounded lion for Ma to shut the door behind us. I take one last look as Ma's smile dissolves, stiffens, her chest puffing out. She tells us to wait in the lobby. We are going home with her.

I run after Jamal, who thinks we are playing a game, laughing, screaming down the corridor until a blue man with a thick accent inquires who are we and where are our parents.

"My daddy's in jail," Jamal says like it's a badge of honor. He makes a gang sign and says, "You step to me, my daddy gonna check you."

I grab him by the collar as Jamal yells at the security guard, calling him a punk. I yank him by the arm, apologizing to the guard for his behavior. His feet refuse to cooperate as I drag him, navigating us to the lobby. As we watch a man in a white uniform and waist-length dreadlocks pushing a stretcher with a woman on it attached to an intravenous bag, I explain to Jamal we must be respectful of people here, who are as sick as Grandma.

"Grandma gonna give Ma a beating?" Jamal asks as his spindly legs dangle off the plastic chair in the waiting room.

"Nah, Ma's too big. She'll give Grandma a beat down."

"She gave me a whipping," Jamal reminds me, referring to the other morning Grandma whipped him for breaking her favorite coffee cup after warning him three times to use a plastic one for his milk.

I playfully slap him upside his shaven head. "You're hardheaded."

He returns a hard arm punch. "Ma's hardheaded too."

We do not wait long. Ma fast-walks out, looking for us like lost children in a store. Her tear-stained face and runny mascara say Grandma has won again as she retreats in defeat.

We quietly follow her outside and sit on the sidewalk in front of the hospital entrance. She rummages through her bags, hands Jamal a box of sugar-coated cereal. I warn Ma of Grandma's no sugar edict for Jamal.

"A little won't hurt him." Her voice is empty of energy and full of defeat. Jamal sticks his tongue at me and indulges himself, victoriously eating the cereal.

Ma fires up a stick, exhales a thought on her face. She's

scheming again. Every time Grandma wins, she has the urge to hide from her. She ain't no match for Grandma; no one is. Grandma does not fear no man or woman, only Jesus. God and his son Jesus are the only forces that can make Grandma cry.

She catches me staring hard at her, returning the stare long enough to take a second puff, then quickly away, fearful of exposure. What happened to her dream date? Was she the dumpee again? Why so early? Where is her pretty Beyoncé-blond wig? Why is her makeup melting? Did the polar bear come out? Did the polar bear frighten him away? Why didn't Miss Tamara come to her rescue like she always does? Did she finally listen to Grandma?

"I'll be back," Ma says.

She does not bother looking at me as she lifts up from the concrete, dusting off her dirty booty jeans. The eye bags snitch—she ain't seen sleep in days; hair electrified, breath smelling of alcohol, and whiffs of Newport 100s escape her reeking pores. She flops back down on the concrete for a second, then shoots up like she sat on a nail, searching the sky, cars whizzing by, waving at strangers like lost friends, ignoring the twisted look on their faces. She stubs her cigarette while rummaging in her bag for a lighter and another Newport.

"You gonna disappear like you always do. You're irresponsible." I'm waiting for the scowl to surface on her raggedy forty-year-old face, what I know she knows I know. She can't handle what Grandma said to her, and she's preparing to run away. She never did fool me.

Ma freezes, staring me down; the truth has paralyzed her. She lies so much she don't know what the truth feels like, looks like. I'm no longer blind. She narrows her eyes, fist balling tight, wanting to slap me silly, but she won't for public display.

If she were standing near the edge of a cliff, I'd push her off.

"Can't I go with you?" Jamal now too hyper from the sugar cereal Grandma and I warned about. I told her not to give it to him, and she, as always, undermined Grandma out of spite. Grandma once said Ma's too childish to have children.

"No, baby, I got business to take care of." She cups Jamal's sugar-stained face while eyeing me at the same time. "Stay with Beenie."

Leaning close to Jamal, I tell him, "She's lying again. You can't go where she going..."

The unfinished cigarette flies across the concrete. She grips my arm so tight the blood flow cuts off. "I'm sick of people dissing me." Ma's grinding her teeth, somehow spit lands on my face. "I'm sick of it! You better respect me, you hear me, I'm not gonna stand for it!" she snarls like Busby's pit bull Tiny, exposing her teeth, the ones Uncle Marsh paid for, now ruined by neglect.

She is hurting my arm, but I will die before I let her know this. We are engaging in a staring match so fierce, I'm thankful our eyes are not shooting missiles; we would obliterate each other before Jamal's hysterical, ashy face.

Jamal is no match in the strength needed to separate Ma and me. I shake him off like a snat. His face is washed by tears while snot runs from his nose. I will not break, neither will Ma. Her grip on my arm is a life jacket in the riptide of lies that will drown her. For a brief moment, I let up, feeling sorry for what she reads on my face. I see the pain in her eyes, knowing how much I hate her, but I redouble my effort to punish her before she hurts me; she can't do that if I don't let her. *I don't need her. I'm better off without her.*

"I want you to respect me!" She is yelling, but it sounds like begging, not caring people in the hospital parking lot are now looking oddly at us. They gather around us like witnessing a terrible storm approach.

I refuse to de-escalate, instigating instead. "You said you have somewhere to go—then go!"

She jerks at me again, still holding on, like a child wanting to be picked up. Jamal jumps up and down, pleading with Ma to stop. The storm picks up speed as more and more people assemble; fear, concern, curiosity, and just plain nosiness are etched on the rainbow of faces before us. Ma quickly releases her grip and steps back, hands raised like an arrest. "What da freak ya'll looking at?" she says to the crowd.

"You all right, honey?" says an old white woman with a cane, fried hair, and bright red lipstick. She gingerly approaches, mindful of Ma's malignant glare. I'm impressed by her bravado, that she would risk her life for me. Ma blocks her, obstructs her view, bucking her eyes at the old woman to not take another step.

"Shall I call the police?" asks a black man, gut belly tearing at the seams of his cotton shirt, a comb-over in full view. Standing next to him, an Indian man with a curious look on his hairy face is wearing a turban and holding a baby.

Jamal shakes his fist at the black man, yelling, "You better not call po-po, you big belly fat pig!"

Ma collars him to quiet, then, over to the crowd picking up in numbers, she says, "We're fine." She shoos them away with one hand, the other firmly on Jamal squirming under her talon grip. "Keep it moving."

People exchange looks, some mumbling to each other like a jury undecided whether to convict or acquit, conferring about what to do. Their gazes turn to me. They are fixated by the suspense I am keeping them in. I appreciate faces of concern about leaving me with Ma, but I'm fine. Ma cannot steady her legs to keep upright, letting go of Jamal, then grabbing his small shoulders to balance her. She has no power, she lost to Grandma, the waiting crowd under my control.

A collection of eyes jumps to Ma, then me, then Ma, and finally at me. My old woman rescuer shifts her cane to distribute her weight as the comb-over black man leans forward waiting.

"All good in the hood," I announced to the relief of the waiting masses, reassuring them with the widest, fakest smile—it almost strangles me—my cheeks burn not looking at Ma.

"Yeah, keep it moving," Jamal steps forward to the retreating crowd, waving them away. "We cool, right, Ma?"

Ma, too, waits for people to disperse, anxious for them to leave, shaking a cramp in her leg left to right, rubbing her face. She looks hurriedly at them, at Jamal, but not me. She won't look at me. "Stay here with your brother," her voice trails as she walks briskly away, nearly colliding with a van pulling into the entrance. The driver and Ma exchange screaming curses, flipping the bird to each other.

I space my fingers in front of me with Ma in view. As she gets smaller and smaller within the space between my thumb and index finger, I press together to squash her like a bug. Jamal watches quizzically, cheeks pocketed with cereal. "Whatchu doing?" he shoots up before me, ready to fight.

"Making Ma disappear."

"Stop." He pulls at my hand.

I elbow him away as my fingers press so tight it burns.

"Stop it, Beenie!" Jamal yelps, ready to cry again.

He has done enough crying for the day. I wrap my arm around him as he resumes his seat beside me loudly chomping away at the remains of cereal. I have no psychic powers, but I know what will happen to Ma.

She gonna die.

I'm ready.

But I cannot share this with Jamal. He'll start hollering, crying, become too hyper for Grandma to deal with.

CHAPTER SIX

The hospital discharges Grandma after a lifetime there. It is late afternoon when we arrive home by taxi. Ma has not been around since Grandma made her cry; she took off running as she always does. Ma ain't for nothing except running. She good at that. Grandma grateful the African doctor didn't admit her; she would not have stayed—no how—'cause she don't trust nobody she can't understand. Dad says she's a racist, but Grandma don't see it that way. She not familiar with people different from her though the doctor was the same color. She still angry at Ma. Don't think she wants to see her for a while.

The seniors in Grandma's building welcome her back like she's famous. Each tenant queues up, kissing Grandma, holding her hands a second too long as she firmly releases their grip with a thankful smile as cover. They all repeat the same remarks, thanking everyone but the sun and the moon she is safely back with them. A few talk about tenants who left, never came back, they went home to be with God, grateful the Almighty decided to give Grandma more time with them.

The long red carpet in the hallway has frayed corners. They

hung a banner overhead with *Welcome Home Eudora* in large, uneven block print. Below it, a long folding table holds rows of home-cooked food and sweets. Jamal's eyes about to jump out of their sockets, me too, mouth-watering foods Grandma and Jamal should not eat: macaroni and cheese, sweet potato pie, spareribs, corn bread, fried chicken, and one of my favorites, peach cobbler.

The last person to greet Grandma makes a great entrance, singing, praising God for bringing her Eudora back. It's Ms. Lulu Bell-Davis. Everyone calls her MissLuluBell like it is one word. Miss Lulu Bell is the seamstress of the building. All the elderly women, young ones too, see Miss Lulu Bell to design, alter, and enhance their church outfits, complete with a hat. She is a tall woman with big hands and even bigger feet. I wonder how Miss Lulu Bell can walk without tripping over them.

"Lord Jesus, praise God, our Eudora is back." She wraps her large arms around Grandma, swallowing her as her hands are holding Miss Lulu Bell forearms like a rafter. "How you feeling, honey?"

"Grateful the Lord saw to it I made it out of the storm, Lulu Bell," Grandma says. "I see you done organized this party for me. Much obliged."

Grandma talks Southern when she says things like "much obliged" or "I sho' 'ppreciated it." Miss Lulu Bell talks the same way to Grandma like it's some foreign language people from the South talk. Grandma is from Opelika, Alabama; Miss Lulu Bell is from Tunica, Mississippi. She says it's the poorest place with the richest people.

I bear-hold Jamal as Miss Lulu Bell orders Miss Gracie Lawson to thank the Lord before we eat. Grandma head already bowed as Miss Lulu Bell telling everybody to "Hush up, we about to talk to God." She then barks at Miss Gracie Lawson to start praying "before the food gets cold and she gets old."

As Miss Lawson begins conversation with God in a voice only

dogs can hear, I'm close to Grandma, resting my chin on her shoulder while she is saying her own prayer, asking the Lord to protect Ma, who she calls by her nickname.

"God, take care of my Doll. See to it she makes it safe in the bosom of your arms in the name of Jesus your son. Father, you know she's my only daughter; I don't want to lose my Doll. Watch over, make her balance, bring her back to me whole, as only you can. Thank you for my grandchildren—thank you, Lord, for keeping them safe. They are my life, Savior, my heart."

Warm rushes into every corner of me. I'm smiling inside, bowed head, swallowing oceans of saliva, praying Grandma and the dogs alert Miss Gracie Lawson to stop praying. I'm ready for real soul food with people Grandma calls "salt of the earth." I love Grandma. I know she worries about us; I know we get on her nerves. I hate her sometimes, but I love her more.

Thank you, God, for bringing Grandma home. Please keep Ma safe as Grandma says, "as only you can."

CHAPTER SEVEN

Old Fart's ghetto ass landlord persistence paid off—we've been evicted out of our crappy apartment. Our stuff, what the fire did not destroy, was splayed all over the yard, and I was not surprised nothing was stolen. Neighbors told Ma that Mr. Cortez tried to neatly organize our stuff on the concrete, but Old Fart publicly reprimanded him, told him to just toss it out. Her beautiful floor-to-ceiling mirror cracked in a million pieces. He did most of the work getting rid of our stuff. We arrived as he spotted us approaching, then he jogged over to his car, leaned against it, arms folded, watching us, smiling full of sun-reflected metal teeth. Ma flipped him the bird several times, calling him an immigrant motherfucker. Ma, just like Grandma, is ignorant of people not like her.

I don't care what the fire left for me. I didn't have many valuables anyway. But Ma—her wigs were damaged, singed, smelling full of smoke, what was left of them. She starts cussing up a storm, rummaging through for a salvageable wig. Her chin drops to the ground, missile fire eyes aim at Old Fart. "See you in court. You gonna pay me for this." She shakes her treasured Beyoncé-blond wig at him. The curls in the wig are gone. The stringy fibers flimsy in the gentle wind.

He grunts, throws his hands at Ma while getting into his car. As he drives away, Ma aims sharply at his car, the wig lands perfectly on the driver's side, obstructing his view. Ma and Miss Tamara are over-the-top laughing, high-fiving each other. "That bitch ain't too upset. Sucka got insurance. He'll get a new apartment with new tenants to jack up the prices for that shit hole."

She enlisted her best friend since junior high, Miss Tamara, to help sort out what to bring, what to leave for the landlord to clean up. The right decision to leave Jamal with Grandma since he'd want to take everything, raise a fuss if Ma told him he can't take damaged, burnt-smelling toys with him. She'll get Penguin to replace Jamal's video games and sneakers.

Where are we going to live? I hope it's not like the last dump. It will probably be with Grandma until Ma finds us a place. We will have to quietly sneak in with our stuff, so the nosy neighbors don't catch us and report Grandma to the housing authority for having non-tenants in her home.

Old people are watchdogs. Whenever Jamal and I come for a visit, an alarm goes off, and every senior citizen is at their window watching and wondering. Ma will yell at them to close their windows, mind their business before a stick-up kid breaks in their apartment and takes their social security check.

Ma is balanced right now. She took her medication this morning and is quiet.

"Girl, why you got an attitude?" Miss Tamara is asking Ma but looking at me.

Ma looks at me, laughing despite the scowl on my face. "Beenie was born mad. She's her father's daughter—like my ex, Ruben, moody, always got a reason for an attitude. You must be getting your period soon. That's why you so moody."

I shoo her hand away, hate the way Ma makes me feel—invisible. I'm just a support check to her.

Ma's laughter dissolves into an adulting face. She leans close to me. "I'm not in the mood for your mood, not today with all the shit on me. Okay?"

My chance to blow her off; we take turns ignoring each other, payback. I stare hard at her. I don't give a shit about the situation she is responsible for. I don't give a shit about her and the mess she gets me and Jamal into with her foolishness. Everything is everybody's fault except her.

I walk over to the car. Ma follows me with a smile on her face, proposing a truce as I continue ignoring her.

We put the remaining few things in boxes ready for Miss Tamara's raggedy car. Ma places the last container neatly so I can sit in the back. "Beenie, I spoke to your father. You're going to Upstate."

I want to jump out of my skin, fist pump her in face, but stop at the thought of leaving my brother. "What about Jamal?"

"He needs to be near his school. The transition would upset him. He'll stay with me and Tamara."

"Educated girl, you got the books smarts." Miss Tamara has a wide gap-tooth smile, topaz eyes, and several jiggling chins when she talks or laughs. Rotund, often wearing age-inappropriate clothes, with a thirty-inch lace front wig, looking like a chubby mermaid. Ma teases her about it. They fight like sisters, but Miss Tamara takes care of Ma when she is unbalanced.

"We so proud of you, Beenie, you got good schooling, making the dean's list. You know, you smart like your Mama, take to education like a fish to water. Doll always had her nose in a book, got good grades while chasing dudes that don't love her back."

Ma laughs, telling Miss Tamara to shut up talking about her business. "You do adapt well wherever you go, Beenie. You're a smart girl."

Ma graduated with a BS in finance, magna cum laude, from City College. Grandma had high hopes for Ma. She'd be some financial wizard on Wall Street, but as the financial firms collapsed so did Ma. It was the start of her descent, and it was Uncle Marsh that got Grandma to accept something was wrong and to go to the professionals who diagnosed her. Uncle Marsh explained to her the reason for Ma's behavior that surfaced her sophomore year in college.

"Did you tell Jamal? He's gonna be upset."

She released a deep sigh at the thought of another annoying unfinished task. "Not yet. I'll have to treat him pizza and soda first before I tell him." Ma wistfully looks up at the warm skies for comfort. She tucks her hands in her armpits. "Your brother hates change."

"He hates change without me."

"Ruben says Jamal is welcome to visit on the weekends. The fresh air will be good for his asthma."

Ma touches my shoulder, squeezes it, then plants a kiss atop my head. "It's going to be tough for a while, but we'll get through this."

She is trying to convince herself using me. I forbid my face to give her what she wants right now: assurance, a smile to let her know she, I, will be fine, that she is making the right decision for my sake, not hers.

Her voice is pathetic, entreating me. "You love Upstate, Beenie: the burbs, the malls. The schools are really nice, not crowded, crazy like the city. Much better scenery. Dad got a really nice house, huge, with a big ass yard."

I refuse to ease her guilt.

I'm happy to get away from her. "Change is good" is all she gets from me.

She deserves nothing more.

CHAPTER EIGHT

Dad, athletic, loves just about every sport except hockey. He is very physical with a rock-hard, flat stomach and muscles that ripple through his shirt. There is nothing soft about him at all. He is real as any man. Grandma says he's a waste; she's so ignorant. There is no hint of sugar in his tank, not a sprinkle or a trace.

Marcus, his husband, is equally muscular, equally good-looking, and I suppose Grandma would consider him a waste, too, if she met him. Ma says Marcus looks like a Calvin Klein underwear model, the kind that's on a billboard in Times Square. He is a Hershey bar, rich, dark chocolate with a very sweet nature. An inch taller than Dad with a sculpted face, white teeth in his wide mouth, he resembles the bronze male statues Dad has in his office.

I gave my father away at their wedding last summer and was as proud to do it as my father and Marcus were proud to have me.

They sold their two-bedroom co-op on the Upper West Side, bought this house in Upstate. Dad picked Upstate because it's close to the city for work, near the airports, and it reminded him of small-town comfort with a twist—it welcomes people no matter how different they are. Upstate was listed as one of the best suburbs for the LGBT community. The annual Pride event draws people from the city and beyond. Diversity was a big decision in buying in Upstate. Dad said hopefully, soon, I will live here too.

The house is a renovated barn with exposed ceiling beams touching the sky. When I stand in certain parts of the house, I can hear my echo. It has three bedrooms, mine is the first one upstairs, facing the street, with window light—that's my favorite alarm clock. The oak tree near my window is so big it feels like a treehouse. My room is 180 degrees the opposite of the fire trap in the city, huge, with my very own bathroom. A palace beyond my dreams, brand new expensive-looking furniture, not that cheap, discount junk Ma furnished our apartment with; it never lasts long because of the quality.

The backyard is a blanket of endless green to nowhere; my eyes cannot see beyond it. Marcus wants to install a pool, but Dad does not want the bother of it. He travels a lot for his job as a marketing manager for a pharmaceutical company.

The house is a decorator's dream, and Marcus makes it the bomb, 'cause he got mad décor skills. He did my bedroom, and I love it. He's a nurse during the day and a lit decorator after five.

Immediately in love with him the moment I met him, I saw how my dad fell for him, too, during my weekend custody visit in the city. He makes me laugh with his over-the-top drama, constant hugs that everything will be all right. I can allow myself to feel safe with him and Dad, that all the difficult things are behind me, but something inside me refuses to get comfortable. I cannot feel too safe.

Dad's eyes light up whenever Marcus comes into view. He instinctively wraps his arms around him, kissing him until Marcus playfully reprimands him. This is how people in love should act, not fighting all the time, cussing at each other; I want to be in love like Dad and Marcus. Ma does not know how to love. I don't think Grandma does either.

They met when Dad came to the emergency room for a basketball injury. Marcus gave instructions for ankle care; Dad gave him his number. I take every chance teasing him for his lame baller moves, but he shoots back, "It worked," winking at Marcus. He's responsible for putting a smile on my father's face I have not seen in a long, long time. Ma says he smiled when I was born, then stopped.

Ma and Dad loved each other since middle school. They fought, broke up, got back together, fought some more, got married, fought again, I came along, they fought some more, then Ma finally left him. They stayed together long enough to see me off for my first day in kindergarten. I was scared to death of leaving my nest of comfort and security. Dad knelt before me, holding my hands in his one big hand, assuring me he would be waiting outside when class was over. True to his word, when the bell rang, I ran out of the classroom like a person escaping an inferno, and there he was. Dad has never let me down.

Ma says he loved Marcus first. I think she meant Dad loved other men since Marcus is originally from Texas. She shrugged it off and moved on to the next boyfriend. Ma is a shark. She just keeps it moving, to where, she don't even know. My parents fell in love again once they got divorced. Dad is tough on Ma, but it is out of love for her well-being, wanting only the best for her.

I'm worried sick about Jamal. Dad repeated what Ma said: I will get to see him every weekend as much as possible. Ma always says definitely, but she don't keep her promises. Dad is more cautious. He weighs all options to be sure he can keep a promise. Dad repeats what his father, my grandfather, used to say: "If your word's no good, then you're no good."

Dad and Uncle Marsh are really cool. They live in the same county, often shoot hoops at the gym. I'm happy I'll get to see Uncle Marsh more since moving to Upstate; his wife, Aunt Nelle, not so much.

Grandma and Aunt Nelle are religious snobs to my dad. Grandma told me she loves Dad but hates the sin, using her bible as a reference to disapprove of his life. Ma says Grandma sinning, too, 'cause she eats shrimp, lobster, and pig's feet, and the Old Testament forbids you to eat scavengers. Grandma loves her ribs, scallops, and gossip—all sins according to the bible.

Even when my parents were together, Dad did not like Aunt Nelle and tolerated Grandma, citing her age, respecting elders, and her ignorance. They would only say "hello," nothing much else, both wishing there was someone to fill in the silence between them. That was where I came in, and Aunt Nelle, more than my dad, was grateful for it.

He said she's emotionally neutered and Grandma is a fake Christian. I overheard him mumble to Marcus, "The bigger the bible, the bigger the hypocrite," a reference to Grandma after he was told what she allegedly said about his marriage to Marcus. The source of gossip sounded like Ma. I'm sure of it. I don't have proof, but I know Ma. She's the type to detonate a bomb, run away, then come back to the scene of the crime, asking what happened, all innocent looking but laughing inside.

Marcus tells me not to worry about using a coaster. I am to make myself at home, but I am careful.

I am happy to be here.

This is what a home should be.

But this is not my home.

Home is not with my grandma, Ma, not even my father.

Home is where my little brother is. Jamal needs me, and I must go where he is to protect him, and right now that is with Ma.

CHAPTER NINE

I've unpacked my things since moving to Upstate. We have dinner at six thirty, sometimes seven if Marcus works a twelve-hour shift at the hospital. Dad and Marcus take turns cooking dinner, though Dad rarely cooks, actually, he sucks at it, and Marcus usually takes over. Dad's idea of cooking is dining out or take out. Ma ain't never been much of a cook either, and if it wasn't for the fast foods, Mr. Chow's, Jamal and I would have starved to death. It was obvious Ma never paid attention 'cause she don't have the lit cooking skills Grandma and Marcus have. They are the culinary bombs.

I follow Marcus in the kitchen like his shadow, bumping into him, getting in his way, watching him make *Epicurious* magic. Finally, he caught on and made me his de facto assistant. Hand him this, hand him that, go to pantry or fridge for this and that. He cannot cook without his music blaring, pots and pans in sync with sauté Patti LaBelle, deep fry Mariah Carey, Janet Jackson, SWV, Snoop Dogg, Backstreet Boys, low on simmer John Coltrane, Billie Holiday, sizzling with Earth, Wind, and Fire and gospel music.

Marcus loves Jesus just as much as Grandma.

He got me to taste foods I never would have tried: grilled

octopus with couscous for starters. It was good. I told him if the food does not look at me, I will try whatever he prepares. He'd make shoe leather taste good.

I cannot sleep. My first day of my new school starts tomorrow. Dad Facetimes to say he is catching the red eye to make it home in time to drive me. My face betrays I am no longer the scared little girl. "I'm not in kindergarten anymore."

Beenie you cannot deny your old, handsome Dad the pleasure taking his little, now teen angel, to school.

I'm nervous and excited. Marcus says the schools in Upstate are like private schools in the city; you pay eight arms, ten legs, and your firstborn with school taxes.

A warm home, a full belly, happily guilty, grateful to Dad and Marcus, my parents in Upstate.

I join Marcus in the office, standing beside him with my arm around him as he budgets the monthly finances. He feels like a safe blanket, a faint smell of his expensive cologne wafting, tickling my nostrils.

"Your father is teaching me to manage money better," he confesses.

"No more shopping?" He is squinting despite wearing prescription glasses. Ma does that too, like they are embarrassed their eyes need help—or getting old.

"We, I, really, have to manage our expenses for this big old house I got your father to agree to buy," Marcus sighs overdramatic with a free arm against his forehead. "I mean he was as tired of the city as much as I was.

"It's nice to have space, to breathe air over city exhaust. I'm finally getting use to the birds waking me up. I'm loving having nature as an alarm clock over sirens."

"The city is nice, but it's nicer here."

The house is lit; I feel comfortable and safe with Dad and Marcus, having a home with no landlord banging on the door for rent; home-cook meals with real food not from a grease-soaked container, out of a box or dented can with a past-expiration date from the bodegas.

It's so nice taking a bath with hot water, no worry of a roach scattering across the room, or worse, on your face. Sitting by the window in the dark, seeing the moon, and listening for crickets that talk only at night.

Is it a dream? I don't want to wake up. I tug Marcus gently around his neck for assurance it is real. I don't talk as his brows create lines across his forehead, attacking the calculator like an enemy, looking at the excel spreadsheet as though it's written in a foreign language he does not understand. I go over to the ledge and stand sentry behind the curtain.

The office is on the ground floor, facing the street, with a large window that welcomes the morning light and at night allows in the beam of a single lamp that nestles between houses and the street.

I stare into the night, street-scanning about, looking at nothing. Suddenly, my eyes zero in on a small form dragging something seeming three times its size. "Do you have coyotes?"

Marcus replies with a faint mumble. "We have foxes, possums, raccoons, and deer," he says without much thought, then stops. "I saw a fox once, beautiful orange-red, nearly scared me to death." He laughs. "He was scared to see me too."

"What is that?" I point at form opposite the house across from us. "I don't think animals walk like that."

Marcus removes his reading glasses and half-stands over the computer, squinting. "I thought they only had boys. What is that little girl doing outside at night without a sweater?"

I refocus again at the form revealing itself to be a small girl wearing flip-flops, a thin gown, and nothing else. She positions the recycle bin, then sprints back to an open door.

"You may have a new friend."

"I'm too old for her."

Marcus puckers his lips, responding to my eye rolls. "She might need a friend. I'll make an introduction just for you."

"You so nosy."

"Hey, girl, my hood, my business. Good night, Beenie."

"You going to bed?"

"No, you are." He logs off the computer, planting a kiss on my forehead. "You might be a blessing to that little girl."

CHAPTER TEN

I finally relented, let Dad take me to school, though it is only a ten-minute walk from home—I'm slowly getting use to the two words, *my home.* The warm morning weather gave me permission to wear a light jacket, so even if I got lost and wandered about Upstate trying to find my new school, I wouldn't have a problem.

Dad looks over at me every chance with no expression on his face. He is a black computer screen, a blinking light waiting for information input to react; a blank canvas waiting for a hand to draw him, put color on, to draw out a reaction, a response that is cognizant, that there is a pulse. Have I said he is hard to read? How do you love someone you cannot see?

Quiet during the drive to school, he struggles to hide his side glances. His eyes flutter away a thought refusing to leave his head as his hands grip the steering wheel. He is fighting something that I cannot see. I never know whether he's sad or worried, but when he is happy, he will smile a half smile, as if a full smile will disappoint him back into not smiling at all.

We sit, parked in front of the main entrance of school in a new

Mercedes he purchased since moving to Upstate, happy to be driving instead of waiting for a taxi that often bypassed his color in the city. It had gotten better since Uber, but my dad is a control freak, Ma always on that about him. Always.

"Upstate is a great place to live—what do you think, Beenie?"

"I like it so far—I'll tell you more after school."

Dad seems satisfied with my answer, but he is thinking of another question to fill the silence between us. "Nervous?" he finally says.

"No more nervous than you."

"You got a new challenge ahead of you."

"You sound like Marcus. Isn't life a challenge?"

Dad lets go of a small laugh, not really a laugh but some form of communication to take up the space in the car.

"I'll be okay, Dad. I make friends easily."

Now his smile is a full one. He seems comforted. He places his hand over mine and gently squeezes. "You are a remarkable young lady, you know that. You take care of everybody for such a young age. I know you'll be fine."

"What are you worried about?"

Dad lets out a sigh that fogs up the window. "You got lunch money?"

I nod, showing him the lunch Marcus packed for me. "Off to work?"

"Yeah." He forces a smile again, this time for his sake as well as mine.

I tell him again I will be ok and not to worry; but I think Dad is worried about something specific, and it is not about me and my new school. This time I place my hand over his, squeezing. "It's gonna be okay."

There is a dim light of hope in his warm brown eyes. "I hope so."

My new school is a complex of several buildings connected to one central unit that has four floors. It feels like a mini city, a college campus instead of a school—massive. I can hear my voice echoing and the sounds of students bouncing against the walls. The ceiling reaches to the sky. I'm packed against people of many colors, but the one constant, dominant, is white. It is a majority student body of more whites than black, brown, or yellow students. We are sprinkled about sporadically in the mix like a little pepper on mashed potatoes, just a little, but not too much, and for sure don't go overboard or it's ruined. Back in the city, it was a mixture of brown kids; we were mostly blacks and Latinos and a few sparse low-income white kids, sprinkled with Asians.

So, this is all strange to me. I feel like an alien dropped off on a strange planet where I must fend for myself. I'm curious, excited about the unknown waiting for me, but cautious of a new environment I have never experienced and outside of my comfort zone.

And living in Upstate is the same. The population is large for a village near the city, but for one face of color, there are ten faces of white. I'm not scared at the sight of so many white people in one place, one town, but it feels unnatural to me. People are friendly, will say hello to a stranger like me when Marcus and I go into town. He seems receptive to the change, embracing the kindness of a stranger, but I am hesitant. I don't trust someone I don't know being nice to me on the street.

"It was weird at first for me too, Beenie," Marcus said earlier while preparing my lunch, "but you'll get used to it. Enjoy the warmth of a town like Upstate instead of the cold city. Look at the shops we walked by with rainbow flags; you feel like you belong here."

"With white people?"

Marcus laughed. "Well, a lot of them are here, but we're here too. But it's LGBTQ-friendly. No one is trying to scam you, or take advantage, or have a hidden agenda, just plain folks greeting one another in town regardless of color, gay, straight, whatever."

"That would never happen in the city, not in my hood."

"Thank God we don't live in the city anymore. The pace here is better for the quality of life, you'll see."

The students at my school move slowly, like herds of cattle. The new kids like me are as invisible as a bull's eye, confused, and looking at a schedule on our iPhone or paper in hand in search of our first class before the bell rings.

My first class is my number one favorite after art—French. I am advanced; I can read and write fluently—no Google translate for me. At my school in the city, I was allowed to tutor classmates and lower classes with ESL and composition. I'd sometimes show off, throwing French at them like a hand grenade when I was feeling myself, mainly as payback to the snotty girls who were dumb but had money and nice clothes when I had none. Ma spent very little support money on clothes for me.

Dad announced last night after dessert that we are going to the south of France for the summer. As much as I will miss Jamal, I am super excited by the thought of seeing my favorite country using my favorite language. I wished I was back at my old school in the city for a day to rub that in those mean girls' faces. I wish they could see where I live now: in a big house with a big room in nice neighborhood with a nice school.

My books at home are in English and French. Dad and Marcus always gave me books to read in both languages, and I read them over and over until I had them memorized.

At my new school, Mr. Borden is my French teacher. He is a small man with milky skin and a face full of chocolate stubbles in need a razor or at least a trim. He looks like an Oreo cookie. When he smiles, I can see his protruding teeth, visible from where I stand. He instructs me to come closer, in full view of the classroom, to make my introduction in French. Mr. Borden is a bit wordy; he uses a million words when only five are needed. I am pumped to show off my bomb Francophile skills. I introduce myself, killing it. I went overboard to the point of showing off by the looks of some of the students. I don't care.

I tell myself another rule of mine: I will not be associated with any group that disses people who are different; designer girls, the sport stars, artsy kids, and ones outside ignoring the smoke-free zones. Dad says we're all the same inside, and the outside is what makes us unique human beings. "Imagine how boring the world would be if we were all the same, Beenie," Dad told me.

I will not be defined by any group. Whoever is nice to me first, I will be nice in return. Period.

On my first day in class, there is very little, if any, English spoken unless a student is stuck thinking too long for the answer. Mainly the entire period is French only, and I seem to be the only one reveling in it. Every chance I am allowed to, I get to show off my advanced French to the amazement of my classmates, some impressed, some hating by the roll of eyes, some fake yawning for show, or some checking for the time and hoping for the bell to release them. In French, I tell them my name, where I am from— New York City. I leave out the specifics. I delete shit they don't need to know about me. I don't say my address. I leave out that I am from a slumlord home. They will be able to Google it and know I'm from a shithole, things about my mother and family life, and the reason I am new to this school and Upstate. Some students appear impressed that I am a city girl.

Mr. Borden smiles, then clears his throat to take over. He is obviously impressed with my skills as he looks at me and then at the students, hinting they need to up their French game to match this city girl. He nods and directs me to an empty seat in the classroom.

All eyes are on me as I navigate to the seat assigned. I managed to sneak a glance at the only black girl in my class, who is surrounded by four white girls, one in particular who seems to be the leader. It surprises me the black girl is not. She looks like she is mixed as her skin is several shades lighter than mine, which is the color of coffee, as Ma says. I take one solid stare at her; her eyes are celery green, and her hair is frizzy brown in color—either she is Hispanic or biracial.

As I plant my butt on the chair, I hear a voice slapping me in the back of the head.

"Oh, Monsieur Borden is so wrong. He's seating the new girl in front of a skunk. The foul smell is behind you, sis."

As I half turn, following the voice, it is obvious the white girl, who I learn is named Amber Mills, is the leader of the four, snarling like a dog with rabies. The surrounding girls are laughing as if a game show host is holding a cue card for them to do so, fake laughing. I stare at her, not expecting her to be nice, as her fake smiles greets me. She rolls her eyes and yawns. She then says to the black girl, clowning in hood slang, "Gwynne, here be one of yo' peeps. We need this school to be basic black."

Gwynne does not respond to the diss about the way some black people from the hood talk. I immediately dislike Amber and Gwynne even more; has she turned so white from living here? She should have checked Amber but did nothing, just focused on her phone, texting like she a boss.

I will be black wherever I go, especially in Upstate. I will not allow myself to turn white from this school, this town, where I can't stand up for my people.

Her minions, Molly Simpson, Sophie Roberts, Lauren Green, and Gwynne Sanders, cue laugh again and commence to texting when Mr. Borden has his back turned. We were told in the beginning no cells in the class, and it is obvious Amber and her gang don't think the rule is for them. Maybe their French is shit.

"Ignore that stupid bitch." A whisperer taps me on my shoulder. "She wanna be black, always tries to act black, fucking culture vulture, wanna be fake ass. She's a hater."

When I turn, she is smiling, a real one. I did not notice her when I came into the classroom. Seated, I can see she is a tall glass of orange juice, orange skin, orange hair, and if I look harder, orange eyes. She talks so fast I have to tell her to slow down. "You got mad French skills," she says.

"Thanks."

"Soyez silencieux!"

"You from New York City? I would love to live there, like Serena, Blair, Gossip Girl living. That's my show when I can watch it. I wanna live like that someday, big ass dope New York apartment with a huge closet to hold my clothes, designer of course! I'ma be banging, rocking my Chanel, Balenciaga, Air Force Ones. I love me some of those threads and shit."

"You into designer crap stuff?"

She checks for Mr. Borden and then, "Not really, but it's all about strutting for the 'gram, Tik Tok building my brand, you gotta fake it to make it, ya know? I'ma be a blogger with a makeup line like Kiley, Rihanna, have a reality show and shit. I'ma be a boss."

"Silencieux!"

"You be quiet!" orange girl barks back at the faceless teacher.

Mr. Borden stops, swings around, not smiling, his eyes scanning for the offender. We are stock still, arms folded, looking straight ahead to throw him off our scent.

Amber and her group also take notice of him, quickly concealing their phones, looking at Mr. Borden with sugar-coated smiles bound to give him a toothache.

When we start talking again, we are shushed by a nerdy boy with an outdated Caesar haircut sitting across from us. Orange girl snarls as she flips him the bird. "Won't you talk shit to Amber, tell her to shut up?" she growls at him.

The nerd glances over at Amber talking to her crew while looking at their phones as if Mr. Borden was not there, not important, then turns back with his massive block head down, catching his glasses before they slide off his nose.

"I thought so. Pussy!"

Mr. Borden whips around scanning the culprits for talking in class. He gives everyone in the room a once over again, waits, then returns to the chalk board. "Last warning," he says.

The orange girl's eyes sparkle as she seems unable to stop smiling at me, happy someone is talking to her as if she has been isolated from humans for decades. "I'm Tiki. My real name is Tashauna. Don't ask why my mother gave that name. It sounds like a hood name, like I'm black."

"You don't like it 'cause it sounds black?" Unsmiling, I'm ready to send her back to isolation but check her first.

Tiki leans back, blinking rapidly at me as if I cursed her grandmother to her face. Her eyes go two sizes too big. "No, no. It's a boss name."

I keep her in suspense, staring at her, watching as she blinks rapidly, biting her lower lip. "It's not too bad a name. You from around here?"

Tiki's chest rises, and she exhales slowly, smiling again. She sucks her teeth. "I fucking hate this school. People here so fake. If you don't have no money, no status, you're nothing. They don't even wanna get to know you. Some of them don't even have money, they put on a front, you know."

"They flexing."

"Yeah, they ain't shit," Tiki whispers loud enough to catch Amber's attention, who flips her the finger as she holds her nose.

"That's foul," I whisper, mindful of the eyes in the back of Mr. Borden's head.

"If you're good at sports or live in the right hood, you get a pass, but—" She nods over to the girls in the back. "I don't even know why they in this class. Most of them don't care anyway. When Mr.

Borden asks them a question, they Google translate the answer. They cheat big time. Stupid bitches."

"Why are you in this class?" I ask.

"I read if you speak another language, your brain gets exercised, and you won't get Alzheimer."

The weight of my narrow, twisting face prompts her to explain further. Tiki checks Mr. Borden has his back turned.

"It's a forgetful disease, like your brain turns into mush and you go back to being a baby. You can't care for yourself; you can't do shit. My grandma—she's in a nursing home, she waiting to die. I don't know what I'll do if that happens.

"My grandma, the best person in the whole world, got it. She don't even know my name half the time, but there are moments when she does—man, I'm so happy she remember me, she knows my name. We can talk, but it ain't much of a conversation, ya know? I'm hoping she'll be okay, but I know she won't. It don't get better, just worse.

"I lived with her 'til I was eight, that's when it started. After that, it was down fucking hill. My family don't care. Ain't right to lose the person who care about you the most. It makes me so mad the way them asshole nurses, those shitty aides treat her. So fucked up, ain't it?"

"So sorry about your grandma," I say quietly. Mr. Borden is looking at me. I offer up a smile and answer his question in French. That satisfies him.

Tiki smiles at him for added coverage. "I wanna buy a big house with a garden. She loved gardening. Hire some decent people who will take care of her. Treat her nice, care about her as much as I love her. Maybe you can help me?"

"With your grandma?"

"No, dumbass, my French," she laughs.

I smile at her bright face, the first person to be nice to me, and say: "Bien sur, je vais vous aider, mais vous devez être dispose à apprendre."

She leans so close to me that I can smell her cherry flavor bubblegum breath as her orange face twists. She says, "Wait, I missed a few words."

I giggle at the confusion on her bright face, wondering how she got into this class, then whisper in our native tongue quickly before Mr. Borden turns to face the class.

"Okay, dumbass, I will help you, but you must be willing to learn."

CHAPTER ELEVEN

The lit moon pierces my window, entreating me to wake up though it is not yet daybreak. I have not gotten used to the quiet of the night in Upstate. My hearing attunes to every sound, the ruffling branches, the rattle of trash critters dining on the neighbor's unsecured garbage cans or recycle bins. From my window, I watch intently as a raccoon and his friends are licking half-filled yogurt and orange juice cartons, one dining a considerable distance from his friends on French bread. His friends spot him, attempt to steal his bread, a fight ensues, with the bigger, the bully, snatching the bread and running off into the woods a few steps away. The suburban critters eat better than city inhabitants, including the humans.

Unable to leave my window, I'm searching for nothing, staring at the night when she comes into view, shuffling, wearing ill-fitted neon-yellow crocs and a sweater two sizes too big. The sweater weighs more than her, more than the bins she is helping the old-looking woman with. Why would a mother dress her kid in raggedy clothes and shoes that don't fit? Maybe she spends money on herself like Ma instead of her child.

The girl is paralyzed, frightened by the furry diners in front of the house next to hers. The woman, impatient, waves the girl forward, pushing her to follow as the woman attempts to shoo away the racoons.

The bully returns. I'm stunned a loaf of French bread can be gone that quick. Bully stands on his hind legs, fur raised, masked eyes enlarged, challenging the woman to approach. He is a badass raccoon, but then, perhaps in afterthought, he backs down and scatters off with the rest of the friends. He may be too full from tonight's meal to fight the challenger, or maybe he's patient and hopeful a careless homeowner will leave a garbage can unsecured for tomorrow's dining.

The woman goes over to the neighbor's side, snatches the lids off the ground as though they were in some imaginary hand, slams them harder than needed to make them secure. She seems annoyed at the neighbor's carelessness.

Her body stands erect before the offending house of her neighbor as if she is waiting for them to come outside for a tongue-lashing. The lights inside the house are off. Only the light to the entrance door shines bright. She does not move for a few seconds. I thought I saw inferno lasers aim at the house. She was for certain going to set the house on fire with just one look.

She kicks the neighbor's recycle bins closer to the mailbox and stacks it with the paper bin the raccoons did not bother to touch.

All the while, the girl stands frozen, arms wrapped around her little body, which does nothing to protect her against the night air. She has nothing to keep her warm unlike the woman, who is wearing a fleece robe and thick slippers. The girl is shivering, moving left to right, attempting to warm herself, waiting for the woman so they can go back inside together. As the woman makes her way to the girl, her erected arm points back to the house like a general in charge of a firing squad. Maybe she is the wicked stepmother.

Boredom, or insomnia, forces me to want more of the show-down between the woman and her neighbor, or with Bully the raccoon, and so I wait, wanting to watch more, but it was over as soon as they entered the home and shut the lights off. I can see the beaming eyes of the raccoons as they slowly make their way back to the dining area. Bully returns, leading his posse, mouth secured around the remaining French bread. He sniffs around the woman's garbage can and somehow, with the dexterity only a raccoon has, lifts the lid off the can. By the size of his girth, Bully is well-fed and knows how to play against homeowners. He invites his friends to join him and successfully knocks the woman's can to the ground to free the grubs, and, feeling generous, feeds his friends too.

I wait, curious to see if the noise from the garbage cans would wake the woman up and make her come charging outside. Nothing after five, ten, fifteen minutes.

She thought she was smarter than Bully. She thought Bully was as fearful of her as the little girl. She underestimated the tenacity of a hungry raccoon and was outsmarted by one.

Scoreboard: old woman, zero; Bully the raccoon, one.

CHAPTER TWELVE

Tiki and I do everything together, have lunch, hang out between classes, go to the mall. She clings to me as if she is the new student, not me; I'm the veteran schooling her. She gets on my nerves; sometimes I have to tell her to shut up, but I'll say it in French under the guise of tutoring her. She talks too much, jackrabbit talk, like Grandma says when a person talks so much, they can't stop or listen. She thinks I'm joking, but I'm not.

Her doctor gave her drugs for hypers, anxiety, but she refuses to take it. "It makes me dopey, Rubena."

"You already dopey."

Her standard response when she does not have a rebuttal is the middle finger.

Tiki sometimes has very little lunch or money to buy it, and I don't mind sharing my meals with her. Marcus, Dad, give me more money than I need, so I don't have a problem buying her lunch.

I've been in her shoes; I know how she feels.

I got very little money from Ma when I lived with her. It was embarrassing getting subsidized meals at school because she needed a new wig, her cell services reinstated, an outfit for Instagram or some random dude she picked up on Tinder. I feel good that I can help someone who is struggling like I was when I was knee deep with Ma and her bullshit; she ought to thank me for not snitching to Dad about what she did with *my* support money meant for me.

Tiki don't get a better meal at home than in school either. In class, her stomach growling so loud, I can't help wondering if everyone, including Mr. Borden, hears it. Her face turns ten shades of orange-red, and she looks around the room, seeing whose stomach is making that noise. I hope I'm the only one that can hear it. Amber and her friends would ride her to the end about it, add more lies to the mix about Tiki being broke, posting shit about her on social media.

I treat her like my child, and she does not seem bothered but embraces it instead. Tiki has several advanced classes, but her dyslexia is a challenge. She's really smart despite her learning disability. I tell her how proud I am of her. In spite of it, she has succeeded; I am patient, but sometimes she is annoying.

Her large eyes cannot absorb my home, amazed three people live in a house like ours. I wonder if she's more amazed *black people* live in a nice house like this. I give her a viewing since she cannot ask but throws grenade-hints at me.

"Your house is awesome." She is turning around slowly, then again, to be sure of where she is. "I wish I had my own room."

"Where do you sleep?" I hand her a napkin with two large cookies, which she takes, both of them; one in her mouth, the other in her hand.

"Anywhere I can—mainly on my sister's couch—way better than my bed at home."

"What do you mean?"

Marcus is off today. He is the perfect host and gives us hot chocolate and his famous from-scratch chocolate chip cookies. Tiki's cheeks are full of cookies like a chipmunk gathering for winter. She slurps hot chocolate loudly and says to Marcus, "Are you a model?"

He half turns his head like a blushing bride, smiling so hard, gassed up from Tiki's compliments. He pours her a second cup of hot chocolate without asking, puts another tray of cookies in the oven, sets the timer for us to take them out when done. He leaves us in the kitchen to study. Tiki's eyes follow Marcus out of the kitchen. "You got two Dads; I wish I had one."

"Where's your dad?"

"Somewhere, out there." She stuffs the large cookie, meant for me, into her mouth. "Can I take some home?"

I raised my hand at her not to talk with her mouth full until she finishes chewing. Tiki takes several gulps and excuses herself for belching. "Can I tell you some secrets? No one outta of the kitchen, outta your house, between you and me, must know, or I'm fucked. Okay?"

Tiki's real home is the trailer park four towns away from Upstate. She lives in constant fear of discovery by the school board. Her sister Sasha, who is ten years older, lives in the only state low-income housing in Upstate. Sasha's address allowed Tiki to attend our school. She stressed someone will report her to the authorities, who will fine her sister money she don't have, forcing her back to her school district, the thought of which horrifies her. The school district where she lives, officially, tested poorly with the state and receives little or no funding from taxpayers. It makes the news often with alleged school board official corruption. There are more black and Latino kids there, who beat her up, tease her about her orange skin. But she is teased, picked on at our school, too, and treated like shit, branded Stinky Tiki, Trailer Park Tiki.

"Upstate has one of the best academia programs in the state. Graduating from this school will give me an edge over the competition, which, you know, is brutal. It will give me a heads up when I apply to colleges." She releases another grateful chocolate burp. "I know I can get a scholarship; I got the grades, just got to improve my French game, which you're gonna help me with, ya know."

Her smile reveals particles of Marcus's cookies. "Despite the drama I gotta deal with, I'll have a better chance for a good future. Yeah, I gotta put up with shit at school with bitch Amber and her fake ass friends, shit at home with my sister, *and my mother*. It's still better here than there. It doesn't stop at school. Weekdays, I live with Sasha; we got the same mother but different fathers. She's lucky, she knows her loser dad is at the nearest dive—he may be a loser, but he loves her.

"Her apartment is a closet with me, the baby, and her jerk-off boyfriend Matt. The rent's kind of cheap, but Sasha is having a hard time paying it. We're always months behind in rent, lucky it's the projects; they don't throw you out like private housing.

"I'm a burden to her; she has no problem throwing bomb hints at me on how hard it is, like why can't I help pay for food, or why can't I get a job to help. Jesus, I'm fucking fourteen, the earliest I can get a job is fifteen.

"I wish I could get a job, the first thing I'd do is move away from her and her constant bitching that I don't contribute," Tiki sucks her breath. "I got matches to light the candles when the electricity was cut off. While she's working, I watched the baby in the dark while asshole Matt was off somewhere getting high. Rubena, he don't help at all, not even to watch his own fucking kid." Tiki bugs her eyes and slaps her thigh. "And she's complaining about *me!*"

Tiki says when Fridays are close by, Sasha's mood improves, smiling more, being nicer to her, not complaining as much. She says sweetly that she has had enough of her and needs a much-deserved break, kicks her out to stay with her mother Lorna.

"They got a mutt, it's Matt's; he's more welcome to live with Sasha than me." The irony of it burst Tiki into tears, evolving into laugher, holding her side so she won't pee on herself. On weekends, she stays with her drunken mother and creepy boyfriend, who has a habit of walking in the bathroom while Tiki is using it.

"He tells me to wait a second, whips his thing out, peeing on the toilet seat—so gross. The first thing I do when I get there is check the locks on my bedroom door and the windows. I have a butter knife with me that I keep under my bed, sleep with my arm under the pillow, holding that knife like a life jacket. Somehow, the bathroom does not lock anymore.

"You asked why I smell so bad on Mondays. I can brush my teeth in the kitchen, but that's it. Taking a bath is not an option for me," she says, twirling her orange greasy hair. "You don't know how bad it is. Speed is mad creepy. Mommy won't do anything. She's too drunk to help me. He's worse when he's on meth—he just stares at me. I'm too scared to even pee there. Oh, thanks for letting me take a bath at your house."

When Marcus and Dad are at work, I sneak her in to clean up before school.

Tiki shrugs, resigned, as I hand her foil to wrap cookies for home. "I'll be free as soon I get the hell away from my family."

A couple days later, it is the start of the weekend, and Tiki is quiet. She folds her arms, unfolds them, sighs loud enough to tickle the leaves high up in the tree. She looks far away, as if a dream has abandoned her, then suddenly looks at her phone, which has been disconnected for nonpayment. Sasha made sure her own phone bill was paid, promising Tiki the next paycheck will go toward her bill. The frame is cracked, yet she caresses it as a lifeline to escape. I wanted her to spend the night with me, but I'm going to the city to Grandma's.

"You gotta hang on, it's gonna get better." My attempt to cheer her up fails. Tiki responds with a large sigh, rolling her eyes at me like I said something dumb. I try again. "Votre français s'ameliore."

She forces an appeasing smile. "My French is improving?"

"You understood me."

Tiki straightens up, surprised, pauses for a second. Her eyes light up in a mind-blown moment as she's suddenly filled with hope. "I understood you. Merci, Mademoiselle."

"De rien, mon cheri." I'm testing her.

"You're welcome, dear!" She jumps up, high fives me, believes she is teachable for French. "Rubena, you the bomb, sis!"

"Now I want you to practice over the weekend, just imagine yourself somewhere lit, a beautiful place with no stress or drama—"

"That would be with Satan in hell right now."

"Come on, other than at your mom's. Talk to yourself in French, think of all the things that's gonna happen when you're free—in French, okay?"

Tiki side-eyes me, a slight smile appears this time, wide, unending. "You know you're so wack, right?"

"No more than you are, dumbass."

"I'll be saying all bad things in French like pervert, asshole, shit head..."

"Pervertir. Cunnard. And don't cheat using Google translate."

"I won't." She inhales and exhales hope. "When I turn sixteen, I am going to escape. I won't have to imagine anymore. I won't have to deal with it anymore."

Our laughter dissipates into painful silence. "It's messed up Sasha won't let you live with her more than during the week."

She shakes her head violently. "I told you she says she has me all week. She wants the weekends for herself, Matt, and Madison. Of course, it's bull crap."

"Can't you tell her about Speed?"

Tiki looks at me horrified as if I cursed in front of the Pope. "Do you know what she would do? Call Child Protective services. They'd throw my ass in foster care. That would solve her problem, having me gone without feeling guilty. One less mouth to feed, which ain't much anyhow. It'll be too easy for her and worse for me. I'd rather jump off a cliff than go into foster care. That's what would happen cause the neighbors know Lorna ain't shit, an unfit mother, and Speed's a pervert. She would get rid of me before Speed, trust and believe."

"How Sasha home on the weekends? What break? Your sister's working all the time. You're useful to her for babysitting only, and you don't even get paid, that's a job. Matt's sorry ass won't watch his own kid. He only in the house to get high. That's a violation in public housing. Your sister could get evicted on that alone."

"Really? How do you know?"

I catch my words before they can escape and reveal my life in subsidized housing. "I just know. No shade, Tiki, but your sister is so foul."

"My whole family sucks. I wish I could move in with you," Tiki says wistfully.

"I wish had a big house where all my friends could live with me, not that I have many friends—only you and Jamal. No adults are allowed."

Tiki jumps up, arms expanding. "Like those houses on Cribs, the infinity pool, big ass yard, kitchens the size of a small house. Man, my fridge would be overflowing with pizza, Marcus's chocolate chip cookies, and Coke." Her orange eyes light up. "You know who would be my neighbor besides you? Taylor Swift, Olivia Rodrigo, Kylie Jenner, BTS, every KPOP band. We all be friends, sipping nonalcoholic martini and dancing."

We begin to play our favorite game between us—one up. It happens when we're at an impasse at a resolution to Tiki's problems, mine too. We feed off each other like kindling for a fire. We know a better life is waiting, a life without irresponsible adults suffocating us. Wanting, but we need to find the road to get there. Adults in our lives do not know the path either.

"And no men in the house," Tiki says evenly.

"Only my brother Jamal," I insist.

"God, a house with no men." Her smile stretches beyond her

face, on fire, at the idea of a male-free home. "I'll be able to breathe, not stress. I can pee in peace, take a bath with no drama. I won't smell anymore. When I grow up, I ain't having no men in my house."

"Not even a boyfriend?" I asked.

"No men!"

CHAPTER THIRTEEN

The hood is the same way I left it; indecipherable graffiti, plexiglass entrance door cracked in several places, sneakers twisted high up the utility pole, overfilled litter baskets, bottles, wrappers, another garbage pyramid piling up, no sight of rats, thank God. Bully the racoon would have a field day dining on it but would be too fearful of the more aggressive city dwellers, rodents and people, to venture out.

My senses take a moment to adjust to the buzz of the city. Honestly, I don't mind it, but I much prefer the quiet of Upstate.

The closer I get to Grandma's, the less dirty, less ghetto-like it becomes, much more pleasant, less garbage, less building tags, less offense to my senses but still noise.

Jamal leaps over three steps, running to me with his thin arms outstretched, runny nose, screaming so loud the dead can hear him. His attempts to neck hug me fail as he still cannot reach my shoulders yet. He holds me, yelling, hollering why I left him for all the neighbors in the projects to hear. He punches my arm as hard as a seven-year-old can. "Why you leave me?" he inquires for the fifth time.

I lock my arms around him, so he'll calm down, hold him each time he tries to loosen my grip, then plant a kiss on his newly shaven head. "I had to. You needed to be near your school in the city. Where's Ma?"

"You got any candy?" He stops smiling when I tell him no. "You got some money?" He is tearing at my pockets as if I'm lying to him.

"Where's Ma?"

He looks around at the neighbors, some with walkers, aided by their home care workers, others with canes, a few alone without walking assistance, all outside on a sunny day perfect for warming arthritic joints and watching us. Jamal yanks at my T-shirt to lean down so he can whisper, mindful of people nearby with their hearing aids turned to the highest volume. "We live with Grandma. Miss Tamara kicked us out."

"Why?"

"You got any money? Take me to the store, I tell you."

As we exit the bodega, Jamal's hyperactivity kicks up a level as he holds his orange soda, a bag of chips, and grape bubblegum with the instruction not to let Grandma see it.

Between interruptions of loud chomping, lips smacking barbeque chips with swigs of soda, he attempts to tell me what happened while licking his fingers; it starts to irritate me. I snap at him to stop eating and tell me what happened.

"The polar bear came," he whispers, spraying potato chips bits on my face. "Ma and Miss Tamara started screaming at each other. Miss Tamara called her a liar, a thief. She say Ma's an unfit mother and a whore. Ma called her a fake fat bitch. She say Miss Tamara jealous 'cause she too fat to get a man. Then Miss Tamara said to get the fuck out."

"What did Ma do to Miss Tamara?"

"She accused Ma stole her rent money. Miss Tamara say she hundred dollars short. They started cussing and fightin'. Ma snatched Miss Tamara's wig off, and ever'body saw Miss Tamara's bald head. She don't got no hair, Beenie."

"I've seen Miss Tamara without her wig. She has a lot of hair. It's cornrowed."

Ma's behavior pisses me off, fighting in front of Jamal, knowing that it would upset him. He loves Miss Tamara like a second mother. She takes care of him when Ma runs away, to where, no one knows, leaving Miss Tamara to make sure he does his homework and has dinner on the table.

I was not there to console him. I know he was hollering, screaming Ma to stop. He told me he did not cry, but I know my brother.

Ma will fight, talk shit to everybody except Grandma. When someone talk crazy to her, she wanna fight, badass, but she's really fighting someone she's afraid of—Grandma.

Ma ain't been seen since she dropped Jamal off at Grandma's on the down low.

I decide to hang outside and talk to my little brother, who I missed terribly, as he grasps the hem of my T-shirt.

"My Daddy's home, staying at Grandma Henderson here. I got two Grandmas, Beenie, you only got one."

"She died before I was born. I didn't know her."

Penguin's mother is two floors up from Grandma. I follow Jamal to her apartment. Penguin greets me with an over-the-top bear hug like a reunited father to his daughter and starts with his lame joking. He is clean shaven with brown sugar skin and high dark eyebrows. His stocking cap secured around his head setting up the tight hair waves. He has on cut-off shorts and a tight T-shirt showing his prison fitness. "Hey, eenie, meanie, Beenie. Miss you, girl. Thanks for looking out for Mally Mal."

Jamal abandons me upon hearing his name thrown at Miss Henderson's screen window. Penguin clears his throaty voice at him. Jamal throws his arms around him, then releases a tight neck hug and dashes out the door, returning to his friends.

"You are still a lame wanna-be rapper. Glad you're home."

"Girl, you ain't telling me you miss me? Not my tough, hard-core, Beenie."

He tosses his head back, showing off a mouth wide opened. I can count the number of caps he's had; penal system seemed to provide good dental service. I remember Penguin missing a few teeth before he left us.

"You and Ma gotta stay out of trouble, you hear me?"

"Yes, ma'am," Penguin salutes. "All good, all right with God."

"You became a Muslim in prison?"

He starts laughing at me again, but I was not joking. "Nah, just right with God the way my mama raised me to be. I'm grateful. Check this out, Beenie." Penguin rises up slowly, mindful of his disabled hip, then sits back down. "See that black bag near the window? Get it for me. You gonna be proud."

I retrieve the heavy bag as he extends his sinewy arm to assist me. He pulls out a plaque, gold-embossed *State University of New York* across it, *cum laude, bachelor degree of Psychology*. He holds the degree up, beaming, ensuring it in my view, waiting.

"I didn't know you were that smart," I nod, smiling at him.

"I got a new life ready to live. I got a job. The next thing to find apartment and get my Doll."

"Good luck finding her. You gonna try to get back with Ma?"

"I miss my Doll."

"Everybody does. What about her polar bear?"

Penguin no longer laughing as his smile disappears. "We gonna get her the help she needs. Your mother got a good heart; she has an illness, needs help."

I want to believe Penguin can help Ma, but he ran away. I cannot allow myself to believe he will be reliable for her even with his degree and affirmation to change. "Have you seen her?"

The thought of a future with Ma returns Penguin's smile to him. "I saw her a week ago when she came to see me. She looks as fine as I last saw her. She told me she'd be right back, but I ain't seen her since."

"Well, you got your answer," I say, folding my arms, wondering why Penguin would dare to think Ma would change for him if she cannot do it for her children or Grandma.

"I want my family back. We can have a good life together."

His heart was broken. Ma disappointed him over and over, like she does with everyone in her path. Penguin seems hopeful to restart again with her, but Ma moved on without a second thought of him. He looks off as his teeth are clenched, fists tight, blinking to prevent the tears. I have to make him laugh again to ease his pain. "You're going straight, right? No more white-collar crimes?"

His eyes thank me. "Nah, I'm not about that life anymore. My mother needs me. It's time for me to be an adult; a little late, but finally, it makes sense to do the right thing." Penguin leans back, erupting into his safety mechanism—laughter. "There's a wise old soul in you, Beenie."

"You got all these old people to watch you," I warned.

"True that. I remember them spying on me, telling Mama when she got home from work. She cooked dinner and whipped me at the same time—them old church ladies make sure you fly right."

Penguin knew about the fight between Ma and Miss Tamara. He says he gonna repay Miss Tamera her rent money, that he looking for a one-bedroom apartment to start. He says he going to find a second job so he can put Jamal in an afterschool program specialized in learning disabilities to help him with his ADHD.

I'm listening to Penguin talk about all the things he wants to do to make life better for us. He wants to give Ma stability, take care of her, and be important in Jamal's life. His parents were involved in his life, but Penguin said he was too stupid to appreciate a family, the stability he was given as a child.

"This sound crazy, but this was the blessing I needed, Beenie. You appreciate what you had when it's taken away. I've been given a second chance, and I want to make it right. I want my son, you, to be proud of me. I wanna be here for my mother. I want my family back."

"I will come back to you, if you stop that lame ass rhyming."

"No guarantee, Beenie meenie. Let's get Jamal—I'll treat ya'll to lunch."

"You paying with cash, right? No more jacking people's credit cards?" I say without a trace of laughter, not an eye blinked.

Penguin leans back in the kitchen chair, his weight on the hind legs, rubbing his chin, laughing at me. He thinks I'm funny, but I'm serious. Ma does not need any more temptations.

He sits upright, the lines around his mouth relaxed. "I never stop loving Doll even when she pushed me away. I won't let her push me away again—"

"Even when the polar bear comes out?"

"Nah, I'ma jack that polar bear up, girl. Believe that."

I hug Penguin, happy he is out of prison, at home, and in Jamal's life. If there is any hope for Ma, maybe Penguin can make her balance. He is more patient, humble, and seems to understand Ma's psyche. He got a bachelor degree in psychology while he was incarcerated. He is less hyper than I remember him when he was committing crimes, always suspicious at the knock of the door.

But the real work begins: he must find Ma first.

CHAPTER FOURTEEN

After much pleading, Dad granted me permission to go with Tiki to see her grandmother. Her grandma, whom she calls Peggy, is in a nursing home. She has been living there for years.

Peggy was a maid at a fleabag hotel until her forgetfulness escalated, and she could no longer work. Sasha and Lorna kept her low-income apartment that the state paid those two for until the money ran out.

The state cut her benefits, but she couldn't be left alone. Sasha and Lorna stopped caring too. Tiki was desperate, begging her mother and sister to help. They refused since the money was gone.

"If we lived in Japan, China, or any other Asia country, my Peggy would be respected, cared for until it was her time to leave here. Asian people take care of their old people. I'm fucking moving there when I get old."

"You curse too much."

"Sorry, forgot I'm in front of a saint. I was weaned on it."

"You don't have any peeps in those countries," I remind her.

Tiki bugs her eyes at me. "I'll find some."

She assured Dad it was okay for us to visit. Lorna will either be there or meet us at the nursing home. If Speed shows up, I promised Tiki that my parents will pick us up.

"I love you—"

"Shut up, weirdo."

Tiki ignores me, outstretching hands towards me. "I can always count on you to save me. My hero."

"Okay, dumbass, stop with the lame stuff." I thwart her hug.

"Bitch."

Marcus gave us explicit, repeated instructions not to touch or take any offer of food from any of the residents there. He told us to make sure we washed our hands so as not to bring any outside germs to the old people. Tiki nodded eagerly, calling Marcus "Mother Hen."

The nursing home smells of stale medicine and spoiled milk, with rows of old people tied to their seats like babies strapped in highchairs, leaning against the rail, drool from the corners of their mouths lengthening into narrow lines of salvia reaching the floor. The smell of soiled diapers, pee make me glad I declined McDonald's before we got there.

Tiki warned me, don't eat no food, wait to eat after visiting Peggy. "I love her so much; I don't smell the shit there."

Nurses, attendants, and cleaning people don't seem bothered by the smells either. They are unaffected by patients moaning, arms outstretched at them, anyone within reach, some babbling, some making sense. One wants water, many want to lie down to die, a few calling for their mothers. Their voices eventually mesh into one in my head, dizzying. I cannot tell one from the other and walk straight down the center line to avoid a brushed hand or fingertip touch.

It's after a long walk down a hallway of misery and despair that we make it to Peggy's room. Her bed is by the window, but she in a chair, strapped in like the others in the hallway.

Grandmother Peggy is quiet, unmoving, non-responsive as

though we never entered her room. Her long yellow-white hair is braided, wisps of it drape around her melted face; obese body puddled, flesh hanging off both sides of the chair. I lean an inch to look at her glassy skin, gray marble eyes that do not roll or move.

Tiki's mom, Lorna, sits on the other bed in the room. Her small frame weighs down the cheaply made mattress. She is thin, with an exposed collarbone from malnourishment, hair fried from too many dyes and menopause, and she reeks of a cigarettes-and-coffee smell that is as bad as the shit and pee from the patients.

She greets me with her bony hand and tobacco-stained teeth. I search her wrinkled skin, which looks like it has been folded a million times then opened. Legs folding the cross, moving back and forth, she says, "Ma's roommate pushing up daisies." Her attempts to humor us fail. I cringe, looking at her teeth, then forcing myself to look away whenever she opens her mouth.

Tiki says, "When did you get here? Did the pervert drop you off with your car, or did the repo man take it?"

Lorna leans forward to say something, then retracts the words stuck in her mouth, navigating to neutral territory. She looks at me. "You and Tashauna in the same class?"

Tiki corrects her.

"When you were little, you didn't mind Tashauna."

"When I was little, I had no control."

Lorna lowers her head with her thumbnail between her teeth. "I'm glad *Tiki* has some friends, I mean, *a friend* in school. Those rich kids make her feel bad."

"No, you make me feel bad."

"She never did have a knack for making friends. Her mouth makes it difficult."

I'm ready to leave the room, leave Tiki and her mother when Tiki jerks her head up at Lorna. "Because I never had a stable home to bring friends or a friend to." She mumbles under her breath but purposefully loud enough for Lorna's ear.

"If you're gonna start with me, I'll leave," Lorna closes her mouth as she narrows her eyes. "You need to be more respectful to Bruce."

I'm grateful she's stopped smiling.

Tiki slams her shoulders against her ears. "I don't give a shit about Speed, Bruce, whatever name he has; you should be more respectful to your mother. You put her here—oh, wait, you don't care—*my bad*."

Lorna side-eyes me, then looks at Tiki, seeming to debate whether to reveal a secret. "My mother was not a saint. She could be cruel, you know." Lorna is shaking her head at me, then at Tiki. "Peggy didn't talk, she hit. You could never measure up. She wanted perfection. To believe; makes her feel better not every family member is worthless. She's done some dirty deeds in her life; her sickness helps her forget them."

Tiki glares at her mother, biting her lip. Her eyes are fire-red, temples pulsing, ready to explode. "You'll never be half the woman she was. You never measure up."

Lorna shoots up, grabbing her bag, checking for her keys, cigarettes, and a reason to leave. "Tiki likes to worship a fantasy; it makes her feel better." She looks at me, then back at her daughter, who now refuses to acknowledge her. "Peggy *did take care* of you at a time with all her heart—and the state paid her for it." She does not wait for a rebuttal, walks briskly out of the room before Tiki can respond. "You got a good friend there, Rubena, great girl with a great attitude." Lorna's sarcasm trails away behind her like toxic sludge.

A half-empty milk carton zooms across the room, splattering the door, missing Lorna by a nanosecond as Tiki yells, "You didn't wanna be here anyway. Stupid old bitch!"

Tiki gently separates Peggy's tightly clenched hands, clasping each one in her hand. "You got a shitty deal for a daughter. I betcha if you could trade for someone you would, right? I damn sure would." She looks at me, then back to her grandmother, smiling. "Peggy, this my best friend, Rubena. I never had anyone as good as you, but I do now."

Turning away from me, Tiki wipes her face with her palms, talking with her back facing me. "You would love her, Rubena. When she was with me, talking, I learned how to curse from her, so sweet and gentle. She took care of me when no one would. I wasn't a burden to her. I was loved. Lorna's a fucking liar. Peggy did it out of love for me. Nobody had to pay her. Bitch. I don't care if she is not here anymore. As long as I can see her, she's here. That's all that matters."

Tiki says it like a chant over and over, wanting to believe Peggy did it out of love, not what Lorna said, as the truth.

Deep in the core of her soul where no one can go or see her real pain, Tiki believes what Lorna said. The pain in her eyes, the truth, its poison, will kill her.

Lorna makes my mother look like Mrs. Doubtfire.

CHAPTER FIFTEEN

The window of my bedroom gives me the perfect view, a high tower to survey the neighborhood and beyond. Despite the massive oak in front, my view is not obstructed—actually, I can hide behind it when I don't want to be spotted, watching any movement of cars, people, and my friends from the woods from very close by.

The digital clock on the nightstand won't let me sleep. I can't, even if I wanted to, despite the early rise to school in a few hours. If I'm running late due to insomnia, I'll take the bus instead of walking or, even better, get Marcus to take me over my father. Dad will lecture me: if I went to bed at a decent time, getting ready for school would not be an issue. After his predictable speech, he would take me to school; Marcus would do it without the lecture.

Where are those two furballs? Bully and his friends will come; they will be hungry after a day of sleeping, away from humans, the neighborhood dogs.

Whoever shows up, I'll watch them until my lids close against my will.

Night is safe for the neighbor girl to breathe fresh air, steal a look at the stars, and make a wish, for what I'm not sure. Maybe for freedom from her stepmother, or mother, whatever she is.

Looking down from the midnight sky to their house, the outdoor light flicks on as a guide to the trash, recycle bins in front of the house. There she is, same thin gown, same flip-flops, same shuffling gait with bins in hands, following the woman. She stops, allowing the woman to take the bins from her, and she rubs her arms like they hurt. Maybe the weight of the bins injured her arms. Maybe the woman has a heart, some type of pity, relieving her of the bins. Maybe she is a good woman after all. They make their way back into the house and shut the lights off.

No mother can be as selfish as Ma. But that woman making her daughter work at night in the cold? Then, there's Lorna, too. So, it's not rare for a mother to be so mean to her little girl. If she starting school, maybe she can snitch on her mom, get her ass in trouble. I'll be a witness for her.

Slipping quietly out of my bedroom and making my way to the hallway, I am betrayed by beautiful, creaking Cherrywood floors. The wood's imported; Dad nearly blew a blood vessel when Marcus exceeded the renovation budget. He wanted Marcus to follow agreed expenses down to the last red cent. He complained Dad is a big-time tightwad. "When Ruben walks, his shoes squeak."

Dad's tight-fisted attitudes toward finance come from the way he was raised. My grandparents were repurposers; they threw away nothing. Dad says they were environmentalists before it became a trend. He was taught to find a way to use something several times before you could throw it away and then give it to someone else who may benefit. He has two older brothers, and he rarely got new clothes unless the moths took away the old ones. That pleased my grandparents; Dad says when the moths got it—no waste.

Marcus is the opposite. He is an only child. His parents gave him everything shiny and new until his father stopped speaking to him. He is a retired military man, a textbook general, and a right-wing conservative. Dad calls him Uncle Tom, and Marcus does not disagree. "I take after my mother. I like nice things. If you work hard, you should reward yourself," he looked over at my father, "don't you agree, Ruben?"

The office downstairs faces the house across the street. Earlier, before Dad and Marcus went to bed, we prepped the bins, making sure the bottles, glass, and plastic were separated from the cartons and boxes, and cans are in designated color bins. The last thing we, Marcus and I, want is for Dad to get a fine from the county for not properly recycling. He would surely look to Marcus and me for an explanation. We carried the bins to the front of the house facing the street.

Looking directly at several bins parked neatly in a row, I'm amazed three people can drink so much. Dad is water, beer, and wine; Marcus, water, beer, wine, and soda; myself, water, juice, and soda. When Dad is away on business, Marcus and me mainly drink soda like kids invading their parents' liquor cabinet while they're away. If Dad had his way, soda would be banned. He playfully scolded Marcus being a nurse with bad eating habits, adding a return to the gym might be a good idea, offering to schedule a time they can work out together like they used to in the city. Marcus gets annoyed by Dad's criticism in the form of joking.

It must be hard to pretend when you love someone. That is a lot of work.

Marcus works very, very hard.

Leaning forward, pressing my nose against the windowpane, I see the house light across the street is on again. I see her. They are outside again. She is pushing a bin with all her weight despite the pain in her arms. They must have overlooked bins left moments ago from the first round. Following her is the evil stepmom or monster mother. The woman trails behind her like the police with an appre-hended criminal. She yanks from the ground a fallen wine bottle, shaking it at the girl as if to hit her with it, finger-wagging at the girl for clumsily allowing it to fall out of the bin. The woman is in a much warmer pattern robe, white fur protecting her against the cool night air. The girl has on covered slippers now and is wearing a sweater. I took inventory of her clothes: two pair of shoes, crocs and flip flops, and a sweater that seems too small for her, fit for a toddler.

What is wrong with that woman?

She is like Ma, selfish, spending money on only herself, except this woman is much worse. Ma did buy me some clothes when I threatened to tell Dad how she spends his support check; she was mad about it, doling out enough dollars to keep me from snitching.

The woman motions the girl to hurry back to the house while looking to her left and right as though she does not want to be seen with her.

Retrieving the ends of bread that no one eats in my house except me, I gently open the door and prevent tripping the alarm, grateful I had enough sense to wear my flannels and robe. That girl in thin rags against the night—I hope the toddler sweater she had on was keeping her warm.

Not too long later, my friend Bully appears, alone, as if his friends have abandoned him. He seems upset, bamboozled by the homeowners' ingenuity to prevent him from stealing the garbage. Why deny him something you don't want? Why does that woman deny the girl the warmth of clothes or the sun of daylight?

Bully checks each garbage bin desperately, searching. He perks at a plastic bag, excited by the prospects inside and attempts to delve it, only to be shocked by something, and he backs away. Defeated, he retreats into the woods in the same downtrodden shuffling like the girl.

I wait until he has fully disappeared and approach his favorite trash bin. For some reason, Bully is partial to the blue bins in the neighborhood, which have glass containers and cans. He seems to like creamy Caesar salad dressing, chocolate icing from the can,

Coke, regular and diet, Doritos crumbs, and, of course, French bread. I liked him immediately for that selection though he absconded it from another French-bread-loving raccoon.

"I'm sorry to disappoint you, Bully, but regular white bread ends will have to do. Like my grandma says, 'Take what you get and thank God for it.'"

I break up pieces of the bread ends and place them around the bins in a single line leading to the wood entrance, then dash back to the front door.

Inside, waiting and watching, with the weight of my head against the office window, I jerk up without reason to see him eating the bread ends alone, one by one, following the trail, starting from the wood entrance, around two bins, and back at the street-light. He likes playing games too, but I make him work for his food.

I rush to the door and slightly open it to watch him dine on discount bread. Staring intently at Bully, I instinctively look up across the street to see her there, the girl, alone, standing near the garage entrance, watching me and the raccoon interact like we're BFFs.

We look at each other forever like aliens from another planet. Slowly, I raise my hand to wave at her. She does not respond, staring at me for longer than a minute, her feet refusing to move. I wave again. She looks over at Bully eating, then back to me and retreats to the house.

CHAPTER SIXTEEN

Grandma and Ma are speaking again. She got back on Grandma's good side by being here. We hug each other more than the norm, tight. Wrapping my forearms around her, I feel she has lost weight. As I rest my face against her bony chest, looking up her nose, she says, "You getting so tall, girl. You might pass me at five foot seven."

"I'm going to pass you in height, and so many other things."

"Still talking shit to your mother, huh, Beenie?" Ma plants a kiss atop my head to prove she is still taller than me and *the mother*. I see a semblance of a twinkle in her hazel eyes, instinctively give her another tight hug, a second too long for Grandma's liking. "Come on, ya'll. We got a lot of work to do."

"I saw Penguin," I tell her as if withholding a secret of interest.

Ma raises an eyebrow as she tilts her head, "Did you?"

"I bet he wants to see you."

"I bet it's none of your business." She taps me on my head.

"Eudora, you best make sure Bette Mitchell don't mess with them collards," Miss Lulu Bell sounds the alarm for all ears in the room. "Last time she made 'em so tough the folks about to lose they dentures. She ain't about to loosen my bridge with them old, tough collard greens."

"I heard you, Lulu Bell!" Bette Mitchell sniffs.

"Then you heard the truth." Miss Lulu Bell shoots back a wink at me.

Grandma, myself, and Miss Lulu Bell along with members of the Good Grace Baptist church—the whole congregation getting ready for the annual fish fry. Actually, the entrées are more than fish. On the menu, available for the community, there's fried chicken, smothered pork chops, shrimp and grits, collard greens, macaroni and cheese, pimento cheese, and garden green salad along with Miss Lulu Bell's legendary peach cobbler and sweet potato pie and Grandma's famous pound cake. Reverend Wright and his trustees received food donations from various corporate supermarket chains.

The church basement flooded with food for miles the eyes can see. Tiki would be elated, slip in a food coma. I can imagine her eyes getting bigger than her stomach, stuffing her face, asking to take food home for her and baby Madison to eat when there is no food in the house and Sasha is between EBT card and payday. She would fete out a little to Sasha to show her gratitude, but Matt would get nothing, not even the crumbs falling to the floor. Tiki would quickly vacuum before he could reach for it. He can starve to death for all she cares.

She hinted big time to join me, wanting to meet my grandma and Jamal. Tiki rarely ventures out of Upstate; Sasha don't take her nowhere, nor does Lorna. They never have any money to do anything. I know she really wanted to come, but she is annoying after a while.

She asked if I could get Grandma's permission to visit. I told her I would though I did not ask Grandma, and I told Tiki she said no. Tiki tends to wear out her welcome with incessant chatter. I know she would get on Grandma's nerves to the point that she would yell, "Hush, child, give your mouth a rest; stop flapping your gums for the Devil." Flapping your gums for the Devil is an old Southern saying, means you talking too much, you're lying.

I'll make it up by bringing her a slice of Grandma's pound cake and Miss Lulu Bell's sweet potato pie.

The church as old as the congregation, as old as the cooks preparing the dinners, as old as the rest of the building in much need of repair. It smells damp, musty despite the aromatic smells of Southern cooking, which alleviate the stale odor a little. Arthritic hands lift pots bigger than themselves, some slicing sweet potatoes in wash basins seated with their walkers safely close beside them, practicing a hymnal for Sunday service. Others leaning against the table for support, too proud to use their cane, stirring as much as their sore, flaccid arms allow them to.

Reverend Wright smiles brighter than a sunbeam in a desert as he approaches the table where me, Ma, Grandma, and Miss Lulu Bell are stationed. "Morning ladies," he says with his eyes fixated on Miss Lulu Bell, who is ignoring us. He catches himself, acknowledges Grandma's glare; lip twisted immediately for her pardon, then the rest of us. "Thank God for the hands preparing this beautiful bounty, raising money to fix the souls in the neighborhood and our blessed house of worship."

They all respond with a resounding *Amen* except me, which prompts Grandma to side-eye me. "Amen," I correct myself to her satisfaction.

Reverend Wright inspects each of us with a nod, a hearty laugh ending with a smile. He stops in his tracks, saving all his wattage for Miss Lulu Bell without shame or care anyone noticed. "Miss Bell, I'm sure looking forward to your peach cobbler, and I ain't ashamed to tell my mama she could learn from you."

"Why thank you, Reverend Wright. I'm sure it ain't nothing like your mama's cooking."

Now, staring too long at her, he says, "No, I don't think so, I'm afraid to say." He laughs, acting like a schoolboy too terrified to ask the prettiest girl to the dance. Funny, Miss Lulu Bell did get dolled up to cook food with her false lashes, foundation, concealer, and coral lipstick. The rest of us, including Grandma, have rags on our head, no makeup, dressed in sweatpants and tees while Miss Lulu Bell got a dress on, high heels, and her hair coiffed.

I dare not laugh, even as Ma walks a few steps away from us with her back turned, snickering. Grandma not smiling; maybe she's jealous.

The Reverend realizes he has to tend to the rest of his flock and leaves with a smile for her so bright the blind could see it a mile away.

"Shameful," Miss Lulu Bell says.

"I'm sure it ain't nothing like your mama's cooking," Ma mimics Miss Lulu Bell as she laughs, waving her away.

"You ought to be respectful, Doll," Grandma says as deep frown lines mark her face.

The smiles melt away from Ma and Miss Lulu Bell's faces. "Eudora, it's all in good fun. Ain't nobody being disrespectful."

Grandma lifts the bin of Idaho potatoes and goes to the sink to wash them. With her back turned, Ma leans over to Miss Lulu Bell, suppressing a laugh, and says quietly, "She's just jealous. Nobody wants to see Ma other than for her cooking except Mr. Cicero Bird."

"Hush, girl." Miss Lulu Bell stops smiling as Grandma returns with the same frown on her face, carrying washed white potatoes for us to peel.

We sit at our table, silent. Grandma's eyes on nothing but the peeling potatoes as Ma, Miss Lulu Bell, and I look at one another every second, uncertain if we should stay silent or talk. We eavesdrop on the next table, watching and listening to Miss Gracie Lawson and Miss Bette Mitchell praying with the Reverend about their sons. Miss Gracie praying her grandson Tevan free himself from gang life and come back to the church. Miss Bette Mitchell asking her son to heal his crack addiction.

"Now, that would be a miracle only God can do," Miss Lulu Bell mumbles. "That boy got a habit even Carlos Escobar can't satisfy. Poor Bette gotta lock up everything in her house. It's a shame you gotta be a prisoner in your own home."

The Reverend now is talking about how to bring young folks, he calls them millennials, back to God and his house of worship.

"Shoot, ain't gonna happen less they can post it on Instagram, get likes for it," Ma says.

"I suppose you would know about that," Grandma says, her eyes focused on the peels in her water-soaked hands.

Ma stops in her tracks, opens her mouth, then looks downward at the potatoes already peeled and ready for the stove. Miss Lulu Bell bites her lower lip. Grandma continues to speak as though she did nothing for anyone to be offended.

"They ain't gonna get none in hell for it," Grandma says, engaging a serious face. I guess she realized Reverend Wright has eyes for Miss Lulu Bell only. Maybe tall, imposing women are his type. He recently divorced from his second wife, who was as tall as he is short. Ma says his first wife was a giant too.

"Child, please, hell gonna be full of young people glued to their cell phones. Satan won't be able to get their attention. He'll send them back, telling, ya'll created this problem, you deal with it," Miss Lulu Bell cackles.

The laughter can't be contained, even Grandma, despite the puss face, starts to laugh a little.

"Go on, Eudora, you know it's God's honest truth." Miss Lulu Bell's laugh sounds like a strangled hyena. Ma and I laugh for no reason other than hearing her laugh.

Grandma waves the knife at us to do less talking, more peeling, time is not on our side as the door for selling will be open starting at lunch time. I am trying to keep alert, peeling what seems like mountains of white potatoes that will bury me alive. Grandma has one eye on her potato and two eyes on me. "Beenie, peel the potatoes with the knife towards you so you don't cut yourself. We out of peelers."

But I'm clumsy with a knife, peeling much to the disapproval of Grandma. She stops and takes the knife from me to show me how to do it correctly. I do it her way, but it is slowing me down from peeling faster and efficiently. Grandma seems satisfied anyway and now targets her next victim, watching for a few seconds. "Doll, you leaving too much skin on that. Trim it some more."

"It looks fine to me, Mama," Ma responds, not bothering to look at Grandma, who is glaring at her.

"You gonna make less potatoes that way." Grandma has steam coming out of her ears. "Now you taking too much skin off."

Miss Lulu Bell watches with a side-glance, shaking her head. She starts humming so the table next to us don't stop and listen.

Grandma stops peeling, watching Ma and the potato. "We can't make enough potato salad to sell if you keep taking off more than the skin."

Ma stops, slowly lifts her head up, back straight, looking ahead, the knife in one hand, the potato in the other. "One minute I'm not taking enough, the next too much. I can't do nothing right in your eyes. Never satisfied, never satisfied with me."

Grandma moves closer to Ma. "This ain't got nothing to do with you. Peel them right."

Ma turns her head, staring eye-to-eye with Grandma. "You look at me, thinking you've failed. Why can't you be happy with me?"

Grandma takes the potato and knife out of her hands. "If you can't do it right, don't do it at all."

Miss Lulu Bell whispers, "Eudora, stop it! It ain't serious. It's about fellowship, not no damn potato salad."

Miss Lulu Bell's attempt to whisper fails. All eyes are on us, and I feel myself melting away from all those people of the church, staring at us like snarling animals in a cage. Grandma regains composure, resumes peeling, not caring if church members are looking at her.

We all resume peeling except Ma. The light in her eyes gone. She moves back and forth like a weeping willow with a stone wrapped around her. Miss Lulu Bell puts the knife down and gently grabs Ma by her waist. "Come on, lemme take you outside for some fresh air."

"We got work to do, Lulu Bell," Grandma says, not bothering to look up.

"Them potatoes ain't going anywhere." Miss Lulu Bell escorts Ma out of the basement.

I look at Grandma to see if she will follow them. She continues peeling, silent, as if no one but her is in the basement, nothing to talk about, unaffected by the looks of Reverend Wright, Miss Gracie Lawson, Miss Bette Mitchell, no one, not even me.

I am in a church.

Ain't there supposed to be peace in a house of God?

CHAPTER SEVENTEEN

The weekend in the city ended horribly, ruined by Grandma and her stupid white potatoes.

I blocked out what happened after the church drama. Ma took off to where nobody knows. She decided against coming home with us, and Grandma seemed not to care as we were swamped with the successful church fry. She was counting the money, smiling, making merriment like nothing happened, singing praise of her Lord, not thinking about Ma. Miss Lulu Bell, the peacemaker, could not fix the rift between them, and if the house of God couldn't do it, she lacked the power too.

I kept my promise, brought church food for Tiki. She squealed like she won money, mouth full of potato salad and collard greens, ripping off the chicken drumstick like a lion first at the kill site. Her sister managed to scrap up a few coins to give her but not enough for a full lunch.

"I don't wanna ever see or hear crack, snap, pop again," she says. "The whole weekend cereal; breakfast, lunch, and by dinner, the milk was gone."

"You gonna eat all what I brought?" I ask. Her jaw seems

unhinged, allowing chunks of food in like a malfunctioned conveyor belt.

"Watch me. Aw shit, here comes drama." Tiki's eyes follow Amber, the designer-wearing, Tik Tok-loving Queen Bee, walking on air like a boss with the girls behind her, minions who laugh when told to do so, agree with everything she says or does like they don't have a brain.

Amber Mills is not tall but walks like a six-foot runway model. Her brown, wavy hair scorched from flat iron overuse, and she dresses beyond her years. A big, busted girl, her boobs make her look older than she is, and it is Amber's biggest asset. A stripper in training with big tits and bigger attitude.

She wouldn't last a minute living with Grandma or Dad; they'd both make her remove all the makeup, too much for someone so young. Dad would sit her down, explain how it is not a good idea, enjoy being your age; Grandma would snatch her up, wipe the makeup off with a wet towel, scolding she is way "too grown for her draws," quoting biblical verses of modesty, self-respect. Marcus would purse his lips, eye her up and down, then give a hard look, arms folded, with a "Girl, please, take several seats."

She begins a stare down at Tiki, inserting a snarl at me without cause so I don't feel left out.

Amber purposely sits one table away from us. She must be bored, so Tiki and I are her source of entertainment for lunch period. Looking at us with disgust for our choice of lunch: fish fry leftovers, a shared burger and fries, cherry soda for Tiki, cranberry juice for me. She and her cult followers have a communal cup of fat-free yogurt. Each of the four girls takes a turn eating a spoonful, monitoring each other's portion control, followed by their very own Calorie 1 Diet Coke.

We hit the floor, laughing at them, taking the last big bite of burger, our mouths wide open for everyone to see, and then squirt a crazy amount of catsup on the last French fry. Tiki dangles a fry in front of them like a horse with a carrot. She takes a massive final bite of the chicken drumstick, tearing off the skin, exposing the bone now stuck in her mouth like a lollipop. We chew slowly, announcing how good it is.

Amber shaking her head with a dead stare. "Who wants to be fat?" The yogurt cup is clean. Amber whips out a banana and, with a plastic knife, cuts it into four equal pieces.

I rest my chin in hand, watching these girls eat, all of them are thin or underweight except Amber, who is full figure. Tiki says she's fat, but she really isn't, she's just not super skinny like the rest of them. I hear their stomachs talking right now, the sound of growling will increase in decibel before the end of lunch.

I'm hoping Tiki will ignore Amber, but she won't. The other girls at the table mind their business, looking at their phone unless Amber needs their help.

"Hashtag eating disorder. Hashtag I'm hungry," Tiki says while checking her cracked, disconnected phone without the bother of looking at them. "Unreal."

Amber pauses, lifting her head high, sniffing the air. "OMG! What the hell is that smell? Oh, it's only Stinky Tiki. Why do you wear cologne de trailer park to school? You will have the entire student body in the nurse's office. I'm going to request the super to seat you outside or get us biohazard suits and masks."

Tiki does not smell anymore. Marcus allows her to shower at our house in the bathroom in my room. He even installed a towel bar for her once I told him about the problems of bathing at home.

I'm in no mood for her bullshit. "Why you gotta start crap? Stay in your lane."

Amber smirks at me, holding her face in hands, elbows firmly on the table. "You keep hanging with Tiki, Rubena, you're going to start smelling like her, too, if you haven't already." Amber looks over at her minions, and they laugh on cue.

Tiki smiles, exaggerates a head move side to side. "Oh, you fat ho, can't get enough of me, living rent-free in that empty head of yours. Stop, before you get checked." Tiki slowly gets up as we prepare to leave. "Don't have enough likes on the 'gram? No Tik Tok love? No attention at home?"

"How would you like it if we dogged you?" I snap at Amber, looking at her friends glued to their phones, silent.

Amber claps back, "I don't stink."

Tiki lunges at her, placing her armpit over Amber's flat-ironed head, rubbing as hard as she can as Amber's hands flail for help. She alternates each armpit harder into Amber's scalp. "Now you do."

We leave Amber shrieking, frantically wiping her head with as many napkins she can get her hands on as her friends sit frozen in their seats. "Why didn't her crew help her?"

She high-fives me. "They don't wanna fuck with the power of Stinky Tiki."

CHAPTER EIGHTEEN

The dinner Marcus prepares for us tonight is creamy salmon with rigatoni pasta. It looks as good as it smells. My mouth is salivating as he places a plate before me. I'm anxious to dig in but wait until he serves Dad and then takes a seat himself.

They sit on opposite sides of the table, and I am in the middle. The mid-century fixture above my head provides enough light to see their faces. I'm waiting for something to happen, like watching a pressure cooker about to explode, spraying anger, sadness, and disappointment all over the ceiling, and on us. Dad is smacking away at dinner like he ain't got no reason to be bothered while Marcus is uncomfortably quiet, an elbow on the table, finger under his nose as his thumb rests on his chin, staring at Dad but quickly diverting when I look at him. There is considerable space at the table as it seats six comfortably. Marcus explained to me the table was one of the finest, imported from Europe, handmade oak showcasing natural imperfections and knots. Without any chairs, the table alone cost $7,500. Dad rubbed his chin, complaining how stupid it was to eat off a table costing nearly $10,000. He will not call you stupid directly, but your actions are. Marcus usually responds with sarcasm, but tonight his arsenal of clap back appears empty.

We are silent eating, and though the meal is delicious enough to not talk, something is missing.

Communication.

Dad and I focus more on eating rather than talking, but conversation usually interjects between mouthfuls of food.

So, it's uncomfortably quiet at the dining room table, like dancing without a partner. The only sounds are light rain pattering on the roof and forks tapping plates. Dad seems to be enjoying his meal without concern. Marcus picks at his plate like a child not wanting to eat it. I have never seen him do this; he brags how good of a cook he is. He breaks away from his barely eaten plate, his eyes on Dad, wanting his attention. Dad fails to comply, whether deliberate or stuck inside his own thoughts, I don't know.

Dad is not an easy person to live with sometimes.

If I could ease Marcus's pain, I would. Instead, we eat in silence.

After dinner, needing a break from adult drama, leaving them asleep, I make my way down the stairs to the door, navigating outside in the dark. The rain ceased earlier before leaving fresh dew on the grass like spilled water waiting for a mop to clean it up. I take in more air than needed to clear my cloudy head.

Stale bread ready for Bully. Earlier, Marcus put it aside for stuffing a roast chicken, but salmon won, and he saw no use for it. I carefully place the bread for Bully, leaving it at his favorite blue bin, then I rush back to the house, a safe distance away, so as not to scare him.

He is a timely raccoon; within minutes, he arrives and starts eating the bread. I worry that feeding him will make him too lazy to find his own food. I decide tonight will be his last free meal, then he must fend for himself. He must return to being a self-sufficient raccoon. Maybe Bully will resume being a thief, maybe he won't, like Penguin, given a second chance to change. "Eat up, Bully. This is your last free meal."

Heavy eyes are upon me as I steer away from Bully enjoying his last supper. She is there, watching Bully, entranced.

We stared at each other for a long minute, two or more. I raise my hand at her to wave and wait.

She looks up at the window of her home. The bedroom light is off. Then, slowly, she raises her hand, waves once, then again after I return a wave. We wave at each other far more than needed, our hands refusing to stop.

She points at Bully, raises her hand, suspended in the damp night air, then touches her mouth, tapping it, looking at me. She wants to talk to me. I wave again. She does not return the wave but raises her hand, touching her mouth. As I take the first step to approach her, suddenly, she dashes back into her house. Bully pauses eating to look at me, then at where she was standing, suspicious.

Bully and I are both confused as to what she wanted me to do.

CHAPTER NINETEEN

It has been a long time since I shared a bed with my little brother, and I'm reminded I'm grateful for it. Jamal is four feet six, but he sleeps like he is six feet six. His little body hogs the sheets on the queen-size mattress in my bedroom. How did he manage to sleep on a saggy twin bed when we lived in the hood? Throughout the night, I had to reposition his skinny body, so I'd have a little bit of room.

Earlier, Marcus surprised him, decorating the guest bedroom with glow-in-the-dark Marvel superheroes bedding. He even put up curtains for him. Jamal started to cry. "Your house is too big for me to sleep alone, Mr. Marcus." He looks at me for help should Marcus deny him. "Beenie, I'm scare of this big old house."

Marcus spent a lot of paper for Marvel superheroes. He was so understanding, wiping Jamal's nose, snotty from crying about sleeping in a big old scary house. "Now, stop crying. You wanna sleep with Beenie in her room?" he asked.

I shook my head violently, crossing my arms *no*, to not offer up my room.

"Your sister will let you sleep with her, right, Beenie?" Marcus smiled at me, not waiting for a response.

He told Jamal he can take the superhero sheets home. Marcus is unaffected by two hundred bucks spent. Surprisingly, Dad is not mad about losing the money either. He even bought Jamal a bike with the promise to keep it safe for him in the garage until he returns to visit. Marcus and I exchanged looks, our mouths dropped to the floor when Dad carried the box inside to assemble it.

Jamal gonna spend Saturday with us for the potluck, then we're going back to the city tomorrow to go to church with Grandma.

I check the hallway and then return to my room. "Where is Ma?" I whisper though Marcus or Dad are nowhere around.

"She staying with Daddy and Grandma Henderson. Grandma Dorie locked her out again."

He is so excited about coming to Upstate, whether it is to see me or ride his new bike or the neighborhood potluck we're having today—my guess is all three.

Marcus prepares a breakfast of grits, sausage, and French toast. Before he sits down to eat, he blinks his unbelieving eyes a boy Jamal's size can consume the amount of food on his plate. Jamal releases a satisfied belch, adding a pardon me, then asks Marcus for some more.

We clear the table. Jamal assists me in rinsing the dishes for the dishwasher. "You scare now of this big old house?" I ask.

"No, it's daylight."

"The dark in Upstate is the same as dark in the city," I point out.

"Nah uh, we got the ambulance noise, police noise; I can hear people talking, yelling, fighting all the time. It's too quiet, ain't no night walkers around here."

"I don't miss those night *walkers*." I hug him tightly. "I will protect you in the quiet of the night, okay?"

* * *

Tiki's cell service is restored, for how long she doesn't even know. Sasha must need her phone active, meaning she'll be stuck in the house babysitting for the duration of the weekend. I invite her anyway to the neighborhood potluck party to atone for the church fish fry in the city with Grandma.

"I can't," she snaps, the decimal up ten levels in her voice. "Sasha gotta work a double this weekend to catch up on the rent. News flash—we're behind."

"I don't even have to guess where the baby daddy is."

Tiki sighs so deeply in the phone my eardrum cracks. "I guess it's better here than Lorna's. I can piss in peace without creepy Speed here. Matt's a loser druggie, but he ain't no pervert. I gotta go, Rubena, baby's crying. Can you bring me something on Monday?"

"Do you have food for Madison and yourself?"

Tiki tells me to wait. I can hear her comforting Madison in a patient, gentle voice unfamiliar to me. She returns to the phone with the baby screaming in my ear. I'm ready to hang up.

"Yeah, we got a few things from the food pantry in town, wasn't much left when we got there late, but it'll do."

"I'll bring you some food on Monday."

"Thanks. She ain't gonna have no lunch money. It's all going to rent. Oh, don't try to text me Monday morning; my cell gonna be shut off after midnight."

* * *

Jamal running like a wild boar in the forest on speed, taking in as much Upstate as his asthmatic lungs allow. Bent over, hands on each knees, catching his breath from overdose of fresh suburban air, his eyes absorbing as much as they can. There is so much green to cover, he can't remember the starting point.

The roadblock is set up; the town gave our street association permission to keep it there for the outdoor potluck. Every year, the neighborhood do the meet and greet for old and new residents. The OGs are stalwart sentries against unfamiliar faces, documenting strangers' license plates, scanning Amazon, UPS, and FedEx employees. The guardians of the hood are mostly retirees or work-at-home residents. They'll retrieve packages (with permission) and hold them until the homeowner arrives. They paternally monitor activities of all residents in the hood. Marcus says they are too nosy for his taste; he's a fine one to talk as he is just as nosy. Dad says it's good to have neighbors look out. They're good citizens. The one bother he has is when the president sees an unfamiliar face who happens to be a person of color. The association president takes the license number down and has the police chief, who we were told is a distant cousin, run the plate.

Bully and his friends outsmarted the residents for a long time, vandalizing the bins and leaving garbage strewn on the sidewalk and streets, and then it stopped, suddenly. I overheard the block association president, Mr. Greenly, tell Dad that mint-flavor garbage bags and moth balls stopped the vermin from their chaotic dining, which explains why Bully backed away from the bins and garbage can as if they were poison a few nights ago. I have not seen him since. I was full of myself, thought I was teaching him to be independent, but it turns out, mint garbage bags banished him from the hood. I'm determined to help Bully again once I hatch a plan.

The target of my ire is the association president, Mr. Greenly, a nervous, color-deprived man with thinning hair and an eye twitch. Though he is of small stature, he can always be seen standing before his window, wondering and watching. He lost his wife to cancer last Christmas and has a daughter who does not speak to him. He opens about it to anyone that will lend him an ear, soliciting their sympathy.

Mr. Greenly extends his hand to Dad, then Marcus, and then looks at me with his hand out. I show him my hands are occupied by a hot dog.

"Beenie, this is Mr. Greenly. He's responsible for the care of the neighborhood," Marcus says, motioning me to hold the hotdog in one hand to receive his. I was going to be nice until I learned what he'd done to Bully. I resent him calling my friend vermin.

Dad pushes on, "Mr. Greenly is a lawyer."

Mr. Greenly interjects, hand up, "Oh now, I'm retired."

"Private practice?" Dad asks.

"No, I was an attorney for Legal Aid."

Marcus nudges me to be polite. "What does Legal Aid lawyers do?"

Smiling, Dad interjects, "They are a law firm that provides various services for the poor, low income like civil rights, immigration, domestic violence."

"You help people with problems?" I ask. Dad nods to approve that I'm engaging Mr. Greenly. "People's rights? What about animals' rights?"

"Well, there are agencies to protect the rights of animals," he says.

"What about the wildlife here? The raccoons, foxes, and opossum. They come out at night hungry. They should be protected too."

A thick gulp holds Mr. Greenly for a moment, his eyes rolling over to Dad and Marcus for help, and in a second, he is conveniently summoned by the grill master.

The warm jacket weather allows people to come out, greeting old and new to the neighborhood. Dad, Marcus, and I are newbies as well as the people across the street. I crane my neck, searching, looking for her. Everyone is out of their homes except her.

"Who you looking for, Beenie?" Dad asks, looking in the same direction.

"Nothing."

Everyone so friendly and helpful even if not needed. I cannot find her amongst the crowd. Jamal, happily talking to the boys his age, including the new neighbor's boys, who are ten and twelve. Their names are Jacques and Dennis. He supplies this information to me as though he on reconnaissance. He returns to me, asking if I can hold his jacket while he plays with his new friends. The two boys, one holding the ball, wave Jamal to join them.

"They talk funny," Jamal says between loud, long slurps of Popsicle.

"That's a French accent."

He quickly takes one last massive bite of blueberry popsicle. Jamal does not care what they are when the boys wave a second time for him to join them in a game of soccer.

Dad motions me back to join him and Marcus. They are talking to her, the stepmother. The monster mom. They are talking to the woman with the girl I have been watching during the night for a long time. I see her from a short distance. My stomach is jumping, the nerves in my body pulsing as the blood tries to pump oxygen to steady my walk. Will she eat me alive? Or cast a spell on me? Is she aware that I have been watching her at night like a stalker?

I straighten up, fearless of her. I will not be afraid. She has no power over me.

I'm from the hood, New York City.

As I approach her, she is standing next to a man way younger than her. Her face is a dull clay brown, old, with deep, long lines in her cheeks and three hard lines drawn across her forehead that could channel sweat. The bags under her eyes are so heavy I can see the white lining under them. She has thick black hair with sprouts of gray, and she is tall and very skinny. She looks very much like a witch.

Marcus mentions her name, but I did not hear him as I could not take my entranced eyes off of her. We are staring at each other. Her smile is cordial. Mine is not. I only heard she is a doctor, of what I do not know. Her husband is a professor. I now know them as the doctor and the professor.

He is way better-looking than her. His skin is the color of hot chocolate, no wrinkles on his face like his wife, but his lips are pencil thin. His hazel eyes smile as his lips disappear. She is a foot taller than him, and it is obvious to me she is the boss as she nudges him hard to extend his hand to me.

When I shake his hand, it is heavy like hardened wax. The doctor's handshake is a wet dishrag, limp. I feel the skeleton frame of her bony hand with very little fat as cushion. The wrist bone is visually protruding.

They were living in London, but the continent of Africa, French-speaking, is where they are originally from. "Tu es d'Afrique centrale?" I asked if they are from Central Africa.

The doctor tilts her head slowly to absorb what I said as her mouth opens wide enough to welcome flies. She then presses her lips together to form a semblance of a smile as her eyebrow raises, looking like a painted-on inverted V. The professor's lips disappear as his eyes twinkle at me, impressed.

"Oh, tu parles français?" then in English, "Congo is my home country."

"Oui. Français est ma langue préférée." I say French is my favorite language.

The doctor exchanges looks with the professor, smiling ear to ear and back to French. "Magnifique. Nous aurons quelqu'un à qui parler." She is happy to have someone to talk to in French.

I tell the doctor and professor I will be happy to converse in French. I tell them I met their sons Jacques and Dennis. The doctor is receptive to me, smiling and touching my head as if I am a good dog. She compliments me that I am a lovely girl, so young and cultured for an American, to speak other than a native language.

Then, she switches to accented English and says, "So sad Americans do not learn another language, why is that? American schools are below standard of France, Europe, the rest of the world, really. They tend to be too arrogant to educate themselves, perhaps they suffer from extreme isolationism." The poison visible on each corner of the doctor's lips. She brightens. "But you, mademoiselle, have proven me a little wrong." She is smiling, ready to bite me. "You are a breath of fresh air."

It is a diss, but I'm not affected. Clearly the doctor is a snob. Though she is an African, she made it clear she identifies as French.

"Où est ta fille?" I finally ask the doctor about the girl.

Suddenly, the light in her eyes shut down like a power outage. She straightens up, not looking at her husband. "No," she responds in English, looking around, hopeful no one's listening to us.

"Tu as une fille, oui? You have a daughter, yes?" I ask again.

The professor side glances the doctor, his eyes still bright, hands deep in his pocket, lips pressed tight. She narrows her eyes like a vulture spotting prey ready with talon-like nails, aiming poison darts at me. "No," she says in English. "We have two boys."

I tell her in French I saw her. I continue to speak in French to the witch, who is no longer smiling at me, aggrieved, as if I have revealed her secret. "Was that your niece? I saw you the other night taking out recycle bins with..."

"Non." Her voice, elevated, quickly turns down with a smile as insurance in case we are being watched. She continues to speak in English so low I strain to hear her. "No. You saw me with one of my sons. They are home for a visit from boarding school." She nods at the professor to cease talking. He was conveniently distracted by an attractive woman to get away from me.

"Beenie, can you keep score? They cheatin'!" Jamal shrieks between gasp of air. "Come right now."

"Who's cheating," I yell back. My eyes are glued to the witch.

"The Frenchie boys." Jamal turns at them, trying to snatch the ball from Jacque as he is spins around with it secured under his armpit, speaking French to his brother Dennis, who is splayed on the ground laughing. "Come now!"

"Did Grandma pack your inhaler?" I tell Jamal to go to my room and get it, then I will join in. He leans over to catch his breath, then sprints inside.

They have left me, escaped further inquisition, the doctor and professor. Looking around at residents of the block, I wonder if anyone witnessed what happened between us. I find them, zero in on the doctor and professor as they speak their heavily accented English to people safer than myself. She's comfortable again, laughing, trying to blend in a new country with new people, trying slang English to charm them. And she succeeds in making them laugh. Probably, they are engaged by her French accent. She is back to fake smiling.

The doctor eases her bony frame through the crowd, navigating to where she is stopped by a group of four, then three, then two, and finally one person, all the while clasping their hands and shaking, until finally, conversation-ended, she leaves for home more quickly than she should need to. She flings her hair back and heads to her house. She has made it to the door.

The professor, stopped by Mr. Greenly, notices the frown on the doctor's face. The doctor stands ramrod straight, arms folded, foot patting, laser-locked on the professor to end his socializing and come inside.

He is stopped a second time by a woman, an attractive neighbor, a model-looking lady with auburn hair and an effervescent personality. The smile on the professor's face tells me he is enjoying the pretty neighbor as the doctor's face twists into knots, huffing as she paces in front of her residence. He does not seem to care that the doctor's pissed, laughing, touching the pretty woman's arm. The doctor, safely at her door, flails her hands at him to end it and come inside. He is cemented in conversation with the model lady whose name I do not know. I am waiting to see how long before he concedes and goes to his house.

"Come on, Beenie!" Jamal screams.

The doctor catches me looking at her, a maniacal smirk surfacing on her face like a monster out of the lagoon. My attempts to replicate her smirk fail as I jog backwards, bouncing, smiling, as she slowly closes her door, never taking her eyes off me. The professor trudges back to the house, head down, hands in pocket, looking at his feet's betrayal.

Jamal assigns me to goalie as he no longer likes or trusts the brothers. The ball is a hair's inch in before Dennis tries to kick it. I throw it as far as I can. He falls backward, cursing at me in French. I respond back as he picks himself up, dusting his legs and backside, blinking several times, convincing his pea brain he heard me cursing back in French at him fluently. I'm having fun taunting the little asshole and his cheating brother.

I complete my second block at the goal post. I see the professor has returned to the potluck group, searching for and finding the model lady, delighted she is still outside, more delighted she notices him as her high wattage smile lights up the neighborhood while twirling her hair.

"We got them good," Jamal says as I hand him his jacket to protect against the evening's cool air.

The neighbors are slowly dispersing as Mr. Greenly and staff begin cleanup. Marcus is wrapping some leftovers I asked for earlier for Tiki as Dad assists with the disassembly of tents, tables, and folding chairs. Not surprisingly, the professor insists on helping the model lady with her tasks.

I high-five my little brother, vindicated against those two, who lost interest playing when they started to lose. Jamal flips the finger. I grab his hand, laughing long after the boys leave.

"Whatcha laughing at?" Jamal pushes me.

The doctor has opened a box that she cannot close. I playfully push Jamal back, then slap him upside his head. "Nothing."

* * *

At night, the neighborhood shows no evidence of the festive block party hours ago. Mr. Greenly enlisted the residents' help, ensured every table was cleared, every party favor removed, all traces of debris, every morsel of food gone like it never happened.

"Bully, come out, I got something for you, your favorite, French bread. It's a gift from Mr. Greenly. He's sorry about the garbage bags. I'll leave it here at your favorite bin. Goodnight."

CHAPTER TWENTY

Grandma's apartment on Sunday mornings has many smells and sounds: iron-pressed clothes, shoe polish, hot coffee, bacon, slightly burnt toast, and a perfectly cooked roast chicken resting on the countertop for dinner after church. Gospel music from her apartment and other old people readying for service blasts throughout the hallway. It's the only time no one's complaining about the volume of music. God in charge of the building, especially on Sundays.

She is ironing, making sure there are proper creases in Jamal's pants at both their insistence. She has on a white silk slip that accentuates her red bone skin and pink rollers in her hair. Grandma wears minimal makeup, only a little pressing powder on her prominent cheekbones and lipstick. Her skin is clear. She has hardly any wrinkles for a seventy-something-year-old woman. Her church suit is hanging on the hallway door, picked up Saturday from the cleaners, under a plastic covering protecting it from the smells in the apartment.

And, of course, her church hat is safely tucked away in a large black and white hat box. No black woman of faith would dare enter the house of worship without one. Grandma has one closet alone for her hats that match each church suit she owns; some she has not yet worn. Uncle Marsh gives Grandma a hat allowance to supplement her church budget. She is able to tithe properly because of Uncle Marsh.

She told me once when God calls her home, I will get them. She never mentioned Ma getting a hat when she is gone.

I am watching her focus on the iron puffing steam and thankful that I have her in my life.

Penguin told Jamal he will be there with Ma. I hope he is able to do so, so Grandma and Ma can at least be nice to each other even if they don't make up. They are both too stubborn to say I'm sorry and haven't spoken since the church fry despite Miss Lulu Bell's help to intervene.

I'm enlisting God's help on this one.

Grandma's favorite church CD is playing as we get ready for our appearance for eleven a.m. services. She never has to force me to come to church with her. Actually, I am always glad to go with Grandma.

Jamal is behaving. He is quietly polishing his shoes the way Grandma's neighbor, old Mr. Cicero Bird, showed him. Grandma hands him his pants as she begins brushing his head. She spurts a dime-size dab of lotion in her hands, rubbing for a second, then smearing Jamal's face as he tilts his chin up.

He looks so handsome wearing his black suit with a polka dot bow tie. Grandma let him select what he wanted as long as it wasn't too expensive. He proudly showed me his new bible Grandma brought him with his name embossed in gold. I'm a little jealous; since I moved to Upstate and he moved in with her, he and Grandma have gotten super close.

"I don't have much electricity 'round Grandma," he says.

He loves Sunday school and is the star pupil of Miss Keisha, who works closely with him. She is a teacher in New York City in special education. Grandma is so appreciative of her working with him. Jamal can be focused; he has little electricity around Miss Keisha. She says Jamal is also calm when he is singing and learning music. He wants to learn to play the drums. Grandma says she's going to ask Uncle Marsh to pay for lessons.

He is singing lead today in the children's choir so we cannot be late. Ma and Penguin promised to be there on time. Dad texts he and Marcus are on the West Side Highway right now and should be there shortly if there is no traffic.

We make it on time, thanks to Grandma's efficiency, and remove our jackets to settle in for ninety minutes of joyful noise. I like being in church. It is a warm place. Everyone is shouting, smiling, happy, and full of light. Grandma motions me to take a seat, giving me her bible and handbag. She has to make her grand entrance, lining up with all the other ladies ready for gospel pageantry. Miss Keisha welcomes me with a kiss on each cheek, then takes Jamal downstairs to join the other children gathering there.

Shortly before service starts, Ma and Penguin arrive, followed by Dad and Marcus. Ma looks so pretty and steady; she is rocking her natural hair, which has grown a lot while hiding under those wigs, and she has on very little makeup. She looks Instagram-ready to me. Penguin holds her hand tightly as they make their way to the nearest available seat, and she blows a kiss at me, smiling.

At church, before services start, any member of the congregation can stand up and give testimony to the greatness of our Lord and his son Jesus and then lead into a song of praising. Penguin is the first to stand up. He gives thanks to God for a second chance and forgiveness. He recites what he is grateful for: Ma, his mother, and his only son, Jamal. He starts singing, tilting back his shiny dome, clapping. Penguin got a nice voice; it is strong, rich, and explodes toward the ceiling like fireworks. He was a part of the music ministry when he was young and played the piano for the church until he started getting into trouble and left. Grandma Henderson was crushed because Penguin took away her bragging rights.

Reverend Wright asks Penguin to come to the piano to play and sing again. With the choir as his backup singers, all fifty of them follow his lead. He is right where he belongs. I slightly turn, looking to my right at Mrs. Henderson, who is standing up, supported by her walker, tears streaming down her face so you cannot see her eyes. Penguin is home with God, and we all can see he has restored his mother's pride that he took away from her so long ago.

He should be on American Idol. Penguin has moved Ma too; she is crying. I want to go over to hug her, but the church is packed, and the ushers, big-boned women in all white, are guarding the red-carpet walkway like prison guards ready to shoot to kill with one precise glare.

Marcus is singing loud enough where I can hear him. He needs lessons.

Church is a fashion show runway. All the ladies, from the youngest to the oldest, take turns strutting down the red carpet, hands raised to God in praise and worship while checking out the competition. Even the mother of the church, ninety-five-year-old Miss Delores Baker, gets in on it with her walker to steady her, a crippled hand on her hip. She brushes away an usher's offer to escort her. The spotlight must be all hers for this one. Miss Delores was an *Ebony Fashion* model back in her day. She is still a looker.

Grandma walks in like a peacock with too many feathers. Her head is held high like she got a stack of books on it, singing in step with the sea of church ushers in uniforms and gloves, marching steady with the beat of the music ministry. No amount of sugar can stop her from church. No stress from Ma's antics, neither.

Uncle Marsh and Aunt Nelle walk in late, quickly taking the nearest seat in the back for members who lack the ability to be on time before the ushers walk. Uncle Marsh winks at me. Aunt Nelle pretends not to see Grandma or me, looking straight ahead like a horse with blinders.

The last church member who makes the biggest grand entrance is none other than Miss Lulu Bell Davis, who has more feathers than Grandma and all the ladies in formation. She has the largest hat with the biggest bow, and she is wearing the highest heels. She looks like she about to lean over but steadies herself. I did not think women's shoes could be as large as Miss Lulu Bell's feet.

I was not alone with that thought.

An unfamiliar churchgoer sitting behind me muffles her laugh as best as she can. The man seated next to her is the responsible party.

"Who knew God was capable of creating feet that big in a woman," she chokes back laughing.

The man shoots back: "What woman?"

CHAPTER TWENTY-ONE

For dinner, Marcus decides to surprise us with a vegetarian dish of roasted sweet potato and a red lentils coconut pot. I look at the dish, wondering where the meat is.

The aromatic smells of spices and roasted potatoes make me forget about being a carnivore for a moment. I do everything within my power to not lick my plate, scrape it clean, and put the spoon in my mouth, sucking it like a vegan lollipop, happy there is enough for seconds. It never occurred to me to eat meatless for dinner. Dad says he enjoys the meal but complains meat of any kind should have accompanied the dish.

Marcus slams his fork down. Though it doesn't make any noise, Dad and I both jump. "Ruben, it's *vegetarian. That means no meat,*" he snaps at him, the volume way up, something bigger than the offense. "I thought it would be nice to do something different, break out of the box sometimes."

Dad repositions himself in the chair to explain, appeasing, "It was good, just missing some type of protein, what I like—like chicken, lamb."

"Lentils are *proteins,*" Marcus shoots back, bugging his eyes as though Dad said something dumb. "I will give you a meat dish tomorrow, okay? That'll make you happy!"

I shuttle looks between Dad and Marcus, unable to break the code between them. Dad needs an out, though sometimes he doesn't deserve one.

"You hate lamb, Dad." I throw him a safety net smile, then shift over to give Marcus a smile like a life jacket. Marcus is not smiling as the tension rises in the dining room like a poison that will suffocate us. No words to pacify or break the tension will deflate it; Marcus is not entertained by the faces I make that he normally responds to.

Dad, too, for his sake as well as mine, is trying to change the mood. "You're right, I don't like lamb." He raises an index finger, a futile attempt to disarm Marcus. "But I do like chicken, beef, and fish."

Marcus purses his lips, elbows firmly on the table, not placated by Dad's entreating smile; it irritates him more, as if Dad is mocking him. I wonder why Marcus blew up. Dad is a serious carnivore so there must be more to it.

Marcus and I are omnivores like the bear that was sighted in Upstate before I moved here. Joy-killer Mr. Greenly spotted him and had animal welfare trap and take him away. It would have been nice to see a bear, but Bully and friends would be the bear's meal ticket. My regret was the bear did not see Mr. Greenly as appetizing.

Marcus and I do like to switch it up every now and then. Dad is not that flexible. Actually, he's not flexible at all.

"He is like cement, unmovable," Marcus joked once.

"Your cholesterol's high, remember?" Marcus gets up clearing the table. "Stop being so ungrateful."

"Here, lemme help," Dad offers as a form of apology, though I can tell he is really dismissive of Marcus's antics, which he finds a bit overdramatic. A peace treaty comes from him without an apology in the forms of a hug, a compliment, a bottle of wine, or an offer to help. It's the only way Dad knows how to say sorry. I don't know why he has a tough time saying it. Like Grandma, his tongue will not allow it.

"I got it." Marcus cuts him off, grabbing the dishes, prepping them for the dishwasher.

I take Dad's plate and glass, joining Marcus in rinsing them. Dad gets out of his chair, carefully sides up to Marcus, gently grabbing his waist as he pulls away. "We're not going to be mad over wine, are we?"

They usually cap off after dinner with evening walks, reading, watching CNN, and a glass of wine. Sometimes Dad will drink bourbon or brandy.

"Sporadic appreciation is needed sometimes," Marcus says quietly, unresponsive to Dad's attempts to cuddle him.

He draws him in closer, hugging him tighter, resting his chin on Marcus' shoulder. "Tell you what, I'll cook tomorrow, and you and Beenie can critique me. You can insult me all you want."

"You're used to being insulted, you were married to Ma, remember?" I chime in, punch him for hurting Marcus's feelings.

Dad holding Marcus, moving back and forth, slow dancing. "I can't go on if you're still mad," he starts singing.

"I can't go on if you keep singing." I place my hands tightly on my ears. "Marcus, please, do it so he can stop." I raise my hand, jumping up and down to the amusement of Marcus. "We'll get him."

There is a long, quiet pause. Marcus side-eyes Dad, then over to me, surrendering, then high-fives me, "It's on."

CHAPTER TWENTY-TWO

The beating of my heart is going faster than I can catch my breath. The girl is outside in the chilly night air, looking in the direction of my house. I am excited she's waiting for me; at least, I hope so since she is outside first.

She has on a sweater more fitting for an adult. If she took it from the witch, she has every right to do so. We are looking at each other, waiting. I slowly raise my hand to wave at her. The girl seems to be smiling at me as she raises her hand to wave back. We continue to wave at each other like two passing on different ships for several safe minutes. I look up at the window I know is the witch's bedroom; I don't see a silhouette—it's safe. Her lights are still off.

A car's headlights betray us. She dashes back into the house, frightened, exposed, like an escapee returning.

Slowly, I go back to hiding behind the high bush, irritated at the intruder in our covert meeting. Mr. Greenly is brought out from the car, escorted by a blond-haired man way younger than him. Mr. Greenly stumbles with an unsteady walk and staggers up the short driveway, giggling like a man in love. The blond man has his arm around him like a boyfriend. At the doorstep, Mr. Greenly has his hands full of blond hair, kissing his neck, while the blond man fumbles under the entrance light for a house key. The lights flick on like stacked dominoes, spotlighting the couple as they seem to bypass the first floor, going to the second floor. The lights in the bedroom flick on for a few minutes, then off.

Mr. Greenly always checking license plates for strangers in our hood. If his boyfriend was driving his car, I'd take his plate number.

I wait for the girl to reappear, twenty minutes, then thirty, now an hour. The heaviness of my eyelids coerces me to call it a night and go to bed.

I will meet her, I will find out why she is only out at night, like the animals from the woods.

* * *

The doctor is a liar.

My plans to see the girl again tonight are ruined by the doctor standing outside with her this time. They are positioning a chair missing a leg, a soiled toddler-size mattress (was that her bed?), clothes in two boxes, and a large, rusted metal table for bulk pickup. On certain days of the month, you can discard larger items, too big for the bins for pickup. If residents put them out on days not designated, homeowners will get a kick-ass fine. Our block president, watchful Mr. Greenly, will ensure the right culprit is fined and warned not to do it again. The hefty fine is a good deterrent.

I could right now run over to Mr. Greenly and report her.

The darkness of the office conceals me safely from the doctor's view. The thick drapes deflect the streetlamp pouring through the large window. I pull the drape over when the doctor looks directly at our house despite the lights being off. The two seem to have difficulty moving the furniture. The girl is too small and the witch too thin. A puff of wind alone could blow either of them away. The girl is better insulated against the night air than the previous time. The doctor said she has two boys. Why don't the boys help? Where's the professor, her husband?

They are from a culture where women are invisible; they don't matter. I did my homework on those countries that mistreat young girls, women. The males are valued. Her country has a long list of human rights violations. If that was the doctor's reason for emigrating to America, why can't she show compassion for the girl?

She shows her predictable impatience with the girl and waves for her to hurry. The table is way bigger than she is, and it is hard for her to balance it while walking. Where does she sleep? Is she hungry? Did they kidnap her? Is that the reason for the doctor lying about her presence?

The weather will be warm soon. Spring is around the corner. In the darkness of the office, I begin praying, asking God to keep her bones warm, her body fed, and to provide protection from the doctor.

"As only you can."

Dad hates mess. He will run away at the sight of it, can smell it like a hound from miles away. He will take flight to avoid it or use an arsenal of silence, walking away without a word. Or he will change the subject, signaling the end of a discussion not to be spoken about again. Or he will deflect and use your words against you. It is never a fair fight. He's the type to throw dirt in your eyes, give the knockout punch, then ask why you're on the ground. Grandma is a considerable match, but Dad will sucker punch hundred-dollar words, toss off analytical thinking like hand grenades; Grandma counterpunches, firing biblical quotes like flame throwers.

As tough as Ma thinks she is, she is no match for Dad or Grandma.

She was no match for him when they were married. She would reach an impasse with him and, fearing another loss, commence cussing, calling Dad every name she could think of. She called him a robot, an unfeeling zombie, called him Tin Man, no heart, no feelings like his mother, his screwed-up childhood made him what he is. Ma hit a new low, attacking his mother, who died before I was born, calling her a colorist, a house negro, and a self-hating black woman.

She was wrong to talk about his mother, whom my dad adored and was very close to. I heard wonderful stories about her. Helen was her name. She was biracial and grew up in the South. Dad spoke proudly about how she came to New York to be a model, then started a successful beauty salon chain business. Her father was the mayor of a small southern town but never married her mother. Ma snickered that Helen was the product of my great grandma being a side chick, a white man's bed wench.

Ma and Grandma Helen did not get along, and she did not have a problem letting everybody know what she thought of her ex-mother-in-law. "Helen would do them dark skin women's hair, take their money. Best believe they can't step foot in her house. Ain't that some shit, a racist against your own people? You might have gotten a pass, Beenie, cause of your coloring," she laughed. "Helen wasn't too crazy about the dark."

Dad wanted to name me Helen, but Ma fought like a poked bear, refusing to name me after her enemy. They compromised with the name Rubena Helen Wilson.

After Helen's death, she bequeathed most of her assets to Dad, leaving his brothers next to nothing, severing their strained relationship. They have been estranged since; I have never met my two uncles.

Dad, unmoved by her malicious attacks, hurled hurtful words back, toppling Ma. He would correct her in mid-cussing, catapulting her into a raging bull. He'd sit back, arms folded, watching

Ma come undone, entertained by her inability to maintain control while he did. It was sadistic.

The teacher called my parents, reporting "dirty words" I'd repeated. Dad pointed to Ma, the source of my potty mouth, and reprimanded, "You see what you've done?" He'd goad Ma for her misbehavior, isolating and ignoring her, not giving her a second thought, like paint on the wall. Ma acted up, had temper tantrums like a child. Strategic planning on his part pushed her away, mindful of potential criticism about leaving a mentally ill woman with a child. Grandma accused him of not helping Ma take her medication. He protested that he had no control.

"Doll ran wild while he did nothing. Ruben just sat back, watching her come apart, wiping his hands of her," Grandma mumbled to Uncle Marsh during a visit while I listened in the hallway. "He done forgot his vows: in sickness and health. If he was what he is, he shouldn't have bothered with Doll."

Uncle Marsh tried to explain to her that Dad did everything possible to help Ma. The polar bear did most of the work driving him away.

Dad used every ammunition against Ma to win just for the sake of winning. Grandma complained of the paltry settlement he gave Ma, a bit more generous with child support but with suffocating stipulations. Ma added she qualified for public assistance because of it. He tried to get full custody, but in a brief moment of compassion, he took pity on her and relented. Ma was on the verge of a breakdown at the thought of getting visitation rights only. Grandma sniffed, "He can't have a child around with his sinful lifestyle."

How can Dad be so loving and treat people like they're invisible?

* * *

They are arguing. Not really; Marcus is doing all the talking. I can hear them from the office though their voices are only a whisper. Adults see me like a ghost, ambivalent about whether I'm in their presence or not, and it has made me a proficient spy. I'm good at listening to whispers, adapted to the skill from my experiences with my parents, Grandma, and landlords.

Against the door, gently opening it without sound, I see Dad silent as a stone, looking straight at Marcus like he is not there. Dad does not see him nor is he hearing him; I can tell just by the look on his face. The Matisse print on the wall has his undivided attention as Marcus flails his arms, clenches his fists, then slams his palms against his thighs.

"Everything has to be your way. How is that a partnership, Ruben?"

Now Dad looks down at the cherrywood floors Marcus spent a fortune on, sulking at the waste of money. He would have purchased fake floors rather than expensive wood.

Dad slowly looks up at him and fires a rebuttal to lock up Marcus like a deadbolt. Without a facial muscle moving, not an eye blinking, he says, "Doll is killing me with alimony and child support. You're killing me with frivolous spending. You got the house, the floors you wanted, that damn ten-grand table we eat off. I earn, you spend, that's our partnership."

I never told Dad what Ma does with the support money for me; he only has to go on Instagram really to see. Grandma told me she was pissed off the support check was reduced to next to nothing since I no longer live with Ma. She does not have to pay any rent, other than a court case settlement with the West Indian landlord. Dad will not give Ma one cent for the back rent. He gives her a little money out of pity and, knowing him, Ma better appreciate it, or she'll be cut off totally.

I see the look on Marcus's face, temple vein bulging, lips forbidden to release words he will regret. He loves him way too much, and it is painful to watch. I wonder if Dad loves him just as much—or less.

Marcus folds his arms, shaking his head. "We're a team. You're not alone anymore. You don't get it."

"I don't want to argue anymore about it." He is pointing at the door with me behind it.

"Why must everything be a fight, a challenge for you to win?"

"Beenie needs to get ready for bed."

I shuffle quickly back, pretending to sleep with my arms under my head on the desk. Dad leans in sideways with a wide smile like nothing never happened. "Wake up, Beenie, time for bed."

I join them in the living room to bid good night. Dad does not hide they were fighting. Marcus half-smiles and plants a kiss on my forehead as he hugs me for comfort. I want to console him, feeling the weight of tears inside him. He reminds me, "I'll get up a little early to make the brownies, I promise. Make sure Tiki get some too."

Dad asks, "Who?" It's a safe topic for him.

We both ignore him. I look up at Marcus, nodding, my arms wrapped tightly around his muscular body, returning his hug, feeling the sadness transfer to me. The burden of his pain makes my knees wobbly.

Dad takes his turn to kiss me goodnight with his hand extending to Marcus, who sighs so loudly he could wake the angels as he takes Dad's hand in defeat.

My father wins, but it is a hollow victory.

If Dad breaks Marcus's heart, I will never forgive him.

CHAPTER TWENTY-THREE

"Rubena, check this out."

We decide to hang out at my house instead of going to the mall because of the flooding, rain, and thunder. Marcus made us lunch of fish tacos with curly fries. Tiki frowns. She don't like fish. Marcus coaxes her to give it a try, and if she does not like it, he will make her a cheeseburger. Tiki wolfs down two, asking for another. Marcus amazed a thin girl like Tiki has the stomach capacity of a linebacker.

Yesterday, Sasha announced that Tiki would spend the weekend with Lorna since they left on bad terms at the nursing home the last time she went to see Peggy, her grandmother. We both knew better; it was her day off from work, and Sasha wanted alone time with loser Matt in their shoebox apartment.

"I'd rather sleep in the rain, die of pneumonia than go there."

"Where you gonna stay?" I asked.

"Under this tree at school until Monday. I'd rather stink than be stressed."

I told Marcus and Dad about her situation, and they agreed to let her stay with me. Tiki wanted to cry when I told her the good news that she gonna spend the weekend at my house rather than with Lorna and creepy Speed; instead, she caught herself, puffed her chest, bearhugged me, and attempted to do the same to my dad, but he was too tall for her at six foot one.

While I rested comfortably in my bedroom, she took a long shower, washed her hair, and then flopped on my bed with its clean, crisp sheets and let out a grateful sigh for what a home should be—warm with love, a full belly, and not strife. She could not stop inhaling the bedding until I jokingly yelled at her we got work to do.

Our teacher discussed slavery in America in the past and today all over the world. Child slavery exists in parts of central Africa and several countries beyond the African continent. In Pakistan and Yemen, girls as young as eight are forced to marry men old enough to be their grandfathers. Children from the poorest families are sold as servants. Tiki told me of a former classmate whose parents kept a slave from Afghanistan. The girl saw a chance to escape when she was with the woman in the emergency room, being treated for a fall. The scandal forced the classmate's family to leave Upstate.

"Man, I can't imagine being treated like that." Tiki shakes her wet head. She is sitting so close beside me that I can smell traces of my lavender shampoo in her hair. "Being forced to marry some old fart like your grandfather you don't even know. Perv country, that's where Speed belongs. He'd be right at home there."

"They don't have a choice," I say as we move on to the next country.

In Mauritania in western Sahara and Morocco, girls as young as five are sent to camps to gain weight in preparation for marriage. It is the practice of leblouh or force-feeding. Obese females are status symbols for husbands. Girls are force-fed like geese are for foie gras until they ready for marriage. They are beaten, abused if they fail to gain massive amounts of weight.

"God, so awful being force-fed like that." Tiki is amazed at the level of cruelty girls suffer all over the world beside America. "I thought I had it bad. It's shitty here, but it's worst there. At least when I'm old enough, I can escape this crap."

We discussed how hundreds of girls and women are kidnapped by terrorists. "You think your neighbor got a slave in her home?" Tiki asks.

"Why would she lie about her? They are from a country with history of human rights problems. The doctor said she had no girl in her house. I saw her a couple of times, and it wasn't a boy. It was a small girl. I stood face to face with her. She has two boys in boarding school. I wanna talk to her. Her native language is French. I can talk to her."

"How?"

"I don't know."

Tiki did not keep her promise to stay up with me. After we watched the second movie, past midnight, she was counting sheep.

I look over at her sleeping sound. A faint snore moves the sheet she is under as she exhales. A blanket thief, so I got a second one to cover myself up with.

Unable to sleep, I quietly slip out of bed so as not to disturb her, retrieve the empty pizza box, cans of soda, and a half-eaten bag of chips and make my way downstairs to discard them. I decide to put them in the recycle bins outside.

Pulling at the collars of my flannel robe to protect against the damp night air and mindful of the puddles from the rainstorm earlier, I go outside. Despite my efforts, my bunny slippers are saturated.

Mr. Greenly's lights are on. He must be a night crawler, a party animal—strange for a man his age. He is more like a grandfather type though he has no one since he does not speak to his only child. He attends mass regularly with his elderly mother, whom he retrieves from her retirement home in the next town. Often, he will bring her to his house for Sunday dinner. He handles her tenderly as he assists her getting out of his car into a wheelchair. She is a typical blue-hair lady with blue hands.

I look up at his window, see him and a male figure I can't make out play fighting with pillows. They pause for a bottle drink. Now they are dancing and laughing. I move a little closer to focus. He is dancing with a short man. Maybe it's a boy; I can't tell. The dance partner appears not to want to dance with him. He is pushing Mr. Greenly away. Funny, little old man, I can't imagine him being playful.

He stops in his tracks, appearing frightened, then spins around, looking out his window, immediately drawing the shades and curtain. I don't think he saw me. Maybe he did or was afraid someone might.

The girl is near the front door of her home—not too far in case she has to run back in quickly, unnoticed. Preparing for flight? Maybe not. She waves at me like we've been longtime friends, or maybe she's asking for help. Praying my eyes not tricking me, I see her take a step farther. Now she on the driveway pavement, smiling. My heart jumps to my throat as I watch her about to approach me when, instinctively, the light in the bedroom flicks. The girl bolts as if she is escaping a fire. I watch the window, waiting for the witch to appear. Nothing, the bedroom light is off again. It is safe for her to come back out; I'm hopeful we may finally be able to talk.

I wait for her to resurface; certain she would see the coast is clear for us to appear before each other. The rain starting to come back like a joy killer, picking up intensity until it's a downpour. I try to make a run for it, but my rain-soaked slippers hinder me.

I go back inside.

First the wicked witch, now the rain. I'm delayed, but I will not be deterred: the girl and I will meet, and soon. I cannot stop; it is unfinished business with us. I want to know who she is, where she is from, why she is here, and what the witch is to her. Why is the witch hiding her?

I cannot reason why I am obsessing—why do I have to know?

Maybe I'm nosy like Marcus. I like to think it's what Dad says is a good point about me—I'm inquisitive.

CHAPTER TWENTY-FOUR

We are at Tiki's real home. If you would like to call it one. It is not fit for humans nor animals. Smells of stale cigarettes, old garbage, beer bottles, and rotting food assault my nose, preparing me for flight. I'm ready to turn around and run back outside, ready to puke on the sparse lawn with plastic flamingos and Santa Claus without his hat and faded from the sun. The stench is stuck in my throat: I'm unable to cough it out.

I feel so sorry for Lorna's ragged Tabby, Mink. The poor cat has to live among filth. It is easy to see how fat Mink is by so much free eating of food on the counter and on the floor of Lorna's trailer. Mink the cat is a pig. I make a mental note to remove my shoes and jacket when I return home.

It took two bus exchanges and a ten-minute walk to get there. I did not tell Marcus or, worst, my father; he would have stopped me.

The trailer park is compact with rows of homes and very little space for privacy. You could easily sit outside or by the window washing dishes while your neighbors watch you to see what you are up to.

Tiki needed a change of clothes for the week. She asked her

sister for help, to drive her over there. Sasha's jalopy needs brakes, costing money she does not have, and couldn't do it, so we were left with no choice but to take transit, which is terribly unreliable. When I lived in the city, the trains ran twenty-four-seven and usually on time. Sometimes.

Sasha claimed Matt needed the car despite the repair. He took the car after he dropped her off at work, refusing to give Tiki a ride to Lorna's. I pointed out that the risk is less if we take the bus than to ride in a car with no brakes and a druggie.

"Look who's back" is the only greeting Lorna has for her daughter. She gets up, unsteady, with one free arm for balance, and walks to the kitchen to get more ice for her face. She removes the ice pack, showcasing purple and blue, the colors radiating down to her lower jaw. Lorna winces, touching her face. "You missed me?"

Tiki frowns at her as though she ingested vomit. "I'm not here to *see you*, I need my clothes. We won't be here long. What happened to your face? Oh, oh, oh, I know the answer; what is ass whipping from a turd boyfriend?"

"Don't start with me," she leans into the small kitchen window, squinting. "Don't say anything to them, you hear me?"

Lorna the loser—what Speed called her and punched her in the face and took off before the neighbors called the cops. She warns Tiki not to tell them the truth. Lorna is clueless; they don't need her cooperation to press charges. The state will do it on her behalf, Tiki informs her, adding Speed has a warrant for his arrest for failing to appear for a previous assault offense.

The Hispanic and African American cops come to the trailer, by rote, as it is routine to them by now. Lorna tries to smile and bullshit them away from what they already know about her and Speed. She was drunk and tripped and fell down the basement steps trying to get to the washer to put fabric softener before the rinse cycle; her attempt at joking warrants crickets. No one laughs, especially the cops, who are unsmiling and unable to hide their irritation at her and Speed. She is so high and drunk, she can't even get her lies straight to fool them. Even the cops think she is dumb with that answer; just by looking at her and her messy trailer, they can see it does not have a basement nor steps leading to one.

No wonder Tiki would rather sleep on her sister's couch or under a tree in the rain.

"At least I can take a bath in peace until the dickhead returns," she says.

Tiki once said her mother was beautiful before ugly assaulted her. I look at Lorna, searching for any trace of beauty left on her beat-up, fifty-year-old face. She looks closer to an eighty-year-old, horizontal lines folding like an accordion. Third runner-up in the 1989 Miss New York beauty pageant, Peggy and Lorna, mother and daughter, were pageant freaks traveling to every contest in New York and other states where Peggy would forge documents to prove residential status.

Tiki showed me photos as proof of what Lorna was, failing to prosper beyond the beauty pageant circuit. I cannot believe they are the same person. The trophies Speed did not break line the top of the kitchen cabinet next to the rusted crock-pot and cast-iron frying pan. Third runner-up Miss Palisades, third runner-up Miss Teen New York, and honorable mention in the local Miss Upstate County.

"You were always runner-up something," Tiki snickers.

"I was robbed," Lorna laughs between hacking nicotine coughs, touching her face.

"They kicked her out because she violated the morale clause," Tiki offers between Lorna's ear-defeating coughs. "Sasha was at the last pageant. Mom covered it up until her water broke."

"Thank God wasn't no swimsuit competition. Called my name as the third runner-up." Lorna leans forward, hacking and laughing. "If your sister didn't pop out, I would have won."

"No, you wouldn't—you would have just been a runner-up. That's what you're good for."

"Stop being so mean to me," Lorna's voice softens as she places the ice pack on her face.

"Stop being mean to yourself," Tiki shoots back.

The cops seem impatient with the frivolous chatter. They speak robotically of procedural protocol, unsmiling, disinterested in Lorna's pleas not to charge Speed. This will be his umpteenth arrest for domestic violence. Her pleas fall on deaf ears; the cops advise he'll be arrested once they find him.

Tiki assists her mother back into her chair near the kitchen. Lorna resumes smoking cigarettes, staring at her trophies and looking at them hard enough to give her the life she wanted when she was young, hopeful, and pretty. The nicotine is burning my eyes and throat. I will have to sneak my clothes in the washer before Dad or Marcus find them and ignite an inquiry of what I've been up to.

No one knows how old Speed really is, including Tiki, but she says her mother got at least twenty-five years on him.

"I heard them last night when I called. He started cursing the cougar, calling her a dumb bitch when she could not find her license. They needed it to buy beer. Lorna hollering she don't have no money left after he stole from her. That's all he does for you, right, Mom? Steal money you don't have and beat you—sounds like a winner to me."

Lorna positions the ice pack again on her swollen face as the cops escort themselves out of the trailer, then says directly to Tiki, "Get your clothes and get out."

We are waiting for the bus to pick us up, glad to get out of Lorna's house and away from her filthy home. Tiki stares at the bundles of clothes thrown haphazardly in three shopping bags. She packed frantically to get away from her mother. I was glad to get away from that trailer park. She tells me Sasha gonna make her leave those shopping bags of clothes outside until they make it to the laundromat for fear of roaches from Lorna's trailer.

She is picking at her nails, tearing off the cuticles, not caring it draws blood. "Peggy's getting worse, won't be around too long. Be nobody left for me."

"Sorry."

She spits out a nail. "The nursing home called Stupid. I'm glad I was there when they called. She's useless. The only time Lorna pays attention is when there's a bottle." Tiki looks down at the concrete, focusing on the weeds sprouting between the cracks. "I gotta prepare myself for life without my grandma. I want them both to get better. I'm tired of hating my mother, but I can't stop. She makes it so easy to do."

"You hate the alcohol, not her, and the drama."

The bus was now two stoplights away. Tiki rests her face in her hands, her elbows supported by her knees, watching the bus at a distance, her back at me. "No, I hate her too. Every mother in the animal kingdom fights to the death to protect their kids. Why can't humans do the same?"

As we hoisted her bags to the back of the bus, ignoring the stares and twisted faces, we run out things to talk about as her mind somewhere else, thinking hard. Brows knit her forehead as she leans against the window, staring out.

"If he was gone, I could really help her," she breaks her silence. "I wish he would go to Afghanistan, run up against the Taliban, someone, get kidnapped."

"Who?"

"Speed."

"You don't want him to be beheaded."

She uses her thumb to scratch off a small window label. "Yeah, I do. They can send it back to me so I can spit on it."

At school, Tiki told me they found Speed's fake ID, got the beer, began drinking, cursing, and fighting again. The trigger word for Lorna is old. Speed calls her old and beat up, how he going to date some chick his age.

"He says to me all the time, I'm going to be way prettier than Lorna, gonna wait for me, with his freaking glassy eyes and stinky beer breath.

"Lorna too drunk, depressed to say or do anything, motionless, like she's dead. Only when the beer is gone, no more weed, she wakes up alert and ready to resume fighting over who took the last beer, who got higher than the other? It ended with Speed punching her on the other side of her face. She looks like a drunken racoon.

"Same shit, different day," Tiki says, shaking her head. "A neighbor dropped a dime on Speed, and the cops finally got him. He ain't got no bail money. Thank God," Tiki says with the back of her hand planted firmly against her forehead, breaking into a fake ugly cry. "She all depressed, crying for her Speed. Dumbass.

"Mom called Sasha bawling like a hoe missing her pimp, begging for bail money. Sasha said, 'Hell no,' so loud every person in Upstate heard her and disconnected Dumbo. I think she blocked her. Oh man, now I'll try to go back there, try to clean that nasty ass house, you wanna help me?"

"Only if you give me a hazmat suit, goggles, gloves, and a respirator and boat load of bank."

"You know my ass is broke, bitch."

"That's your answer, dumbass."

A hopeful smile appears on her face like a rainbow after a terrible storm. Tiki sighs. "Lorna never cooperates, goes mute when bad things happen that she can't deal with. This time will be different, her chance to be normal, maybe we can talk nice to each other." She shrugs. "It's never happened, but we can try, right?"

CHAPTER TWENTY-FIVE

Carefully navigating in the dark to avoid using lights that might wake up Dad and Marcus, I succeed in reaching the front door without a sound. Outside, I see a different raccoon dining on uncovered garbage and a possum waiting his turn, unfazed by a barking dog that is safely behind a gate. Where is Bully? What reaction would he have seeing a competitor invading his turf? The possum can play dead if Bully shows up, but there will be hell to pay for this rogue raccoon. The invader perks up on hind legs, showing she is a female, but I don't see any babies. Maybe she is Bully's girlfriend. Maybe he's watching the babies while she shops the garbage for food. I'll call her Bebe. As long as I don't see a skunk, or a fox, my plans are in motion.

She should be out soon, after midnight, to take the garbage out. Looking up at the bedroom window, I see there are no lights on. If the witch entrusted her to work alone, it will be good for us.

My welcome gift included a note along with a piece of chocolate. I'm sure it is nothing like the chocolate she had in Europe, but Kit Kat is the bomb too.

Welcome to America. My name is Rubena. I live in the house across the street from you.

Bienvenue aux États-Unis. Je m'appelle Rubena. J'habite dans la maison d'en face.

Stealthily, quickly, I avoid watchful eyes and the streetlight and slink over to the garbage can in front of their home. I place the chocolate and note, secured in a brown lunch bag and weighed down with a stone, so the wind does not sweep it away.

A beaming light blinds me. Upon seeing Mr. Greenly staring, holding a flashlight, and looking curious as the night, his eye tick at full volume, I give him a high-wattage smile and wave. "Hi, Mr. Greenly."

"Good evening, Rubena. What are you doing? "

"I was taking out the garbage, and I saw from a distance that somebody, maybe from our hood, or maybe not, left a bag on the side of the bin. I want to be a good neighbor like you, making sure there's no straggling garbage on the sidewalk."

He tilts his dome, purses his lips, and manages to release, "You're not leaving goodies for the vermin, are you?" He lowers the flashlight, spotting the bag, then looks back at me blinking like a prime suspect failing a lie detector. "We work very hard to get rid of them, not to kill, but to send back to the woodlands. The vermin have plenty to eat in the words, no natural predators to—"

"What about the coyotes and the foxes?" I interrupt him.

"Where they belong," he cuts me off.

I pick up the bag. "You did a great job with the potluck. Everyone was raving about it, how every year you out do yourself, Mr. Greenly. Everyone talked about how grateful they are to have you as the block president."

His face melts like a glacier in hell, smiling now, the flashlight off. I can still see his shiny dome; his eye tick relaxes a little. "Really? I'm happy the neighborhood appreciates my efforts."

"No doubt. My dads loved it."

131

"Marcus is a superb cook," he says. An amorous smile plasters his cherubic face mentioning his name. His taste goes beyond beach-boy blond. Maybe he likes chocolate, too, though Marcus calls him Pillsbury dough boy. "You're a lucky girl to have a good cook in your home."

"Why didn't you bring your son to the potluck?"

"Son?" His body shifts as his smile melts away from his face, quickly creating a toxic sludge.

I push on. "Yeah, the blond hair kid. He's your son, right?"

He mulls over the question, not to provide a response, he's thinking about what I said, more important what I seen. He eyes me evenly, taking in more air than his lungs need, generating a cough stuck in his chest, nervous, but more so annoyance at my intrusion on his rights to privacy, to live his life without surveillance. "Young lady, you need to mind your business."

"You mind everybody's business." I ignore the scowl on his lobster-red face.

"*Goodnight,* Rubena."

"Oh, can I ask you a question?"

Mr. Greenly folds his arms, impatient. "What is it?

"You help people in need. You're a lawyer, right?"

"Retired attorney for Legal Aid," he emphasizes "retired."

"If someone is being held against their will, like a slave, what should they do?"

"You know of one who's a victim of enslavement?" he asks as my head shakes violently not to betray the girl. "Well, first, run to the nearest precinct to inform them. Next, contact agencies that help victims find temporary shelter from their abusers. Legal Aid's available to assist the victim. Now that I've given free legal advice, in exchange, you must be a good neighbor to help keep our block pristine, fair enough?"

"Night, Mr. Greenly."

"Please make sure that bag goes into the garbage, not to the critters." His voice raises then trails off as he positions his garbage can, securing it.

I walk quickly to the front door, feeling the weight of his eyes on my spine, ensuring I am near the entrance to home to his satisfaction. I manage to catch his back turned and sprint behind the brush, waiting for him to disappear into his home. Mr. Greenly straightens the bins in formation, then double-checks the offender's can is secured. He does a panoramic search one last time and finally makes his way inside, lights off.

Quickly, I run back across the street, dropping the bag away from his view, then dash inside, standing behind the curtain in the office to watch and wait.

I see the girl. She's fearful of Bebe the raccoon, keeping a safe distance away as she places the trash in the garbage. I see Bebe, standing defiant on hindlegs, my kind of girl. "Screw Mr. Greenly" is her rebuttal as she maneuvers the lid, knocking it off.

The girl pauses, looking back at the doctor's home and then spots the lunch bag. I force my feet not to jump, my hands not to clap; they defy me. I do a two-fist pump and a hell yeah as she reading my note, stopping to check that she is not being watched.

She inspects the candy like a bomb waiting to explode, smelling it, and then licks it and takes a bite. The smile will not abandon my face; it will not stop, watching her read my note. She is reading my note again, happy someone speaks her language. She is not alone. Then when she looks in the direction of my house, I open the door and step outside, and we begin to wave like crazy until my hand hurts. She gives me a thumb's up as I close the door, mindful of Mr. Greenly.

Tucked inside the office, I watch as she stuffs the Kit Kat in her mouth, chewing quickly. She reads the note again and stuffs it down her underpants before going back into the house. Luckily, the doctor is nowhere in sight. The lights are off in her bedroom.

I will send the girl another note.

Next time, I will include Marcus's famous cookies.

CHAPTER TWENTY-SIX

We are on the stoop in the back of the school building, facing the parking lot and watching kids line up for the bus.

We are glad it is the start of the weekend. Tiki, though, she bummed out about it because I'm going to the city to Grandma's. She hates Fridays because she won't have me around. I'm her only true friend.

Sasha needs babysitting services the entire weekend so the bright side is spending it with Madison, whom Tiki adores and will fearlessly protect from predators on four legs and especially those on two. She will not let Madison nowhere near Speed though his preference is preteen, girls with buds—that is what he did time for.

I once asked her, "Did he ever—"

"If he did, I wouldn't be here talking to you. I'd be in juvenile hall or tried as an adult 'cause he would definitely be dead."

She is resigned to another dull weekend. "Well, I don't have to stay with Stupid; least gotta a couch to sleep on and my baby Madison beside me." She shrugs. "It won't be that bad, but I'm gonna miss you, bitch."

"I know, dumbass."

I promise next weekend we will hang out, go to the mall for lunch and a movie. My treat: Tiki does not get an allowance from her mother or her sister. They always cry poverty; really are—from what I can see. Her sister gives Tiki bags and bags of bottles to return at the supermarket, but she can only have a third of the money. They regularly drive to neighborhoods in the exclusive side of Upstate to ask residents if she can take deposit-return bottles from their bins.

"Most of the people are nice about it," Tiki says, "but when I reach Sophie or Gwynne or Molly's hood, I stay in the car, hiding. I'm not giving them bitchy snobs tea to spill about me. They'll run to Amber faster than they can TikTok it."

I offer, "We got plenty of bottles you can take. Marcus finds them a pain to return. I don't think my neighbors care if you take theirs either."

Tiki laughs at me like she got a secret. "We did a few times, long ago, but this short chubby turd, blinking fast like he got something stuck in his eye, came charging out of his house, running like an overweight puppy and threatening to call police if we came in his neighborhood again. His eyes followed us out 'til we got on the main road. He kept walking behind our car 'til he disappeared." Tiki sucks in some air, adding, "Those people don't need the money for bottle returns—the fat fuck."

Mr. Greenly, the neighborhood overweight puppy watch.

"I'm lucky if I get to keep five dollars," Tiki says. "See, that's why I want to be sixteen so badly so I can get away from this shit."

"It won't be so bad now your mom kicked Speed out the house. You'll be able to have a hot shower without drama."

"We'll see if he makes bail," she says. "Screw that, I'm taking a nice long bath. I might stay the weekend in the tub." She bugs her eyes, poking me, laughing. "No telling when my mom gets hard up for a replacement or takes that asshole back."

Seniors get into their cars, some used, many spanking new,

while others brave the walk home despite skies warning of rain to follow. Tiki and I shoot for cover under the large oak as sudden, drizzling rain tickles us. We're watching for Dad, who is off today. He's taking me to the city but first treating Tiki and me to burgers and fries at the new Shake Shack in town. This will be a good meal for Tiki until I return. I'll make sure she has extra burgers for her and Madison.

While I'm checking my texts, Tiki nudges me, "Rubena, look!"

A large black SUV swings up to the curb with a slight sound of a skid, and out comes a tall girl, who looks young but is dressed older. Her hair is blond with screaming dark roots, and she wearing platform heels and skinny jeans with a midriff exposing pale skin and a belly ring. Tiki and I squint, focusing on the girl as she talks to a slim-built black man with a goatee in the driver's seat. The girl nods crazy like her head is about to snap off. She is standing outside the car, texting with the fastest fingers while getting peed on by the rain. The man seems unconcerned the girl getting wet. He looks over at us like possible prospects, staring hard enough for us to remember his face, then looks straight ahead as if he made a mistake, dismissing us as rejects. We double our efforts, staring at him. He looks in his early twenties or more, cream brown skin with slight acne that does little to diminish his hip-hop rap star look.

"The music is so loud; how can she hear him?" Tiki says, snapping her fingers as our favorite hip-hop artist is blaring loud enough to wake Grandma up in the city.

From behind us, the clicking sound of heels in a hurry is Amber Mills, running like she is avoiding an avalanche.

"Hey losers!" She speeds past, gifting us a middle finger.

The dirty blond girl is smiling ear to ear like she won a prize. The man is happy too, like he got a fertile golden goose. His demeanor tells us he has replaced the blond girl for Amber, the new target of his affection. Amber is fresh-faced compared to the seasoned blond girl, who probably was once his favorite bae.

He is acting like he got the most popular girl, more pretty than the blond. The blond girl holds the door for Amber like she's royalty. The man's really cheesing now like it is the first time meeting Amber. He turns around to face her, says something, making Amber toss her hair back, laughing. As the door closes, she is bopping, snapping fingers, and seat dancing.

"What a bitch," Tiki says.

CHAPTER TWENTY-SEVEN

Ma and Miss Tamara still friends, but she refused to have Ma live with her ever again. She broke the trust that cannot be repaired. "Doll makes a mess, then leave it for everybody else to clean after her," Grandma rants to Uncle Marsh, who don't say much, just, "Uh huh, really? Seriously?" Grandma vents frustration about Ma. He gives Grandma eye contact, a slight nod, but his mind somewhere else with an eye on his Rolex.

Ma staying with Penguin and Miss Henderson, who is getting on her nerves with constant nagging and ailing health. "That old hen keeps stressing me and Penguin 'bout cleaning her apartment already clean, make sure the door is locked, the building safer than Fort Knox," she complains to me.

Grandma is two floors below, living with Jamal. All of them living illegally in the seniors' complex. It's a good thing their neighbors are church people doing God's work and don't care for housing authority people who make sporadic inspection visits to ensure the rules are enforced.

The neighbors alert the building when the housing authority arrive, moving evidence of clothes not belonging to a senior citizen.

The offender will go to the neighbor's apartment, lay low until it is time for their own apartment to be inspected. If caught, the lie is they left clothes overnight, my elderly parent fell or just got out of the hospital, and I'm staying overnight to watch them. The tenants and family members use every rule in the playbook to fool the housing authority. "Snooty black folks following the white people like slaves," Grandma sniffed once after her inspection. Even the super aids and abets them.

Ma has been hounding Penguin to find them an apartment so she can get away from Miss Henderson before the polar bear attacks her.

She and Grandma are cordial to each other; Grandma had Ma over for dinner last night. That made Jamal so happy. "You the only one missing," he told me.

The weather allows Ma and me to walk a safe distance away from house-bound people watching from the window. We walk several blocks, pick up water from a bodega, and find a stoop to sit and take in the sun and each other. We navigate to safer topics like excellent grades, my large bedroom, eating good food, and school. I also tell her about my new friend Tiki and her situation.

"Well, you keep on being a good friend to her," she says. "They hard to come by."

"What's up with you and Miss Tamara?"

Ma mulls over my question for a second. "We good, just need to heal first."

She gut-laughs over stories about Mr. Greenly. "Nosiness is a global thing, Beenie. You got one in every city, state, country, and continent. Nosy neighbors are good for one thing, bad for many."

Ma stands up, dusting her backside, extends a hand to me, and dusts me off like she did when I was little. We are back at the seniors complex, navigating to an empty bench, looking away from each other at the surrounding neighborhood now full of grandchildren of every race and reflective of the residents in the building. I close my eyes as rays warm my face, taking in as much vitamin D as I can. Without reason, I half-open them to see Ma looking at me as though she has never seen me before. Do I look different to her? How, I do not know.

"You gonna get better?"

She places her arm around me, gently squeezing. "I'm trying, Beenie."

CHAPTER TWENTY-EIGHT

Mr. Cicero Bird is a mad cool old dude sweating Grandma. He posts himself outside of his apartment every morning, waiting for her passing like a dog for its owner. A big, wide cat-grinning smile appears, overtaking his old brown face as he tips his signature fedora at her. He serenades tenants, really Grandma, with his saxophone, like a big, comforting, reassuring hug; the music brings to mind lost youth, loves long gone, sad hearts, arthritic souls, heartbreak echoing through hallways, neighboring apartments above and below.

He performed with jazz greats of his time: Charlie Parker, Dizzy Gillespie, and his friend and competitor, John Coltrane. Grandma chastised, "Boasting ain't God-like," but I enjoy listening to him. I didn't know jack about jazz until I met Mr. Cicero Bird.

I love hearing stories about his life on the road, travels all over the world, interesting people who crossed his path. His apartment tells of a man who witnessed change for black people. He marched with Dr. King in Selma, helped register voters in the South, performed as reward for people registering to vote, especially his home state of North Carolina.

He tells me about pretty ladies in his path but none as pretty as Grandma. He gave me that information. I took the liberty of passing it to her, who responded, I need not mind "grown folk's business."

"Love is everybody's business, Grandma."

Whenever Grandma can't think of comeback, she tells me to "hush girl."

He has been a widower for twenty years and has no children. Grandma told me she'd never witnessed a man so sad, so pitiful when Mr. Bird lost his beloved Minerva. Grandma said she was a fine God-fearing woman. Grandma always recall people who have passed away as a fine God-fearing person even if it was not true. Miss Lulu Bell once corrected her over tea with me and Grandma's famous pound cake.

"Now Eudora, you know old Minerva was ornery, tight-fisted, barely helped the church in tithing. Always worrying about Cicero and his wandering eyes so much she couldn't stay longer after praise and worship." She rolled back, laughing so hard I noticed the caps in her mouth. "She devised a plan to keep an eye on him volunteering his services for the music ministry for Sunday so she could watch him." Miss Lulu Bell pointed a finger up at the ceiling, then down to the floor. "Don't rightly know where she is, but she probably watching him now."

"Hush, Lulu Bell, don't talk mess in front of Beenie." Grandma threw her hands at Miss Lulu Bell, still laughing. "Woman, you know better than to speak ill of the dead." Grandma pursed her lips, but a small laugh escaped. She side-eyed me, then over to Miss Lulu Bell with a flatline mouth to stop.

Mr. Bird continued to play first Sunday at church long after his wife's passing, teaching sax at the youth center. Even at his age, Mr. Bird still gives back to the community, particularly the young.

"Morning, Eudora," his voice is big and wide as the endless sky.

MARGARET BUCKHANON

He barely contains his enthusiasm at the sight of her. "God saw to it to give you a day as pretty as you."

Ma says his voice is like the sax he plays so beautifully; it'll make a woman slip off her panties. It hasn't worked for Grandma as far as I know, at least not when Jamal and me are around.

Jamal and me helping Grandma with laundry, heading to the laundromat, a five-minute walk from her building. She enjoys the exercise but does not trust the cleaning ability of the washer and dryer in the apartment, often in need of repairs. Grandma says the illegal tenants are at fault; they are irresponsible, careless, do not pick up their laundry timely so the real tenants can use them. The damp, musty smell and lack of ventilation make her dizzy, and it is poorly lit even during the day.

Grandma does not fool me. She acts like she doesn't care, all dignified, back straight, tight-lipped, and proper. "Morning, Mr. Bird," Grandma says like she is the Queen of England without the hand wave. She pretending to be indifferent to Mr. Cicero Bird's charm, but she's falling for it.

Miss Lulu Bell leaning out of the window, sipping and watching, laughing as she teases Grandma. "Stop that nonsense, Eudora, when's the last time you had a gentleman caller?"

"Mind your business, Lulu Bell. Grandchildren are with me."

Miss Lulu Bell laughs her signature strangled hyena laugh. It is infectious as Jamal and I start laughing, not at Grandma or Mr. Cicero Bird, but at Miss Lulu Bell's strange, cackling laughter. She closes her window and joins us outside.

Grandma parks the shopping cart full of dirty laundry, joining Miss Lulu Bell. She offers us cupcakes, telling us to go to her apartment and get them on the kitchen counter.

"Don't ya'll forget my key, or I'm gonna move in with you."

Jamal and I enjoy the gooey cupcake with sun warming our faces, mouths pulverizing the sweet, seated beside Grandma and Miss Lulu Bell. "Lulu Bell, I got chores to do, can't stay too long."

"Oh, sit down for a spell, woman." Miss Lulu Bell gulps hot coffee without a concern for her tongue.

The seniors are up and out of their apartments to take advantage of the warm weekend's spring-like weather, including Ms. Bette Mitchell, who does not hide nor is shameful of libidinous behavior in front of us minors. She conveniently appears right on cue when Mr. Bird greets Grandma each morning like a deprived old dog needing to pee. She zeros in on the object of her affection, none other than Mr. Bird, now seated beside Grandma and Miss Lulu Bell.

"Lord, look at Bette. Trifling." Ms. Lulu Bell shakes her head.

Ms. Bette is Grandma's biggest adversary for the affection of Mr. Bird and being married to a man with dementia is not a deterrent. Grandma and Miss Lulu Bell commence to talk how whorish, common Ms. Bette was, a married woman acting that way as if her husband is invisible.

"It's just scandalous how that heifer is shaking her sagging old stuff like its hot sauce on a pork chop in front of Mr. Horace Mitchell. She ought to be ashamed," Miss Lulu Bell says, leaning over to Grandma, whispering loud enough for an unfazed Ms. Bette to hear. Miss Lulu Bell shakes her head. "Poor Mr. Horace Mitchell, a sad sack of a human lopped over by stroke and broken heart."

Mr. Bird's eyes are glued to Grandma, prompting Miss Bette to up her game, a thirsty woman in the worst drought. She starts dancing with a bag of garbage to anchor her. "Hey Ba-beee," she drags a mile and a half, wearing a satin slip in an open housecoat with no bra on.

Grandma mumbles under her breath, then grunts, pulling us along, leaving Miss Lulu Bell and Mr. Bird burning a hole in our backs.

"Beenie, you owe me a visit," Miss Lulu Bell shouts out. I give her a thumbs up.

It's funny watching the drama of old people acting like teenagers.

I keep my promise to Miss Lulu Bell Davis and stop by her place before I return to Upstate. Her apartment is a kaleidoscope of colors, patterns, prints of every shape and size beyond imagination. It is dizzying as I make my way to sit down to enjoy her famous peach cobbler and sassafras tea. Miss Lulu Bell has tea with me but enhances hers with rum, talkative like a woman who has been in isolation for decades.

Grandma and Miss Lulu Bell became fast friends on their first day on the job at the Department of Social Services in 1970s Harlem. She says they both had helmet-size afros, raised a black power fist to each other in the morning and the evening to the horror of the few white people in the office. The minority whites later realized it was simply a salute, a greeting in the newfound "Say it loud, I'm black, and I'm proud" theme of the time after centuries of white oppression.

They socialized after work, partied, smoked weed, and dated.

"Eudora don't want nobody to know how wild she was," Miss Lulu Bell hyena laughs at the past. "Girl, your grandma use to cut up, be the first on the dance floor, the last to leave, called her Dancing Dora. She could dance, honey, be the first one to start the soul train line. That's when you gather a heap of folks, line 'em up, start dancing down the line until it's your turn. You could have a partner or dance by yourself. I'ma hog light so I always danced down the aisle alone. I had skills back then until arthritis and hip replacement stopped me."

Miss Lulu Bell puts a little more rum in her tea and throws her head back. "Oooo wheew, we had fun back in them days. Eudora could've put Josephine Baker outta business, that's the truth.

"Smoked weed more than anybody I knew until she got married, went back to Jesus. I joined her in church, shortly later on. After a while, you know it's time to leave the party when your number's off the calendar. You too old to be in the club then, but Beenie baby, God knows we had fun." Miss Lulu Bell leans in close to me. "Lord, girl, don't never let Eudora know what I done told you. You hear?"

I cross my heart to keep Grandma's crazy days to myself. "Did you know my grandfather?"

Her smile suddenly melts away like bad news. Miss Lulu Bell falls back to taking her tea, a hot-pink-painted pinky raised, then she inhales, taking all the oxygen in her apartment, and exhales.

"Now, I am a God-fearing woman, your grandma is too, but that man, he came outta the womb holding a bible full of judgment. He was a good, very good, provider, loved his children. But he took the fun outta the word fun, and that's all I'm gonna say about your late grandfather."

It's better to move on to get Miss Lulu Bell talking again. My grandfather silenced her.

Grandma does not talk much about him. Ma adored him; she told me home fell apart after he died. Their lives were never the same; Grandpa was the glue that kept the family intact in happier times but also bad times. Ma never forgave Grandma for leaving him when he needed her the most. She won't tell me anything more like Miss Lulu Bell.

"Miss Lulu Bell, is that your brother?"

The man in the photo has on army fatigues and one foot on the lift of a jeep. He holding a machine gun with bands of bullets draped on him like a necklace. The background looks like a desert with the American flag rippling in the wind. Sunglasses atop his head, the man has a mean face, ready to kill. The second photo is the same man smiling with a group of fellow soldiers in pressed uniforms.

Miss Lulu Bell gets up and retrieves another photo neatly placed behind the jeep photo. She runs her slender fingers over his face, smiling. It was her brother Richard who died in Vietnam the summer of '66, a polaroid of him in a hospital bed receiving the Purple Heart, bandaged head to toe, received for disarming a booby trap that saved his platoon. She says he died shortly after he got it.

"You look so much like your brother, Miss Lulu Bell."

There was a spark of light in her eyes while staring at the photo. Her hand languishes over the man's face for a long while. "I've heard that all my life, Beenie. He did not have the blessing of old age."

I look closer at the photo. "Ya'll got the same scar near the corner of your mouth and the sparkling eyes."

Miss Lulu Bell's topaz-brown eyes smile similar to the man in the photo as the scar disappears slightly. "Let me show you this one. This is Richard when he was a baby. Rambunctious, he kept Mama ripping and running." She points out several photos of his short life: young Richard with a baseball bat resting on his shoulder, on the debate team, a teenager in a suit with a girl beside him ready for prom night.

"That was the last picture before he enlisted. Mama didn't understand the need to get out of Mississippi back then. Those were desperate times, Beenie. There was a vast migration to get out of the South, go up North, the promised land for good jobs, opportunities, get from under segregation laws, freedom from Jim Crow and his nonsense. I understood he had to leave for a future that was not gonna come to him in Tunica," Miss Lulu Bell says. "He had to leave, the risk of dying in Vietnam was just the same as dying in Mississippi. So, I understood it had to be done. But looking back, the true heroes, the brave ones, stayed fighting the good fight and won. So many lives sacrificed. If they had left, what would it be like today?"

She asks herself the question but cannot find the answer. She takes a pensive sip of tea, staring at nothing.

"Mama cried until she had no more tears left. She couldn't understand why her only male child wanna go over to Asia, fighting folks that ain't done nothing to him for a country that ain't been right to him since he was born. It didn't make sense to her. She figger he oughta be fighting against America."

"Oh," Miss Lulu Bell says, "you gonna love this one." She retrieves the photo of young Grandma holding Ma as a toddler. Grandma looks so pretty wearing a big Afro, Cleopatra eyeliner, and pink lipstick. She has on a knitted poncho, bell bottoms, and cork platform sandals. Ma was as wild-looking as a baby as she is today. I wonder, looking at her, when did the polar bear show up? Was it when she was a cub or later?

"Oh honey, your grandma loved her baby girl so much," she says. "She had me make all kinds of dresses with ribbons and laces, frilly stuff for Delilah. That's how she got the nickname Doll 'cause Eudora dressed her like one, parading about, showing her off like a prize, telling us every little cute thing your mama did, how good her grades were in school.

"Anytime you saw Delilah, she had her nose in a book. Oh, she was such a smart girl. We was so proud when she got that scholarship for college. Your grandma couldn't stop smiling even if you had a gun at her head, ordering her to stop." Miss Lulu Bell laughs.

"Eudora thought a whole heap about Delilah, maybe too much; she forgot she had another child. I felt bad for your uncle Marsh. He worked so hard to please her, harder than Delilah. She'd glance at a book once, passed the test. Marsh had to study really hard to get good grades but not nearly as good as your mama. But they were good enough grades for your grandfather.

"Sometimes you can't put the burden of your dreams on someone else," she wistfully adds.

"Thank God, he did pretty good for himself. Eudora is proud of him now doing so well, his beautiful wife, expensive cars, trips around the world, living in that big old fancy mansion in Upstate."

Miss Lulu Bell side hugs me tightly. "I hear you smart like your mama. Eudora told me you in them advance classes in school, speak

French like a native. How you save people from that fire in that old shack of apartment y'all was living in. Eudora proud of you too.

"I gonna pray hard just like Eudora, you be successful, but most important, Beenie, be happy."

The smile refuses to abandon my face. When I am in the company of Miss Lulu Bell, I'm hopeful that it's not so bad, like everything is going to be okay no matter how hard it is—anything is possible if you believe.

"You are the grandest lady I've ever met, Miss Lulu Bell-Davis,"

"Oh Lord, bless you child." She places her hand on her exposed collarbone, smiling. "Why, thank you, Miss Beenie." She leans in as she whispers as if there is a room full of people, "Grander than Eudora?"

I nod.

Miss Lulu Bell winks. "It'll be our secret."

CHAPTER TWENTY-NINE

Everybody hates Aunt Nelle.

The cleaning people working for her maintain the massive building called a home: the pool man, the gardener, her employees (she is the president of her IT company). The hate parade includes Ma and Jamal—he always sides with Ma, no matter what, but Grandma makes sure he minds his manners and is respectful. Grandma can't stand her either, but she talks nice to Aunt Nelle to her face.

Grandma's so two-faced; she over-compliments Aunt Nelle, sugar-coating her so much we eye roll in pain from a toothache. I've never seen Grandma begging anybody the way she ingratiate herself to Aunt Nelle, who treats her like a doormat not deserving of a foot wipe. It is embarrassing watching Grandma groveling for Aunt Nelle's friendship, then with considerable distance from an earshot, Grandma mumbles how highfalutin', stuck up Nelle is acting, like her "shit don't stink."

Uncle Marsh is under the influence of Aunt Nelle. Maybe he harbors some resentment to Grandma though he responds to her calls for money, supplementing her income and giving without asking. He increased the amount for groceries now that Jamal is living with her. But his visits are sparse with the exception of holidays; he will visit her in the mornings, then spend the majority of time with Aunt Nelle and her family. He will drop off a store-catered dish for Thanksgiving, mindful of the spread Grandma, who is a kick-ass cook, spent hours preparing, but will not stay beyond an hour or eat a morsel. Christmas morning Uncle Marsh, without Aunt Nelle, comes to the city, drops off presents, takes a cup of coffee with Grandma, and leaves.

Grandma is hurt by this, and it probable she blames Aunt Nelle for his sparse visits. Ma gets mad at her brother for the way he treats Grandma.

Aunt Nelle's mother—this is Grandma's speculative gossip—cannot stand her daughter either. Ma gets on my nerves, but I don't treat her the way Aunt Nelle treats her mother. I saw her talking real nasty to her mom on the phone. And last year, at their annual Fourth of July barbeque, in front of guests, she berated her mother. The poor old lady cowered like a cornered mouse to a hissing cat ready to pounce and kill. Uncle Marsh stopped in mid-conversation for a second, looked over at Aunt Nelle, and continued talking to his guests, laughing, joking, like it was nothing abnormal screaming at your mother in front of people. Grandma was embarrassed by Aunt Nelle's behavior.

Uncle Marsh sometimes acts like a strange black man. When he's around Aunt Nelle's family and her friends, he acts like he grew up the same as Aunt Nelle: privileged, spoiled, and entitled. The difference is when he's with my dad at the basketball court playing with dudes from all levels: the postman, the garbage man, the factory worker, the finance guy, the lawyer—all equals, all home boys to him playing hoops. Only higher educated teammates, the lawyer and the businessman, would be welcomed by Aunt Nelle to his house, providing they removed their sneakers, rinsed off their sweaty gym clothes. I would not be surprised if she made inquiries into their backgrounds first: what college you went to, what is your fraternity affiliation, stupid shit that don't make a good person, as Ma would say.

Aunt Nelle's tongue is mean, but her eyes are sad. She is not rude to me though she says very little, but her eyes twinkle when there is a moment of happiness. I don't see it too often though.

Uncle Marsh invited me at the request of Aunt Nelle. He told me she's impressed with my academic achievements, always asks about me and when can I visit her. The dim light in her eyes sparks a little upon seeing me. She sits in her office with the biggest window I've ever seen in a house looking out to oceans of lawn over a hillside, a sad princess in a castle.

"Beenie, good to see you," she approaches me like a business associate present for a corporate meeting.

She tells me I'm a pretty girl with an interesting name while she touches my hair the way a loving owner pets a cat. It is not a compliment as she covers it with a fake laugh that does not even sound like laughter. It is more like coughing, as if she is choking on a piece of candy or something.

I'm not offended, though Ma would curse her to hell if I told her. She asks me to have Olga make a cup of tea for her and hot chocolate for me without inquiring if I want it or not. I follow her instructions and head to the kitchen where I approach Olga.

"Hi." I introduce myself to Olga, a young girl of twenty or so, short, with feathery bangs draped around her oval sunless face. Her heavily accented English is good for someone who has been in the country less than a year, she tells me.

We connect immediately as she wants to practice her French, which she is now learning. It's her third language after her native one and English. She was hired to be an au pair in a household without children and not wanting to leave America, she accepted this assignment, which she says she preferred over children. "Madam Nelle allows me to have more time for myself. I never wanted to work watching kids." She smiles at me like I will keep her secret.

"Everybody says she's mean," I test her for entertainment, for loyalty.

Olga shrugs it off, "Mean, no. She's the boss." She lets slip that Aunt Nelle cries a lot. Uncle Marsh warned that she has a delicate nature, and Olga should pardon any crying outbursts or sudden fits of rage. Olga, ever obedient, nodded eagerly that she understood, assured Uncle Marsh she knew how to handle Aunt Nelle.

"She needed me more than I needed job," Olga says. "Mr. Marsh always away somewhere, at work, at play. Nelle alone a lot. Her mother called, she don't answer, her father got a new young wife, so he busy. Nobody wanna talk to her except me."

I decline Olga's offer of help as I steady the tray of tea and shortbread cookies and make my way out of the kitchen to the bedroom.

Aunt Nelle, sprawled across the massive oak bed in her cavernous room, appears lifeless until she hears me. She sits up, takes the tray from me, places it down, then pats the bed for me to sit. I remove my shoes and join her as she passes my cup to me. She gently lifts the cup to her lips, looking out the window, saying nothing to me. I drink my hot chocolate, careful not to slurp as Aunt Nelle drinks her tea quietly.

I watch her watching the groundsmen with an occasional eye-blink that lets me know she is here. She is a frail porcelain doll susceptible to break at the slightest touch. Neither of us touch the shortbread cookies. I don't like them. Aunt Nelle is rail thin; skin drapes over her collarbone like clothes on a thin rack. Her skin is several shades too light to be identified as black with thick weave-less hair.

The weight of her sadness is infectious. I want to leave, but my feet refuse to move. She places the cup down; I follow suit though I am not done with mine. She motions me to lay beside her as we stare together out the window with nothing to say or talk about. She clasps my hand in hers, rubbing my fingers as if I can make her better and take away the pain. She seems lonely, desperate for company, thankful I can lay beside her and not talk. My eyes scan her room, then stop at the door, planning escape.

Their master bedroom is way too big for two people. Uncle Marsh and her are children lost in a room so big they can't begin to decide what to do, what games to play. There is so much room to hide—what they both do best is hide.

I gently remove Aunt Nelle's fingers clasped in mine. "I have to go Aunt Nelle—Aunt Nelle, I have to leave you."

She perks as if poked in the flanks, looking at me as if I am an intruder, blinking hard to shake the confusion away. "I'll walk you out," she says flatly.

"No, no, I can see myself out." I ease off the bed, locating my shoes.

She sits up, watching me in wonderment, like a child staring at an alien and smiling. "I enjoyed your visit, Rubena. I know they call you Beenie, but you're a young, beautiful lady. Rubena is more appropriate, don't you think?"

"Yeah."

She offers up a half-smile to correct my English. "Yes?"

I look at my feet to get away from her smile, which looks like she is trying too hard to be nice after whipping me with a flower. "Yes."

She eases off the bed. Her coral pedicure gently touches the fancy carpet bought from some world trip, and she stands before me, then instinctively hugs me with her head resting atop mine. "Come see me again," she says in a voice so low I barely hear her.

I nod as I make my way out of her room, leaving Aunt Nelle climbing back into her bed, back at staring out the window. That's how I left her. I went back in, grabbing the tray, returning it to Olga in the kitchen, who invites me back again. I advise Olga, "Keep practicing French until we see each other again."

"Oui."

Dad texts that he'll be there to pick me up in five minutes, but it's way too long to stay in a cold house.

Outside, the sun warms my craning neck as I search for any signs of Dad's car. I walk a few yards away from Uncle Marsh's house, pushing on for some distance. Without explanation, I start jogging, then instinctively run, my heart pumping oxygen to keep up with me, unable to stop.

The farther away I get from their house, the more I am warmed, resurrected, alive again.

CHAPTER THIRTY

I completed my homework of a current-events essay to be read in French tomorrow for school. The topic I chose was the survival of feminism in oppressive countries. After my searches of countries with human rights violations against women, I've been obsessed with the topic. Why are girls worthless in a male-dominated society? Why are men allowed to mistreat women and not sent to prison? Why is female circumcision happening to girls as young as five? Why is honor-killing allowed? I can't imagine living under the thumb of men, wondering if it's possible to have a moment of happiness, to smile, to know what it is like to have the freedom to choose, do whatever you want. The horror of living like that makes me grateful I was born here.

Tiki and me would be in big trouble living in a male-dominated country, especially with her toilet mouth, clap back, and smart-ass remarks.

Her phone is shut off again. She told me about her essay on domestic violence, adding that she has a well of information using Lorna as an example. Her French is improving so much we are conversing fluently. She is bound to get a scholarship with housing if she keeps up her grades, then she will be free.

Dad and Marcus proofread my essay, impressed I chose a heady topic at such a young age. I informed them now is as good a time as any. "Marcus, I think the next Gloria Steinem is in front of us," he beamed. "Great job, Beenie."

Dad kept his promise and cooked dinner as Marcus and I sharpened our knives, not for eating.

The rubbery steak slaps me in the face. Undercooked potatoes, along with the broccoli mash, look more appealing than they taste. If we had a dog, he would rather starve.

Dad almost burns the house down with all the smoke clouding the kitchen. Marcus and I gag, fan the smoke, and run outside. Minutes later, Dad calls us back in, laughing, accusing us of being over-dramatic. We have to open all the windows as Marcus disarms the alarm before the fire department and Mr. Greenly arrive. I order Dad to hand over his apron, announcing he is banned for life out of the kitchen. He agrees, surrendering the apron to a vindicated Marcus, whose arms are folded, muscles rippling in his tee shirt.

"How did you survive before Marcus came along?" I ask, knowing Ma was not much of a cook either, but she did not smoke up the apartment. Ma was a frozen-food cook; the only food that was not frozen was the drink, and it was Kool Aid. Grandma Helen, I learned later, was not much of a cook either.

"Take out," Dad says.

"And it cost him a fortune," Marcus adds. "Imagine, Beenie, Ruben spending a fortune, *a fortune*, on take-away meals, every day, when he was a bachelor alone in the city."

"But my stomach, my life, got better when you came along," Dad says, planting Marcus with a big kiss on the lips.

"I'm going to break the cycle of bad cooks in my family with Marcus's help," I announce.

Dad treats us to dinner at an Italian restaurant in town. He lost, and we gloat well into the entrée, dessert, over wine and coffee, the ride home, and until bedtime. I go overboard for team Marcus.

I lay out clothes for school tomorrow and make plans to leave some goodies for the girl tonight. This time, it will be my all-time favorite: Reese's peanut butter cups. I chose it because peanut butter is used in African cooking, especially stews, though it would be too sweet with the chocolate from the Reese's.

My two problems are the witch in her bedroom watchtower and Mr. Greenly. Provided he is distracted by his secret red-headed boo, I can easily slip the candy and note near the bins where she can see it. He has been watching me ever since he suspected I am responsible for feeding Bully, Bebe, and company.

It is a little after midnight. Outside, looking to my left and right, ensuring no one catches me, my neck begins to ache. Neither enemy's bedroom light is on. Slowly, gently, so quiet I am afraid the smallest blade of grass will betray me, I make my way across the street and place the candy and note on the side of the bin where she can see it.

I'm near the foot of the woods, a safe distance from the entrance, throwing stale bread and lettuce destined for the garbage to Bully and Bebe. They need to eat, too, despite what Mr. Greenly says. I have not seen the couple in a while. They are probably married now, having babies. I decided against giving Bully and friends the food Dad prepared for us. I'm against animal cruelty.

I take a few steps back as a fire-red fox approaches the bread, smells it for a second or two, grabs it, and sprints back into the woods. Red the Fox may be Bully's competitor.

The sound of an oncoming car pushes me to dash quickly across the street, back to my house. I press the door closed with my weight, then shuttle to the office window, waiting. It is the professor getting out of his car. He grabs his briefcase and jacket, slams the door with a free foot, and heads inside his home. Kind of late to come home from work. He must have lots of papers to grade. He teaches in New York City. I rarely see him.

It does not take long for her to appear on cue.

She slowly walks down the driveway, looking left and right for the coast to be clear, then gently pushes the bin and retrieves the bag. She looks across the street for me. I make myself visible, giving the thumbs up. We will talk soon; I just know it.

We are friends without words, without exchange, but I feel the love from her.

CHAPTER THIRTY-ONE

We impressed most of our classmates and Mr. Borden with our essays. Tiki went before me and killed it. I am so proud of her; she spoke almost like a native. Owen, the shusher, went next with a boring subject about his bug collection. I went after him and knocked it out of the park with my bomb French skills.

We both know there is an A-plus waiting for us for our efforts.

The terrible four—five minus one now that Amber has been reported missing. The tea is she's disappeared, no one knows where. Her crew sit in the back of the classroom next to an empty chair near the window with long faces and wet eyes. No words were exchanged this morning. They are out of character, eerily quiet. Everybody talking about Amber Mills missing is the news, and it spreads quickly in our school, gaining traction, fueling speculation about what happened to her. Gossip and made-up news spread throughout school. Her parents out looking for her, stapling posts on every block, passing flyers to anyone with a hand everywhere.

Owen, a small boy with big glasses that swallow his face, is my only competitor in class; his French skills are nearly as good as mine though I will never let him know it. He is the most studious kid in our class, back ramrod straight as he listens intently to Mr. Borden, like a cult follower. He gets visibly annoyed when anyone talks in class, but he only tells kids who do not intimidate him to be quiet under the guise of conversing in French. He is terrified of the fearsome four, especially Amber, who is deadly with the word *loser*, throwing it like poison darts at him. Owen is relieved she has not been in the class recently as the trio are less powerful in our classroom without her.

He leans over, his eyes jumping between me and Tiki. "Did you hear about Amber?"

We both shake our heads in sync. Owen turns around, checking, watching the terrible trio, then at Mr. Borden, then back at us. "She's a runaway."

Tiki rests her chin in her hand and fires at Owen like the barrel of a gun, "To where?"

"I don't know."

"How do you know?" I ask.

"My aunt's a clerk at the police department, her parents are members of my church," Owen whispers. "They reported her missing, think she was kidnapped. I hope she doesn't come back to school."

"That's foul, Owen," Tiki shoots. "You told me you wanted to become a priest. You should act like one."

"I don't care," he sniffs, rolling his eyes.

"Silencieux!" Tiki barks at Owen.

* * *

With her services restored again, Tiki and I are preoccupied with our phones at our table in the cafeteria, which is crowded for first-period lunch. Molly Simpson and the remaining crew of Amber Mills's mean girls are seated one table across from us, so close we can read each other's texts. I do not think it is deliberate the way Amber would do it; there is simply tight seating.

Molly is a quiet girl who always has a worried look on her face as if she is expecting something terrible to happen. She is obedient to Amber like a dog.

"Missing your master, Molly?" Tiki says, not bothering to look up from her phone. "Where's your leash?" She stops, looks over at Molly, then at the rest of the girls: Lauren Green, Sophie Roberts, and the token Oreo, Gwynne Sanders. "Guys, where's your fearless leader? Oh, look, Rubena, each girl got their very own cup of yogurt. Make sure it's fat-free." Tiki is clapping incessantly like a seal on stimulants. "While Amber's away the girls get to eat food; she's not here, why not burgers and fries? Do you have your very own banana too?" Tiki strains, craning her neck, searching their table.

I tell her to stop, but it falls on deaf ears. Tiki has been in the school system with them longer than I have, bullied by Amber and those girls for years.

"Molly, you lit girl, you should take over, push Amber Mills out since she ain't been around. Guys, look how generous Molly is."

Molly ignores her, staring at the girls' and making eye contact for help. She will not fight back. Amber usually comes up with the ammo of insults and put-downs, and there is no one in the group that can replace her.

"I see you have lunch today, Tiki." Sophie Roberts rests her chin on her hands. Molly shakes her head at Sophie to ignore Tiki. She is a petite girl with huge expressive eyes and large ringlet curls that look like an afro smothering her face. "You can have this when I'm done." She dangles a plastic water bottle at Tiki. "You get five cents back, right? I saw you and your sister at the supermarket last weekend at the bottle returns, surrounded by *bags and bags and bags of bottles*. I thought you guys were homeless people, drowning in bottles and bottles, I almost missed you. Does your sister have an EBT card?"

"Die, bitch," Tiki growls.

"You don't smell today. Did your sister pay the water bill with the bottle returns?" follower Lauren chimes in. She's a ginger with so much makeup on that a paint scraper is needed to remove it. Spineless girl follows the mindless majority, she was no match for the sharp tongue Tiki, queen of the comeback—no one was.

Tiki claps back, "And you don't smell like your father's cologne, Absolut. He's paroled, right? Too bad your crew know how to read the news, he's in it *a lot*—DUI, DWI."

Lauren's chin drops, bangs against the table. Molly's face is red hot and twisting, looking at Tiki, ready to say something, but Gwynne clears her throat to stop her.

"Careful, you might gain weight." Tiki is firing missiles everywhere. "Gwynne, how can you ride with Amber and those bitches when she dissed black people in French class. Didn't she, Rubena?"

I'm not interested in this drama, but I must support my friend since Sophie made the crack about the welfare card. Sophie Roberts has a lot of balls. I hear her home life ain't popping anymore since her lawyer father is in prison for stealing people's money. She doesn't live in a mansion anymore, just a lowly rental with her mother and two brothers.

"Mr. Borden was talking about French-speaking countries in Africa. That's when Amber said she would never date an African from Africa. She's ignorant, too dumb to realize black Americans are descendants from Africa," I say.

Gwynne seems indecisive whether she wants to be black like her father or white like her mother. "She likes black boys," Gwynne offers up, then stops short.

"She likes anything with three legs," Tiki says, cracking up.

I cannot withhold myself from bursting into laughter. The weekend bath made Tiki clean, but she still got a dirty mouth. Thank God, saved by the bell.

I feel sorry for Gwynne.

She is so mixed up.

CHAPTER THIRTY-TWO

no one leaves home unless
    home is the mouth of a shark
    —Warsan Shire

Ma got arrested for shoplifting. Grandma refused to post bail, screaming at Uncle Marsh on the phone not to put up a penny when she called him.

I hate Grandma.

I don't want to spend the weekend with her or go to church. How can she be asking God for help but not help her daughter? Dad was right, all the devils are in the church, calling God, judging others. I will not be a hypocrite like Grandma. I will be spiritual like Dad and Marcus, who love people without judgment.

"More wars are fought over religion 'cause everybody think they're right and will use quotes from the Bible to prove their point," Marcus once said over breakfast. "The God I know is loving and merciful."

Penguin stopped by the house to speak with me and Jamal. He

wants us to go with him to see Ma. He knows it will make her happy. Grandma said no at first, but Jamal's electricity was at full volume, jumping and hollering. The neighbors turned up their hearing aids as her blood pressure rose. He, too, refused to go to church with Grandma, who surrendered with her hands raised up. She's at her breaking point, giving in, the first time I've ever seen her do so. But she refused to give us tokens or money for the train ride to the detention center downtown. As we are leaving, Grandma says over and over she's doing this to help Ma get help. I slammed the door behind me as her voice trailed sounds like crying.

Penguin tells us not to worry; his mother helped with what little she had even though she ain't too crazy about Ma. She decided to help for Penguin and Jamal's sake. Grandma Henderson gave him her last twenty dollars assigned for the collection plate for church. He warns Jamal in advance there is no money for candy, chips, or soda.

"I don't care, Daddy," he says, trying to hold back tears as his nose is running. "I wanna see Ma."

We follow Penguin as he exits after three stops to the projects near the train station. He has a good friend who will loan him bail money. Inside the friend's apartment, I notice a scale and little plastic packets on the kitchen table. I refocus my eyes to see a gun partially hidden in a hurry under newspaper.

As he waits for his friend to get the money, Penguin looks at me looking at the newspaper. "Beenie, we gonna get it right this time. Please believe me. We gonna get Doll help so she can be okay."

I want to get away from this apartment, away from that gun.

I want to believe him, but I don't. "I know you will, Penguin."

* * *

Ma looks like a decaying building about to crumble at the sound of a whisper. She seems listless, unable to focus as the judge rambles on with words I cannot hear. A plus-size woman is leaning in her ear; Ma rubs her eyes with the palms of her hands, nodding, pretending to comprehend what the woman is saying to her.

Outside of the building, Penguin rubs Ma's hand and gives her a second-too-long kiss, not bothered by the scowl on my face while Jamal bear hugs her legs.

She is received by everyone except me. "How you doing, Beenie?"

"Why can't you stay out of trouble?"

Penguin is startled by a volume of my voice he's never witnessed. "Girl, that's your mother."

"Then she *should act like one.*" I want to hurt her as much as she hurts me. Jamal pushes me, I block him and push him harder. He almost loses his balance.

Ma is biting her lip, drawing blood for an answer. "I don't know, Beenie. I wish I had an answer that would make sense to you." She attempts to extend her arms to hug me as I back away from her.

"I'll never be like you!"

Penguin raises his voice, "Stop it, girl."

Her glassy eyes release a single drop. "Promise me you won't."

CHAPTER THIRTY-THREE

I'm glad to be back in Upstate, away from the drama. Dad picked me up earlier after I FaceTimed him upset. He was surprised I decided against spending the rest of the weekend with Grandma. I did not want to tell him why, but big-mouth Grandma did, cussing as she prepared for church, adding the same old lame quote, *she's tired.* I ignored her when she attempted to bid me goodbye, giving her the air when she tried to kiss and hug me. Dad stayed silent, mulling over the incident of Ma's arrest, refusing to be Grandma's ally, but giving her a sigh and nothing more.

Marcus welcomed me back with his over-the-top greeting, preparing breakfast, making my favorite chocolate-chip pancakes. A Sunday morning in Upstate is a comfortable quiet, schools of cyclists from the city, a warm doughnut, fresh from the town's popular bakery, a wave from the shopkeeper sweeping the front of his store. The morning light streams through the kitchen like a kiss on the cheek. Dad hits the remote to his favorite news channel and resumes reading. I almost drop my glass of orange juice upon hearing her name.

Amber Mills, a fourteen-year-old girl from Upstate, is missing.

The FBI issued a BOLO for a black SUV with a man and another young girl.

Marcus lifts the griddle away from the heat to watch the news. "Beenie, isn't she one of the mean girls you were talking about?"

...last seen getting into a car at her school on Friday...

Dad lifts his nose up from the newspaper. "Mean girl? What girl?" Dad is clueless about my life, too busy to pay attention. His eyes are glued to the news. "Is that your friend, Beenie? I thought her name was Mickey."

"Ruben, *that is not the same girl*," Marcus says, exasperated. He instructs Dad to be quiet and turn the volume up while placing my slightly burnt pancakes before me.

Despite the slight char, it tastes good as I drown my plate with maple syrup, eyes locked on the television. "Dad, Amber Mills is a girl in my French class. Tiki is my friend from school."

Amber's father is talking in a whimpering voice on the verge of cracking. He is a large man with a large head and not enough teeth in his mouth. Behind him, the woman identified as Amber's mother is unable to stop crying. She is frail with thin, pallored skin and fading blue eyes. Amber's parents appear elderly, more like her grandparents.

Another woman identified as Amber's stepmother speaks as the father, who begins to fall, is caught by two policemen. She looks old, too, but not as old as Amber's parents, and looks much younger than her husband.

Everyone is crying except the stepmother and her little brother whose shoulders are held tightly by a priest. He is the strong one, holding the family together.

I tell Dad and Marcus about Friday after school when Tiki and I saw Amber get into a black SUV with a blond girl close in age and the man with the goatee. Marcus notifies the police, and I repeat the narrative to Detective Norelle Phillips. I wanted to talk to her some more as I had never seen or met a black woman detective, but it was obviously the wrong time to do so.

Before bed, I decide against watching for the girl across the street. I forgot to leave her a note and a treat. I keep thinking about Amber, where is she, is she safe. I ask God to take care of her and the girl across the street.

I will keep praying for Amber. "Mean girls need God's love too."

* * *

There is heaviness in school, our classroom, a sadness hard to define, put a finger on it. Our teachers talk about grief counselors available for us, encouraging us to discuss our fears and how evil does exist, and no one is immune to it. It can happen to anyone, anytime, anywhere.

News about Amber arrived at school before we did. Whispers, conspiracies of what happened to her. One kid claims she saw her at Hunt's Point in the Bronx with an old man. Another says Amber texted him she had a modeling job in Europe and did not want to tell no one but him. Another rumor: she was kidnapped by Hank, the big mush-mouth janitor at our school who's a snitch—everyone calls him the eyes of the principal. He's not as creepy as the lies about him are. He drags his left foot like a burden. I heard it was an injury from a second tour in the first Iraq war.

Tiki tells me the last time they had grief counselors was when a three-hundred-pound girl named Ranisha Cannon was fat-shamed so much that she committed suicide. "Bullied to death. Sometimes, Re Re—that's what she wanted to be called—was nice, but when she got mad enough from teasing, she'd catch an attitude, start fighting, not speak to no one, not even the few kids who tried to be nice to her, including me. You can't fight an army of haters. It stressed her out. Even after she died, Amber and a whole bunch of kids made foul comments about her fat ass fitting in a coffin, or, like, she was buried with a happy meal instead of flowers—Fucked up, ain't it?"

Some classmates go about their business unaffected like it ain't a big deal Amber's not around. There's a mixed reaction to Amber missing; the ones she was shitty to, don't seem bothered that she's gone. Past rejects, hopeful, are competing to be Amber's replacement, stressing to be part of the most relevant girl group in school. Gwynne and Sophie don't seem to put high demands to accept new prospects, not bitchy like Amber. Some drama queens who also hated Amber are freaking out, knowing they too could be victims of some random kidnappers.

Tiki and I have a free period. The weather is so warm we decide to sit on the stoops in the back, the same spot where we witnessed Amber leaving several Fridays before.

"The cops came to my sister's house yesterday," Tiki says while pulling weeds out around a dandelion, tossing them onto the concrete sidewalk.

"Why are you pulling weeds off around a weed?"

"Dandelions are flowers." She continues pulling.

"It's a weed."

"That's what you see." She stops, then looks at me with hurt scrawled on her face. "You know what it's like to be looked at as a weed?" she says without waiting and continues, "Matt took off when he saw the cops approaching our apartment, hauled ass out the bedroom window, running like the caught bitch he is—dumbass." Satisfied the dandelion is free of grass around it, Tiki draws her knee up close, resting her face, scanning the parking lot, focusing on nothing. "I can't stand Amber, but I don't want anything terrible to happen to her, not that Amber would care if it was me. You know girls get kidnapped and become prostitutes—white slavery."

She releases her grip around her knees to fold her legs. "We had a speaker, this girl, she was like, sixteen, seventeen, spoke to us a few years ago. She ran off with some dude she met in a chat room and was sold from state to state until she found the strength to run to the police. She speaks all over the country about predators like that."

"It's not just white girls," I correct Tiki.

"Facts. Any girl, young girls, with problems. They know how to spot them. I don't want them to see me," Tiki dry laughs.

How horrible to be in bondage, whether you're an American like Amber Mills or that girl from Africa working for the doctor and the professor.

"Facts. I knew you had a heart, Tiki."

"Don't tell anyone. They'll say I'm soft."

"No, they'll say you're human."

Gwynne breezes by us, alone, with her head down like a wounded animal. Tiki calls out to her. She ignores her, picking up speed away from us. I jump off the stoop, running after her with Tiki close on my heels.

She stops short, spins around, jabbing her face so close to mine I smell mint breath. "I'm not in the mood for drama with you two," she barks at us.

"We're not here for drama," I offer.

"Gwynne, we've had beef in the past... I want to say how bad I feel for you guys," Tiki says.

"For what?" Gwynne's eyes enlarge as if Tiki spoke gibberish. "You're so full of shit." She eyes us evenly.

"We mean it. I feel bad about it. We saw it on TV, her parents, little brother—"

"What's going on? Anybody hear from her?" Tiki cuts me off.

Her eyes move slowly, starting at our feet, then up to our faces as though she had never seen us before, debating to her inner self if we deserved to be in her presence. Gwynne then checks her surroundings for Sophie, Lauren, and Molly, and then back at us, indecisive.

"Amber lies a lot. She created this life like she's Kylie Kardashian, her idol. All lies." Gwynne shakes her head. "The truth came out on the news. Her father is not a diplomat in Europe. Her brother does not play for the NBA. He's a kid, and her mother does not look like a supermodel, past or present. She's a prune, a nice one though.

"She said she was going to London to see her father. Her chauffeur and the nanny were picking her up after school to take her to the airport that Friday she went missing.

"She always came to our homes to visit, stayed the night with either me, Molly, and Sophie, *never* Lauren," Gwynne smirks, "because her father's mad creepy, always wasted, the mother's a freaking cuckoo.

"Amber always had to say slick shit about our house, how her house cost more than ours, or her mother use some big-name New York City decorator to design her home. That use to get on my nerves.

"But she always had a reason why we couldn't come to her hood, stay at her place. If anyone challenged her, you'd be out, talked shit about on Tik Tok and reels.

"I followed her home; now I know why we couldn't come to her place.

"Her crib is a rundown shack in a shitty hood with no grass. She lied to make us feel bad. Some random secret dude bought all those designer clothes, new iPhone, every color of Kylie's make-up, shoes, and jewelry she strutted for the 'gram. Imposter, a fraud."

"Who bought that stuff for her?" Tiki asks.

Jerked, Gwynne suddenly takes a step back, looking at us, her cream face cracks like broken glass, regretful. "How the fuck would I know? Does it matter now?"

"She's your friend." I'm shocked at Gwynne lack of empathy. "You and Amber were tighter than Molly, Lauren, and Sophie."

Gwynne leans forward, head tilted at me, her lips pressed tight. "Not anymore. I said too much already. She flexing, but I ain't no snitch. She'd never speak to me again."

"You may never see her again if you don't," I warn.

Gwynne is fighting not to tell us a secret, her eyes fluttering like she got something in them, as if she is forbidding her mouth to open. She looks around again, then at us, contemptuous.

And it hits her. Her face grimaces as her hands shoot up with her palms facing us. "Why am I talking to you two? I've said too much already," she repeats, torpedoing away, leaving debris of questions and no answers scattered about.

CHAPTER THIRTY-FOUR

A little after midnight, Mr. Greenly out on night patrol, surveying the neighborhood, then inspecting recycle bins as he checks and rechecks like a sergeant of a platoon. Satisfied, finally, he heads inside. Lights flick off. The professor and doctor's lights are still on, so the coast is not clear for us yet. It's really chilly. I made sure to wear thermal pajamas under my nightgown in case I have a long wait for her.

Where are those Frenchie brats, their kids? Then it hits me, remembering both the witch and Marcus said they go to private school out of state somewhere. That explains their absence. How do parents have children only to send them away? Marcus said some people want to be part-time parents.

That's Ma's mindset too. She texted me yesterday, left a voicemail this morning. I read it, then hit delete. She needs more punishment; I'm just thankful her bullshit crime was not reported in the news in Upstate. It would be a bitch to go to school with that hanging over me. Despite that, Dad still would force me to go. I'd be putting paws on anyone talking shit about her.

Marcus and Mr. Greenly are the nosiest people in the hood.

Marcus claims to know what's going on, don't think he misses nothing, but he did miss the girl across the street.

The lights are off now; I make my way across to the bins, leaving some buttermilk biscuits with apple jelly from this morning and a note in French. I hope Bully and his friends forgive me. I did not provide for them this evening. Buttermilk biscuits are Dad's all-time favorite and, being from Georgia, he hoovered most of them until Marcus snatched the last two from the pan before he could reach for it.

An hour passes as the moon seems to dim, pushing me gently to go home.

Defeated, I position the note and biscuits safely away should Bully smell it, praying she gets it before the witch or Bully:

"I am a friend. I speak French. If you want to talk, fold this note in half and bend the corners, then I will know, and we can meet in a secret place."

CHAPTER THIRTY-FIVE

Dad petitioned for sole custody. He'd had enough of Ma's antics, felt she was incapable of providing a stable home life for me. He kept a laundry list to support his case, the constant evictions and her lack of ability to hold a job and keep a roof over my head, clothes on my back, and food on the table. Her additional crime—thanks to Grandma—was the misappropriation of funds from a former employer whose lawsuit is pending. She has not kept a record of my expenses to support her request for more child support. Her greed for more wigs and makeup and shit sealed her financial fate.

Stupid. Sometimes, I hate her more than I love her.

Ma should have had the sense to keep track of her spending, knowing Dad is a finance wizard and knows where every penny is spent. She was dumb to ignore it, and now Dad wants account-ability for *his money*. And being currently homeless with no address has not helped her.

He enlisted neighbors from the various places we lived. The condo owner repeated she's a professional squatter. The West Indian landlord and others echoed this testimony; they all spun the same narrative about Ma. The back rents, excessive shopping online for herself, the number of packages delivered to our apartments, even Mr. Ali joined in to get back for non-payment for the stale food from his store. Dad had his investigator speak again to the West Indian landlord and his super, Mr. Cortez, who provided all the ammunition needed to win. I doubt Mr. Cortez wanted to snitch on Ma; he probably had to do it to keep his job. Dad added again that Ma has a pending court date for shoplifting. She'll probably be assigned community service since this is her first offense.

He failed in enlisting Miss Tamara's help. She dropped the assault charge against Ma, refusing to speak to both Dad and the investigator, threatening to call the police if they don't leave her alone. They kissed and made up, but Miss Tamara has kept Ma at a distance. "They little cool again, Beenie," Jamal told me. "She don't live with Grandma Henderson no more. They fight too much. Ma upset Grandma Hendy's lung cancer."

"Prolly sick of Ma's drama," I tell him.

Dad's biggest advocate, I heard, was Uncle Marsh, which will upset Ma once she finds out about the betrayal from diarrhea-mouth Grandma. She wants what's best for me and keeps Uncle Marsh close to her so Aunt Nelle don't cut him off from the rest of the family forever.

I'm not surprised by Grandma's support; she's just following Uncle Marsh to be in his corner. It will be one less child living with her, and a removal of jeopardy from having Jamal there in violation of her lease agreement. He's shuttling between her and his Grandma Henderson, but Penguin is there illegally too.

Dad assured me I do not have to be involved with this drama.

Ma is not easy to love. I care about her, even when she does reckless shit, but I'm tired of living with question marks: where will I sleep, what will I eat, will there be heat and hot water?

I now realize all this time I wanted a safe place, a warm home, and food on the table. I wanted security—my father and Marcus have given me that.

A family... I got that too, though it's not complete without Jamal.

I want to hurt her the way she has hurt me. And it will hurt her but not from my doing. She won't get over this. She will not recover from this.

She wants her family back. It may be too late.

CHAPTER THIRTY-SIX

My promised treat for Tiki was a date at the movies and lunch at our favorite place, Shake Shack. We wanted to take the bus like we've always done, but now with Amber Mill's abduction, Dad and Marcus insisted on driving us. Marcus this time dropped us off at the mall entrance, foot on the brake, yelling over the car engine—no shame at all while I looked away from people looking at him, then us—with specific instructions:

run fast out of the mall if you hear shots fired

don't talk to strangers

don't fall for the scam, your parents were in an accident, come with me

don't run off with random boys

go immediately to security if anyone or a pervert bothers you

Tiki folded her arms, shaking her head at Marcus yelling like someone stepped on his foot. "How old does he think we are? Ten?"

"I have to text or FaceTime him or my father my every move. It's getting on my nerves. I had more freedom in the city. My mother didn't stress me about it."

"Oh, I love Marcus. At least you got people that care for you," Tiki said. "If I was Amber, my family wouldn't give a shit. I'd be one less person to spend money on, which is nothing since we ain't got any. Thanks for treating me."

"Come on."

"Facts!"

There has been no good news regarding Amber. The latest: her cell phone was abandoned in Chicago; there has been no trace of her since. Her parents desperately try to keep her in the news. A Facebook page was set up by her stepmom. "Finding Amber" got about three thousand shares and likes. They've posted photos and flyers of her everywhere. Some jerk off scribbled in Facebook comments: "Yo! That ho's on Backpage!"

We gather our containers, ready to leave the restaurant. As I text Marcus to pick us up, I see a familiar face and quickly sit down. Tiki tilts her head, frowning. "What's wrong?"

"Don't look now, but that man in the blue stripe shirt and hat three tables across from us?"

Tiki is about to turn halfway in that direction. I repeat to do it slowly, so we are not spotted.

"My Uncle Marsh." I position the Shake Shack bag to conceal my face.

"So, go over, say what's up, Uncle?"

"I can't."

Tiki takes a slow peek again. "She's pretty."

"She's basic, looks like a crane, long and beak-like."

"Hater," Tiki shoots back. "That's his wife?"

"No."

"Oh—my bad."

Uncle Marsh is smiling a smile that is lame, full-on cheesy, over-the-top. He is holding her hand like a love-struck nerd, sealing it with a kiss on the lips. I don't think he would notice me anyhow as he is glued to this woman like a zombie.

She looks tall as she is head-to-head seated with Uncle Marsh, white, blond, Egyptian-lined blue eyes and smiling as much as Uncle Marsh is. Her wedding ring with a big diamond is large enough for me to know what they are up to.

"We gotta slip out unnoticed."

Tiki turns back again to look. "I don't think he would notice us anyway. Damn, he fiending for Becky with the good hair."

"Not funny." We slip out as quickly as we can without Uncle Marsh seeing us.

Uncle Marsh is foul.

Aunt Nelle—*who* is responsible for her sadness?

CHAPTER THIRTY-SEVEN

The blood pumping so fast my heart gonna explode. My jellied knees, dancing feet refuse to stay still, face hurts from what I see. She is outside. I see her from my window, waiting for me, standing in front of the garage, waving at me.

There are no lights on at her house, so the coast must be clear for us to meet. I make my way, mindful of the crazy-money cherry-wood floors Dad flipped about, pass their bedroom, and tiptoe down the stairs, which are doing their best to betray me. And for a second, I agree with Dad, resenting expensive floors that make noise, something I would never reveal 'cause Marcus needs more backup than Dad, who is a one-man warrior and needs no one in his corner to win.

I slowly open the door to the blinding lights of a car obstructing me. Suddenly, she bolts inside, running like she is being chased.

I take refuge behind a bush as the car parks itself in front of her house and spits out a man. The professor grabbing his briefcase, doing a little dance like he is still busting a move at a party. He appears not to want to go inside his house, still dancing, spinning, hyped before a pretend crowd. No one watching him except me, I think, and maybe the midnight sky, and the girl hiding from him somewhere, and probably Bully and his friends.

His basic moves ain't no competition for the contestants on *Dancing with the Stars*.

His spastic dancing seems like a man who don't know how to have fun.

CHAPTER THIRTY-EIGHT

I'm still mad at Grandma, and the only reason I decided to visit her this weekend is 'cause I missed Jamal more than my anger at her, her stupidity, her backwardness. I think sometimes Ma and Aunt Nelle are right about Grandma and how narrow-minded she is. Right now, I know she needs me. She needs me not to be mad at her. So I will pretend but not for her sake.

I brought his favorite candy, warning him not to let Grandma see it. He nods eagerly. "I miss you, Beenie."

Ma was admitted to the hospital for her nerves. She does not want to see Jamal or me until she gets better. I suspect she did not take the news well that Dad wants sole custody and to withdraw financial support, which stressed them both: Ma getting the news, Dad delivering it. Grandma told Jamal she is going on vacation with Miss Tamara.

"You miss Ma?" I ask.

He is so focus on his treat; he barely responds. "Ma and Miss Tamara friends again. She—they went on vacation to Bahamas. Uncle Marsh paid for Ma and Miss Tamara. She came by Grandma's with a suitcase, told me she meeting Ma at the airport."

How long will that lie last?

Jamal will eventually start nagging Grandma, Grandma Henderson, and Penguin about Ma. The safe bet is to keep him pumped up with candy, drum lessons, and Sunday school.

Sometimes I think Grandma just wish Ma would go "on to glory," so she can mourn the loss of her daughter, move on with her life, and focus on Uncle Marsh. He is her favorite anyway.

For a long time, Grandma has been talking about leaving the city and moving in with them in Upstate. They have more than enough room, but Aunt Nelle will have none of it. She tolerates Grandma the way a patient tolerates a root canal, bearing her visits, checking her watch until she leaves. They seem to be embarrassed by Grandma. I don't know why; Grandma is just as educated as Uncle Marsh and Aunt Nelle— well, almost; she never finished college. She was a social worker for the city. Grandma did do a semester at Fisk University, but she had to leave when her mother got very ill. Her parents divorced when she was fifteen, and her father's visits were sparse from then on.

Grandma left Alabama once the earth was tossed on her mother's coffin and got a job with the state of New York. She proudly told me how she was one of the few blacks in her department in the early seventies and did not allow racism or a "cracker" to stop her from career advancement.

"I was not a cook, or maid, nor a domestic," she says broadly. "I come from good stock, high-minded folks."

The cooks, maids, and domestics at her church respected Grandma. Some of them were illiterate, and Grandma would help them with paperwork, read letters for them, help them complete a money order to pay their bills, translate documents to help them buy a house or pay taxes.

At work, Grandma got promoted several times, she was even Miss Lulu Bell's supervisor, and their friendship was never strained by it. Budget cuts offered her early retirement. She reeducated herself and did office temp work until her arthritis, diabetes, and Ma's nonsense made her eligible for her pension and retirement.

Aunt Nelle would one-up Grandma—her mother is a retired judge, far more uppity than a lowly supervisor in the department of social services.

I wish Uncle Marsh and Aunt Nelle would let Grandma live with them. She deserves a peaceful life. She is so tired; I often think she wants to die and be with God.

But I don't want Grandma to die. I want a happy ending like the shows on TV-land that we love so much and that bind us together when we are not mad with each other. Marcia Brady, even Jan had a happy ending. In the worst of times, the Evans family from *Good Times* had a happy ending; even after James was killed off the show. They lived in the Detroit ghetto: James, Florida, JJ, Thelma, and even little, abused Penny.

I want a happy ending.

That is how I want life to be for me, Jamal, Grandma, Ma, Tiki, the African girl across the street, and, back in the hood, for LaShonda Biggs and her little brother Keshawn from the gangs.

Even Amber Mills.

Everything neatly wrapped up, ending well, like an episode.

Why can't life be like a sitcom?

Why is it so difficult to do?

Grandma prepared my favorite foods to greet me. That will be the only apology I'll ever get. Grandma's too proud to say I'm sorry. She only says sorry to Jesus and God.

No one else.

Happy endings do not exist in real life. Fairytales are exclusive to TV-land only.

CHAPTER THIRTY-NINE

Dad and Marcus are quietly arguing, again, but I still hear them from my perch at the top of the stairs, away from view and listening in the dark. They think I'm asleep.

My plans are to bring food and a letter to the girl, but the sound of their voices stopped me.

Dad concerned about the renovation budget Marcus has exceeded with his lavish taste. I don't see what the big deal is. He wants to make the house beautiful 'cause he got mad decorating skills. Dad is too crazy about money.

"Ruben, you wanna bury your money with you or be cremated?" he snaps. His voice drips toxics repellent to Dad.

"I want you to be more fiscally responsible."

Marcus changes the subject, saying Dad is hardly here to make it a home. Dad shoots back he has to work to pay for the upgrades Marcus has done. Marcus counterpunches, reminding Dad of their dreams for a home with me when they left the city.

It hits me like a brick fall: Dad's plan to move, buy this house, and get custody of me. He picked Upstate for this reason besides gay-friendly family life, diversity, and good schools—to remove me from Ma's house of chaos. But am I only with him because he got tired of paying child support? He knew what Ma was doing. He was tired of paying child support that Ma spent mainly on shopping for herself. Grandma snitched on Ma. I don't understand her doing that. One minute she bible-thumping him for his life, the next she wants to make sure I have a home, so I don't have to live with her or Ma.

"You wanted this change," Dad reminds Marcus. "We could have stayed in the city and put Beenie in a private school."

"I wanted this to be a start for a family, Ruben. I want us to be a family."

Dad lowers his voice, "I don't want to start over. I do not want any more children. I have my daughter..."

"Beenie's my daughter too."

"We've discussed this."

"No, Ruben, you discussed it."

Dad deflects, steering the subject back to frivolous spending (his words). He says he will review the budget spreadsheet to reel in Marcus's spending. I cannot catch what Marcus says, but now my dad is quiet, meaning it is the end of the discussion. He does not argue, really. He says what he says, then retreats to the isolated island in his head—that is his way of winning.

I don't want to lose them. I'm happy here. I don't want to lose Marcus.

I don't want to lose this home, the first real home I've had in my life.

I wish the adults in my life would grow up.

My bedroom window serves as a watchtower for surveying the terrain of the hood. I'm on the lookout for lights and for the girl to appear. Dad and Marcus, asleep now in the master bedroom, have kissed and made up. Marcus says it is never good to go to bed angry. He's a real peacemaker. Dad was familiar with being kicked out of bed to sleep on the sofa. When he was married to

Ma, they argued, and she kicked him out so many times, he finally kept a pillow and blanket hidden behind the couch. I never heard him raise his voice at Ma. He'd just walk away, ignoring her as she aimed curses at him like a dartboard, following him around until she was weary. Ma never learned Dad's art of war: wear them out and down 'till they tired. Dad is a wolverine, a honey badger, tenacious. He keeps them running until the prey falls from exhaustion.

Tonight, I will approach the girl in French again. I wrapped two sugar cookies Marcus made earlier today, a Kit Kat, and a bag of Fritos.

Quietly, I make my way down the steps and gently unlock the door, careful to leave the stopper so I don't get locked out. The weather is finally changing. Though a sweater is still needed for the evening, cotton pajamas are enough.

Sitting on the steps, waiting, staring straight ahead, frightened I will miss her. There is no need for this fear as she has never missed a meeting with me. I strain to make sure the doctor is nowhere in sight, don't see Mr. Greely's car. He must be out dancing with his blond secret boo thang.

No sight of the doctor, only the girl carrying a bag of bottles. She sees me, and if my eyes do not lie to me, I see a smile on her face. It is my sign to approach her. We are friends without knowing how we will be, an unbreakable connection between us. She is smiling at me, feeling the same way. We greet each other like long-lost friends.

"Bon jour. Salut. Comment allez-vous?" I extend my hand as I step on her driveway, my eyes jumping from her to the doctor's bedroom window like a sentry.

"Bon jour. Merci pour les bonbons, Kit Kat." Her voice is above a whisper, thanking me for the candy and biscuits. She stuffed the sugar cookies in her mouth, chewing fast, while inspecting the Fritos like a booby trap.

I ask if she wants to speak in English or French. We share a laugh at her enunciation of Kit Kat. I ask her if she likes America.

"I want to practice my English better, but if I mess up, we can talk French," she responds in broken English. "I not see much in America."

"Do you go to school?" I ask in English.

"Non," she stops then switches to French. "When I was home, I went to school, but it was not the best in my village."

"Are you far away from home?"

She lowers her head like a sudden headache. "Oui, no, yes."

I want her to smile again. "Well, yes or no? French or English?"

She jerks her head up, releasing a smile, laughing. "Yes, I am far from home. At first, I thought life would be better. I would get a good education, but..."

I am so focused and waiting for her to say something that I do not monitor the bedroom window, do not see her swoop down like the Wicked Witch and her flying monkeys.

My French friend must have eyes in the back of her head or a special hearing device allowing her to feel the Wicked Witch's presence without sight. She freezes like an injured wild animal, paralyzed by fear.

"What are you doing here!" The doctor's voice is full of venom dripping off the sides of her wrinkled mouth ready to bite me.

The girl drops the Fritos and bolts back into the house. I'm ready for the wicked witch, chest out, ready to give her a taste of *my venom*. "You're a liar!" I snarl back, yelling, refusing to move as she comes close. I can see the whites under her sagging eyes. "I'm not scare of you!"

The doctor's shadow towers as she looks down her nose at me, ready to turn me into a bug she can squash. "You should be," she switches to French.

I jerk forward, shaking my head, scolding in her native tongue. "And you should tell the truth."

Her eyes enlarge, pupils shrinking several diameters, then slowly the top and bottom of her eyes form a slit, turning to a snake before my eyes. The Wicked Witch/snake leans back as my words stabs her in the chest.

"You insolent child, how dare you? I shall speak to your father," she hisses in English.

I show my fangs, pantomiming leader of the wolf pack, correcting her with contempt. "J'ai deux pères avec qui vous pouvez parler; *I have two fathers you can talk to.*"

She raises her hand to mock hit me. "In my country, you would never speak to me that way."

"You're not in your country. You're in America!" I bark, backing away, eyes locked on her, slowly, fearful she might grab me.

If only I had a bucket of water in hand, I could melt her away like Dorothy did.

CHAPTER FORTY

If things were different, Amber Mills would be so pumped from all the attention she is getting.

There would be followers beyond her imagination—organic, no fake followers on all her social accounts—maybe the attention of her idols, the Kardashians. She would get real money by playing the professional victim on social media, talk shows, vlogs, and a chance, though slim, she could become a nice person, make up for all the mean, foul shit she'd done to Tiki, Owen, and so many others she hated on.

But first, she must be found, hopefully alive.

She has made national news. ABC, CBS, NBC, CNN, and even Fox News are talking about a missing child kidnapped from school. The headline subject is child exploitation. She made it to the ID channel show *On Pursuit, John Walsh*, who was seen in Upstate talking to the police and her parents. Tiki was annoyed they did not request to speak with us since we saw her last getting into the van with that girl and the man with the goatee. Tiki just wants to be on television. She denies it though.

Her missing has brought the discussion of global trafficking of children into mainstream news with segments focusing on girls in America as victims of sex traffickers. Her family was on as we watched the *Tamron Hall* show along with panels of experts on trafficking: a psychologist, law enforcement, and two victims. And, of course, Amber's cloud-chasing, media-hungry stepmother and father, minus her real mother, offstage at home due to recent chemo.

One girl is shadowed, and the other girl is visible as they talk about their life as underage sex workers. Both girls say it started in a chatroom with what is called a Romeo pimp, then on Messenger with long talks about an unhappy life at home, freedom from parental rules, wanting a boyfriend, just wanting to fit in. Their confidence gained, the next step is an invite them to a party, a place to stay, drugs, food, clothing, and shelter. Often, it starts with a girl luring you, talking to you on social media. "The bait" was what the police called her.

The Romeo pimp then discards the boyfriend façade, turning the tables and saying she must repay him. He is still her boyfriend, for sure, and he has a great idea how she can make the money to pay him back. It turns violent if she refuses. One girl said nude photos were taken, and she was threatened with them posted on social media for friends and family to see if there is no cooperation.

Me and Tiki cannot take our eyes and ears off my iPhone.

Amber Mills was not kidnapped; Tiki and I saw her happily jump into the SUV like she was going to party with some random dude and a girl.

The segment pans over to her father, who is quiet in the background as the stepmother, Pam Mills, speaks for them, hogging the mic time for her own ego. She has on a lot more makeup than before, and her hair looks recently colored, not the brassy tin from the last time. Gwynne told Tiki and I that Amber hated her stepmother, calling her a thirsty bitch.

Tamron is now talking to Amber's real mother on Zoom. She is as thin as a whisper, the cancer eating her alive as her voice is jumpy, halting, like she needs a moment to cry, but then she gets back on track to answer questions. Pam interrupts her, to the annoyance of Tamron and the audience, judging by their faces.

They are showing photographs of Amber at certain stages of her life. Pam is telling the audience how Amber wanted to be a doctor and travel abroad to help people in third-world countries. She makes us laugh. Amber barely came to class, was doing poorly in school. She wanted to be the next social media superstar like her idols.

I want to reach into my phone and give Amber's real mother a hug, give her my love for her loss. It is visible that she wants none of the media nonsense, just her daughter and their life back to what it was before Amber went missing. She is the only one, besides those two girls, who really appears to be in pain. I see the life in her face draining, thinking of terrible things that could be happening to Amber based on the trauma these girls lived to tell.

No mother should be subjected to that.

CHAPTER FORTY-ONE

Grandma was hurt by my decision not to accompany her to the supermarket. I think she made plans for my weekend visit. I'm not mad at her anymore. I just wasn't in the mood for pushing a shopping cart at a snail's pace behind her while she takes forever to decide what to buy, all the while complaining about the price of milk, her medication, the sorry monthly social security, and measly pension checks she receives, how Aunt Nelle is so mean to her, how Uncle Marsh don't stick up for her about Ma, Jamal, her diabetes, her life. She wouldn't really be talking to me. I could be the produce section while she is whining. There would not be a difference as long as someone, or something, was listening. If I'm on my phone while shopping with her, she'd get mad, talk out loud so I can hear how disrespectful children are today with no manners.

Told myself I will make it up to her tomorrow when we get ready for church. I will hide my boredom when she takes several church hats, suits, shoes, trying out several outfits until we, well, she decides on the perfect Sunday outfit to make her grand appearance during the procession.

I decide to visit Miss Lulu Bell Davis in the living room of her whimsical apartment, drinking tea and spilling it, enjoying her sweet potato pie, which is just as legendary as her peach cobbler. She forgoes dessert again, opting to pour a little bourbon in her tea instead. "Miss Lulu Bell gotta leave them sweets alone," she jumps up, rubbing her palms up and down her waist to the sides of her thighs.

"No rum today?"

"I don't want bourbon to feel left out. Old girl's been alone too long." She sits down, straightening her housedress. "Rum doing all right now."

I tell her about Amber and the African girl in Upstate.

She takes a sip of tea, clears her throat, coughing to cool her tongue. Somehow, she manages to suck her teeth and shake her head. "Lord Jesus, we gots to pray twenty-four seven 'cause the devil don't take no time off. I saw the news about that missing girl from Upstate, horrible. It broke my heart to see those parents, all three of them, pain written on their faces that should never be. You don't never expect that to happen to your children." Miss Lulu Bell is wigless, wearing a mustard yellow headscarf with a side bow in a matching housedress that she, of course, made.

"How come you never had children, Miss Lulu Bell?"

"Honey, for the same reason your friend is on the television news," she points out. "Somebody mess with my child, I'll kill 'em then ask the Devil just to come on up and get me 'cause I will go to hell and pay for it."

I can always depend on Miss Lulu Bell to provide laughter over sadness, light over darkness.

"You miss your call as a fashion designer. Your clothes are styling."

The slight eye wrinkles have not diminished her beauty. She takes a long sip of bourbon tea and then daintily places the fine China teacup down, preparing to tell me a story. All of sudden, without notice, she stops, the left side of her face droops, and her speech slurs like she is drunk. She is trying to speak but cannot. I immediately call 911, telling them to hurry, providing information about where we are, what happened. The operator tells me to place a spoon in her mouth to keep her from choking. I follow the instruction as the operator is telling me to remain calm, the paramedics are on the way. I hear her say everything will be all right, but she sounds far away and unconvincing.

With her head nestled in my lap, I place my hand on Miss Lulu Bell's golden-brown face. "You can't leave, you know that, right? You got to finish telling the story why you disappointed the world by not being a fashion designer. You make so many people happy when we are sad, you make us laugh. Don't you go nowhere, Miss Lulu Bell... We're nothing without you."

Her eyes are smiling as tears manage to escape her face. She musters up the remaining strength in her right hand to rub mine.

I gently lay her head on the pillow and let the paramedics in, and they begin to work on her. There are three people, a stout man with a big gut, who is stabilizing her. He is huffing like he needs help. The second man is skinny with stick arms that do not look strong enough to chest press a branch. The lady is petite, her hair pulled back so tight I worry her eyes are going to pop out. She instructs me to locate Miss Lulu Bell's ID while they prep her for the ambulance ride to the hospital.

I locate Miss Lulu Bell's Gucci bag, rummaging to find the information the paramedics requested while they are working on her. As they are about to lift her onto the gurney, I return to the living room, breathless, with a driver's license and insurance cards showing her name as R. Bell Davis. Without wasting a moment, I hand them to the woman, who slaps the handbag over her shoulder.

"I've known her all my life. Her name is Lulu Bell Davis. She has lived in the senior citizen apartments for over twenty years. She is a fashion designer, the best there is. A fine lady who makes the best peach cobbler and sweet potato pie you'll ever taste. She's from

Tunica, Mississippi, *the poorest state with the richest people.*" I repeat Miss Lulu Bell's words, smiling, knowing she is proud of me mimicking her.

They take all the medication bottles. As they make their way out of the building, the fat guy says, "Hang on, Miss Bell, we're gonna take care of you."

I'm allowed to hold Miss Lulu Bell's hand for a moment. It is hard for me to let go. "You get better now. I'll tell Grandma when she gets back from the store. You owe me a story, Miss Lulu Bell."

Somehow, through her pain and paralysis, Miss Lulu Bell's eyes smile at me again.

CHAPTER FORTY-TWO

The ramp at the end of the West Side Highway puts me onto the George Washington Bridge, now the Palisades Parkway, northbound, taking me home to Upstate. Concrete buildings, state-owned houses, line the city with the Manhattan skyline a distant view. The city's filth, smells unique to New York City, and the graffiti have disappeared, replaced by green foliage ready for spring. The unending two-lane highway unfolds between grass, bushes, and trees. Sporadic woodchucks and ground hogs are determined to cross the parkway to greener pastures, standing on hindlegs, impatient at passing cars.

I'm unable to stop focusing on the miles and miles of tall trees tickling the heavens, blue skies, white clouds. It is as pretty as I can imagine. I'm amazed at the height of them, limbs brushing against the sky, pulling on them like a child playing with a kite. Clean air. You can see it, smell it. It feels good for my lungs as I take a deep inhale and exhale out, cleaning my mouth. Though I miss the grimy film of the city sometimes, I always look forward to Upstate. The suburbs are now my home. Now I know it, I can say it without hesitation or fear of losing it—it is my home.

Jamal beside me, slumped forward, mouth hanging open as drool saturates the pocket of his favorite Spider-Man sweatshirt near his armpit. I watch intently, waiting to see where the saliva will park itself. He is all sugared out from the cotton candy ice cream cone Uncle Marsh gave him, ignoring Aunt Nelle reminding him of his sugar hyperactivity. Aunt Nelle more concern about the car interior than Jamal's hyperactivity from too much sugar. "He'll be alright," he dismissed her concerns like swatting an annoying fly. I hear Ma talking through Uncle Marsh.

The window slightly cracked. His asthma lungs grateful for fresh air. A barely audible snore bubbles saliva on his lip. I gently wipe his mouth, dabbing the saliva so it won't touch the car seat.

Uncle Marsh is driving us to his home for the day. He offered to pick Jamal up from Grandma's. I did not want to go, but I saw the light in Aunt Nelle's eyes dim a bit when I stammered without an answer. So, I lied to them both and said I would like to come over. Aunt Nelle's enthusiasm waned drastically when Uncle Marsh said we were going to the city to pick up Jamal to join us for a visit also. He never felt comfortable with her, and Aunt Nelle never bothered otherwise and isn't about to start now. I warned him to be on his best behavior; don't touch, don't even look at anything in her house, wipe your feet ten times, and sit on the edge of the couch. He nodded eagerly, inhaling the ice cream as we neared the car. Aunt Nelle put her foot down for Jamal to finish the ice cream cone before getting into the car. She did this while Uncle Marsh excused himself to answer a call a good distance away from us.

The plans were set for the entire weekend visit with Jamal and me, but Aunt Nelle reminded Uncle Marsh of a previous commitment for a dinner party on Sunday in Scarsdale. I'm not disappointed at all for the one-day visit—grateful and relieved are better descriptions. Jamal was not the least bit disappointed. "She's mean, Beenie; she didn't say hi to me when she came to church last time."

"She's sad."

Jamal took a large chomp of ice cream and turned his nose up quizzically. "What she so sad about?"

"Life."

Aunt Nelle greeted me like a favorite child, chatting about something as if we were girlfriends picking up where we left off when I last visited. I was a captive audience, listening to her without a care for what she was talking about. She treats me like I am her only friend, and by the way she behaves towards people, I may be.

Last time we visited, Aunt Nelle nearly fainted when Jamal spilled water on her rare Persia rug brought home from her Saudi Arabia trip. She became angry when Olga consoled Jamal, reassuring him it was only water and not a big deal.

"You travel halfway around the world, pay a fortune for a rug, then tell me it's no big deal," she snapped at Olga while looking at Jamal, who was near tears. Her anger was directed at Uncle Marsh for bringing a child to her expensive, cold home that was not child-proofed. I did not speak to her for a long time, giving her the cold shoulder for yelling at Jamal.

We are tolerated for a day visit, which is fine by me. Their house is a museum; they should rope the rooms as far as Aunt Nelle is concerned.

Uncle Marsh's massive head blocks the frontal view of the Palisades Parkway scenery. I can see perfectly out of the passenger seat behind him. His expensive-smelling cologne and the smell of a new Range Rover make my nose itch. His car is spanking new, leather seats barely creased under my weight, and no trace of Jamal's saliva or cotton candy ice cream on it.

Aunt Nelle sits upright quietly beside him like a statue. She is a glacial beauty, remote in self-imposed isolation. Occasionally, she will make a remark I cannot hear clearly or ask him something. He either nods or ignores her. He ignores her mostly.

I look at him, thinking about the woman at the food court

smiling to light the world, and now he quiet, maybe in a bad mood, maybe missing his red-headed boo. Maybe thoughts of his redhead babe occupy his mind. Aunt Nelle is way prettier, dark, with thick, shoulder-length hair complementing her beige skin and celery-green eyes.

They seem uncomfortable being in an enclosed space like a car. At their cavernous home, they can escape from each other. They tolerate each other the way you would an unwanted family member, stomach them long enough, counting the seconds until they leave, grateful you do not have to see them again for a long time. Lucky for them, their house is big enough for two people who don't want to be in the same room.

It's weird to be married to someone for so many years you don't like. Years ago, they seemed to really like each other as people, in love as a couple; Uncle Marsh was smiling then, the same smile at the food court. Aunt Nelle was still distant back then but nice enough to fool Grandma. But not Ma. At their wedding, I was one of the flower girls on an afterthought. Ma cussed Uncle Marsh out for being a wuss for not insisting I be a flower girl. "That fake-ass bougie bitch." She never neglects to bring up the flower girl incident to Uncle Marsh when she can't get a dollar out of him. She calls him Uncle Tom to his face and behind his back. "He's a wanna be white boy 'til his ass got stopped by the police in his brand-new ride," she laughed. "Now he knows what he is to them. Marsh ain't nothing but an Oreo. Can't believe he didn't marry a white woman. Ma and me was shocked when he first brought Nelle to Grandma's crib."

"You sound like Grandma. Aunt Nelle could pass," I say, referring to her light eyes and pale skin.

Ma grunts knowingly, "Not white enough."

I asked what secret Ma has about Uncle Marsh; she then became the responsible adult for a moment to reprimand me. "Don't be getting up in grown folk's business."

Ma's jealous; she fell out favor with Grandma because she's a fuck up. Grandma realized she put her dreams on the wrong child, and now that Uncle Marsh is a successful adult with a successful life, Grandma is trying to make up for the years she ignored Uncle Marsh in favor of her. It may be too late. I see by the way Uncle Marsh and Aunt Nelle treat her that they still hold a grudge. Uncle Marsh gives Grandma money, but very little of his time.

Grandma gassed up Uncle Marsh the way she used to about Ma, but it has fallen on deaf ears. Ma has not given Grandma any reason for bragging.

She's hating.

We are almost at their home. I've set the timer on my phone to see how long it will take before Aunt Nelle wants Jamal out of her house. I'm doing this for myself as well. I will be glad to end our visit.

It's chilly outside, but much colder in their home.

It is sad to be in a house with no warmth.

CHAPTER FORTY-THREE

I survived another visit, glad to be done with Aunt Nelle and Uncle Marsh. A trip to the dentist for a root canal is less painful. Uncle Marsh slipped me twenty dollars just because. He always does that when Jamal and I visit, slips us money for no reason. Ma called it hazard pay, gratitude for putting up with Aunt Nelle. Jamal's electricity was at high volume at the thought of buying candy and treats with his; he knows how traumatic it is to be an unwanted visitor. The money lessens his pain.

Uncle Marsh dropped me off first, kissed me goodbye. He tells me to remind Dad of their hoop date tomorrow at three. He is not able to stay for a visit because he has to take Jamal back to the city to Grandma. He definitely isn't going home after dropping Jamal off after taking that call away from us. It made logistical sense to take Jamal home first then me since we both live in Upstate; Uncle Marsh did the opposite; the next stop is off to the mall to see his redhead side chick. Maybe they gonna hook up in the city away from suspicious eyes. Did he see me at the food court that day?

The doctor has been like a guard dog since our confrontation, making sure I am nowhere in sight—but I've watched her watching me.

I instinctively look down at the welcome mat, and I see a white piece of paper with scribble on it. I recognize misspelled words in English. A rush of excitement floods every artery in my body, and my hands make tight fists at the start of something happening with us—what I don't know. It is her note I find under the doormat of my house. And more, I'm surprised it was not noticed by my parents, especially Dad, who hates litter, and Marcus, who is A-one nosy.

How was she able to get away from the doctor to write it, sneak away from her prison to place it here? Did she do it at night? She was probably able to do it when she was taking the garbage or recycling out under the cover of night.

I read it again and again. She is practicing her English. I can tell by the misspelled words.

Hallo, my name is Ninah. I from the Africa. Tank you for treats, smiling friend smiling for me. Pease be kind to bring me more eats, piece of fruit. Merci. Tank you.

I double-wrap the requested items: an apple, an orange, two bananas, three sugar cookies, a Kit Kat, and my last Reese's peanut butter cup. I get a small container to hold chocolate milk. If the candy is not too sweet, she might like the milk too.

My obstacles are the doctor and Mr. Greenly. I hope his boo comes over for a visit to occupy him while I watch for Buddy and Bebe, who I have not seen in a while. Praying they are not victims of roadkill somewhere or the coyotes' or fox's supper.

The bundle of goodies should last until Sunday night when the recycle bin has to be put out for the morning. I am hopeful we can talk. I write a note in English and French.

Hello my friend, my name is Rubena. If Rubena is too hard for you to pronounce, just call me Beenie.

Bon jour, mon ami, je m'appelle Rubena. Si Rubena est trop difficile, tu peux m'appeler Beenie.

CHAPTER FORTY-FOUR

We will finally get to talk, meeting face to face after months of sending covert signals of friendship to each other. We are stunned, looking at each other in silence as though we have never met, like aliens, except we share our race: skin color, hair texture, two arms, two legs, not different but not the same. It feels strange to see a new yet familiar face for the first time, reluctant to say anything, whether to speak the first words in English or French.

She is small in stature, with sparkling black skin and diamond eyes. I want to say something special, welcome her with a hug, but instead, I say in English and then in French, "How were you able to get away to meet?"

Her melanin face reveals pearl-white teeth, which beautifully complement her skin. "I put sleeping pills in her tea."

My eyes jump out of their sockets. "The first time?" I ask in French, happy we are starting to communicate, though it was an awkward start.

Ninah laughs. "No. Every time we saw each other, it was because I give Madam her tea with sleeping pills. I was so excited to see you, I forgot to do it when she caught us together, I had to run. I did that many times; I was able to watch you looking at me. *I was watching you.* I was fearful the man with the blinking eye was going to kidnap you."

It is my turn to crack up. "Uh no, that's Mr. Greenly. He's just nosy, in everybody business except his own. Trust me, he's harmless."

"I watch you feeding the animals. I was afraid the rat would attack you."

"Rat?"

"Yes. You were feeding many rats breads. They were big like a little dog, furry with large dark circles on their eyes with hair on their tails." She expands her arms wide. "I never see such a rat so big. I watch you wondering are they pet rats."

My flanks are bursting with laughter. I bend over, closing my eyes for a second so it will stop. Ninah leans forward, looking at me, smiling. It evolves into uncontrollable giggling like she had not felt so good in a long time.

I inform her, "They're not rats; they're raccoons. They are native to the United States."

Ninah attempts to pronounce the word in her heavy French accent. "Ratcoos?"

I explain that raccoons are North American animals. Most people consider them vermin. And no, they are not my pets. I was just bored, so I fed them until Mr. Greenly stopped me. "Oh, before I forget, this is for you." I hand over a small paper bag filled with the food she requested.

She takes the bag gently as if holding a baby, opens it, and sniffs so hard the paper crinkles. In English, she says, "I so hungry all time. She does not eat much."

Our conversation trails off with nothing more to say than to look at each other, grateful for this meeting to talk. We both look up at the bedroom windows of the doctor and over to Mr. Greenly.

"I must go before the spell is broken. She will wake up soon before dawn looking for him."

"Who?"

"Her husband." Ninah's eyes shift up to the front bedroom window with a slight laugh turning into a wistful smile. "We will meet tomorrow, yes?" There is a plea in her voice.

I extend my hand to her and then clasp them tightly. "Yes, we will meet tomorrow at the same time."

"She has a lot of sleeping pills, so we will be fine." Ninah squeezes my hand tightly again for reassurance. "The moment I saw you, my heart told me you are the friend I was praying for in America."

CHAPTER FORTY-FIVE

"Good morning, we're here to see Miss Lulu Bell Davis, B-E-L-L D-A-V-I-S," Grandma says in a highfalutin tone. She acts grand around white people, making sure they know she comes from good stock. It is so funny watching Grandma act like she's the Queen of England, waiting for a red-carpet rollout. I don't know why Grandma needs to flex and put on a front. Seems to me that she is trying to impress people she don't care for. Grandma professes to love God's people. She's just selective of who she wants to love. She don't need a reason to like anybody who don't like her. She worked with people of all races when she was a social worker. Grandma indicted a whole race based on her life in the South, and when she first came to New York, how rude they were to her.

"Some people just assholes, Mama, nothing more. It's not always racial," Ma tried explaining to her. I tried to reason too—it's simply "folks with no manners, no home training," as Grandma calls it. But if you're not black and rude to her, it's racial. You don't have no reason to dislike her the way she sees it.

The receptionist looks up from her phone. "What?" With green hair and streaks of pink and purple bangs, she looks out of place at the hospital front desk, receiving visitors who may find her a bit odd. I like her hair color. She has a visibly chipped front tooth, a small snake tattoo on her forearm, and a snarky attitude to match.

Grandma looks at this girl, then me, to support her contention that she was not raised right. "I'm here to see Miss Lulu Bell Davis."

The chipped-tooth girl bangs on the computer like it is her enemy, her eyes scanning furiously. She is anxious to return to her iPhone. I tip over the desk to see what she was looking at: TikTok; explains her impatience. "I don't have anyone with that name."

"Well, you need to check again." Grandma's patience is shorter than Miss TikTok's. The girl is flustered by Grandma's menacing stare; it is a prelude to a whipping—Jamal could have warned this girl if he was not at Grandma Henderson's.

Now the girl is deferential, double-checking her computer and then scooting over to a second one to appease Grandma. "I—I'm sorry, I don't a have a Lula Davis."

"Miss Lulu Bell Davis," Grandma corrects her for leaving out the title and misspelling the name. Her eyes scan so quickly they run off her computer, splaying against the wall like cast-off blood from an assault. Tapping the keys for mercy to free her from Grandma's optical choke hold. Now she on the phone, pretending, so nervous she fumbles and drops her phone to the floor.

I cannot bear the girl's torture anymore. "Try checking for R. Bell Davis."

Grandma breaks away from the relieved TikTok girl, looking at me. "Who?"

"R. Bell Davis," I repeat to the multicolor snake-haired girl, ignoring the massive question mark on Grandma's face.

She is beyond grateful for the life jacket rescue from Grandma's tsunamic scorn. "I found it. He's in intensive care," Miss TikTok shrieks as though she found Grandma's lost million-dollar winning lottery ticket. She draws in more air than her lungs need, thankful.

"He?" Grandma's face twists. "I'm looking for a woman, not a man."

"Come, Grandma." I'm holding her forearm as she is suddenly wobbly. Sweat beads around her forearm as if she is home in the Alabama heat. I loosen up her sweater, remove her scarf, and carefully untangle the crucifix with Jesus on it. It was a birthday gift from Miss Lulu Bell for Grandma's sixty-fifth birthday five years ago. Miss Lulu Bell was in charge like always, bossing and barking orders with a smile at everyone.

I gently wipe her forehead, unsure whether she is more shocked by Miss Lulu Bell in intensive care or the revelation about her friend.

"Lemme sit for a spell," she says.

I navigate her to the nearest chair in the lobby. She is catching her breath not from distress but surprise. She looks at me, asking to repeat what her ears did not tell her. "Lulu's brother been long dead. We ain't here to see no Richard Bell Davis," she snaps.

"That's her name, Grandma." I don't know how to explain, teach her about people she does not want to know about, people not in scripture good or bad, the Bible, the church, her environment. To Grandma, if it ain't what God wants, then it ain't no good, and you don't need it. She never accepted Dad and Marcus, never bothered to learn about people who are not like her.

How do I make her leave that Christian bubble? She don't allow no one in unless they think like her.

How do I explain and make her understand what I learned in school about people different from her? She would brush it off as nonsense, not wanting to know. Even I am at a loss for words to tell her. Even if I explained transgenderism to her, she would not allow herself to comprehend it.

"Beenie, you can't change your grandma, she still living in the

Old Testament. It's like pleading with granite," Ma once said, laughing, and added, "She only see what she wanna see."

It is as foreign to her as my dad's sexuality, something she may be too religious, maybe too backward, to accept. But I have to try to explain this to her.

In a whirlwind of confusion, her eyes heavy, she leans forward, massaging her temples. Grandma knows about people different from her. The squinted eyes tell me she don't want to process about Lulu or Richard. She don't care to understand.

Now she's talking to herself. "Lies, lying on her, didn't believe then. I never believe that gossip, but a liar will tell the truth sometimes."

We sit as time abandons us. She processes it slowly. The truth hits her as ugly as the rumors she did not accept, but now Grandma has no choice. "You mean to tell me, my friend of over forty years ain't what she's supposed to be? That makes no sense to me. I've known Lulu Bell all my life. There must be a mistake."

"No, Grandma," I say gently. "That is her in intensive care. Let's go see her, visiting hours end soon."

She shakes her graying hair fervently. "No, that can't be her. Richard Bell Davis is her brother who died in Vietnam."

I gently tug at Grandma. "C'mon, let's go. She may not be able to look or hear us, but we gotta let her know we're here, that we love her."

Grandma falls back in the chair, looking at me as if I spoke a foreign language. She covers her mouth; if only she could also cover her ears and eyes to the truth about Lulu. She does not want to believe. She snaps out of the trance and side-eyes me, unsmiling. The truth, as much as she hates it, has sunk in. "You knew about this?"

"Grandma, she's your friend—your best friend, remember?"

"He lied to me."

"She's always been a good friend. You said friends like Miss Lulu Bell are rare."

"He ain't told the truth for a long time," Grandma talking to herself again.

"She's family. You say that all the time. It doesn't change anything, Grandma. She is your friend," I chant.

"What other lies I've been told?" She does not look at me.

"C'mon. Let's go see her before visiting hours end."

"Stop saying that. That ain't no woman. That's a man, you understand?" The volume of her voice startles a toddler holding a bottle as the mother looks at Grandma, who returns a growl twofold. She shoots up like a rocket, steadies her balance, and puts her hands firmly on the chair for support. "Let's go."

"What about loving God's children as he loves you?" I'm throwing her words back at her as she blocks them.

Grandma leans so close to my face, I can see her pores, and in a voice turned down several volumes to a whisper says, "I'm not gonna say it again—let's go."

"Grandma, please—"

She leaves me sitting in my chair, walking a few steps, going ramrod-straight ahead toward the exit and Miss Tik Tok happily engaged in her phone. She stops, then slowly turns to me. Her tone is firm. "Beenie, you best stop being disrespectful. I said, let's go."

As we walk, I silently repeat in my head what Grandma usually says: *Please keep care of Miss Lulu Bell, for my sake but most importantly for Grandma, as only you can, God.*

* * *

Grandma did not go to church that Sunday, the Sunday after, nor for several Sundays after the hospital visit despite Reverend Wright's offer to come to the apartment for prayer for the sick and shut in.

She sent us to Sunday school dressed, but Jamal kept pestering me and Grandma with questions about why she wasn't going with us. She did not answer him but said aloud to the walls of her apartment that she did not feel like talking to God lately. Jamal put up a fuss. Grandma uncharacteristically surrendered but slipped away the moment she dropped us off, not greeting her friends and fellow parishioners, even dissing Reverend Wright as he stood long-faced with a hand extended to her.

Church did not seem right without Grandma, Miss Lulu Bell, and their big church hats strolling in during the procession.

Nothing feels connected anymore.

Grandma stayed by herself the remainder of the weekend as I packed my bag and got ready to go back home to Upstate. Dad FaceTimed that he'd be here in ten minutes despite weekend traffic on the West Side Highway.

Grandma carrying a heavy sadness I have never seen in her before, not by Ma neither. She did not say much after the hospital, only to make sure Jamal and I cleaned our plates.

Jamal was on his best behavior and tried to comfort her. He leaned against her, rubbing her gray head with one hand on top of hers.

She sitting now at her favorite spot: the kitchen table in front of the window, providing a full view of the senior complex. She listening to Mr. Cicero Bird's saxophone, the salve needed for her soul. It is the same kitchen window where she would holler out to Miss Lulu Bell to join her for coffee, dinner, scriptures, and gossip. Her Bible in her lap as she looks from the window to her Bible. Jamal runs off to get her favorite sweater as a breeze sneaks in.

"We should go back to see her," I say.

"Child, you don't know anything."

"A friend in Christ is a true friend—that's a blessing. You said that."

"It's different."

"Why? Because Miss Lulu Bell is different?"

"That's not his name."

"Yes, it is her name."

Grandma does not look at me, preferring to stare out the window. She hears me, but she don't want to. "Your father's here."

I give her the tightest hug her frail body allows. After a few seconds, she reciprocates, placing her hand over mine, grieving for her friend. She don't know where to put her anger even though it should be God for making the rules preventing her from accepting her best friend and allowing Miss Lulu Bell's friendship.

"Miss Lulu Bell Davis is a wonderful, *God-fearing woman*," I whisper in her ear using her favorite three words.

Penguin called early this morning as I got ready to meet up with Tiki to walk to school. I heard Ma crying in the background. Penguin and Jamal there to care for her. My heart crashed to my stomach, bracing myself for the terrible news.

Miss Lulu Bell Davis died peacefully yesterday, moments after I arrived home at Upstate.

She never recovered from her stroke.

The phone still in my hand, unable to believe what Penguin told me.

If I start crying, I will never stop.

Chest hurts, blood pooling at my feet, forcing me to sit down before they give out.

Heartbroken for Grandma.

And though she is twenty miles south of Upstate in New York City in the senior citizen complex she and Miss Lulu Bell shared for a lifetime, I can hear the wailing, the tears of Grandma, grateful I am not there.

She prefers to grieve alone, with only God to comfort her.

CHAPTER FORTY-SIX

Early morning before school, gentle, rippling winds tickle the tree in front of the house. I find a piece of crumpled paper weighed by a stone. On it is scribbled: *Je vous remercie*—then in English: *The doctor not feeling well; she been sleeping night. I will give her medicine make her sleep more. We can meet when the moon is out. Ninah*

Ninah—the elf of the night.

I prepared the usual request: a banana, cookies, and an orange. At first sight of the moon, I gently close the door behind me. She is waiting near the garbage in front of her house with no lights on.

"Hey there!" I hand her the package and say, in French, "We finally meet in peace again."

She clasps the package under her small arm, grabs my hands, and kisses me on each cheek. "It is a hard life during the day." Ninah's eyes light up in the dark as she inspects the package's contents.

A hard look at her face for the first time lets me really see the features I'd overlooked; she looks like Spanky, Grandma's dearly departed cocker spaniel, with wide, frightened eyes and a shivering little body. Her black face is taut, strained with visible lines of anguish the dark sky cannot hide. Her sun-kissed skin is rich against the night, with hair in defined spirals resembling curly fries. Her English is not bad but is heavily accented by her French. She tells me she wants to continue to speak in English so she can improve.

Ninah hugs me again, unable to let go. Her gratitude and warmth transfer to my body. "Thank you for the food. Madame not so generous. She does not eat at all."

Her rib cage, upon hugging, reminds me of the children of Darfur. I must continue to feed her. "Will she sleep long?" I ask, recalling my confrontation with the doctor.

"*Non*. She will sleep long enough so we can talk a little."

"Where is the professor?"

"With his mistress. C'est pourquoi elle est méchante—that's why she is so mean." Ninah laughs, peeling the banana and stuffing half in her mouth. I'm amazed someone so small can consume food bigger than her.

"They fight all the time. He uses it as a reason to run off—stays away sometimes for days. His lover lives in New York City, teacher at university. Pierre and Dennis think their parents are perfect, but they do not see what I see. They hate her too. She is not even their mother. She is cruel with words to them. Their real mother ran away when they were en enfant. The doctor makes them cry, says she is a better Mama. Their mother does not love them like she does."

Ninah pops the second half of the banana in her mouth without the convenience of taking a bite, then attacks the orange. I make a note to bring water next time.

"Madame, a doctor, takes many, many pills for her sadness, but it does not help. Some days when we alone, her tears flood the house like the river. She is mean because her heart is broken. I feel sad for her when she is nice to me. Her family do not love her, the professor do not love her, Pierre and Dennis do not love her."

Ninah, a dam-full of silence that has burst from solitude, is unable to stop talking.

"He will leave her, that is for sure. He followed his mistress to America, why we are here. When he is home, he goes to the garage to talk to his girlfriend in peace. He talks to her in English. He does not think I understand." She beams. "He talks to her with me there. I will never betray him; he is so kind to me when he is home, but he is not often here."

She puts the orange back in the bag, then test bites the sugar cookie, taking a large bite in approval. "He is a good man with a bad woman. He gives me extra when Madame is not looking. But when he is not at home, it is so bad for me."

Ninah unable to stop smiling at me like I'm a ghost, a mirage that will evaporate the moment she touches it. I touch her arm to reassure her.

"I told you I saw you from the beginning watching me. I knew you would help because you have a kind face. But I had to be sure. That is why I ran when you first approached me."

"I was more curious about you because the doctor is a liar. I told her so."

Ninah's eyes enlarge as she opens her mouth, in awe of my bravado. "She did not hit you?"

I lean back, eyebrows arched, folding my arms. "Why would she hit me? She wouldn't dare. My fathers would pulverize her, then call the police to arrest her."

Ninah paralyzed to silence, mouth agape, blinking to breathe. She snaps out of it, attempting to pronounce the word *pulverized*. I explain the definition. Ninah more curious the doctor would not strike me.

"She would go to jail for hitting me."

"You are so fortunate. She is a beast."

"Why do you call your mother Madame?"

Ninah shakes her head violently, spiraling black curly fries whip in the wind and hit her in the face. "She is not my mother; this is not my family."

"Where is your family?"

Ninah looks up at the window, searching. "I will tell my story, my journey, but I must go. Daylight will be here soon." She instinctively holds my hands again, plants a kiss on each cheek, then suffocates me with a hug.

"You are my angel in America. We will talk again much soon, oui?"

CHAPTER FORTY-SEVEN

Mr. Borden is discussing human rights issues, including child exploitation stateside and abroad. He talks about children exploited in Asia for sex tours funded for the pleasure of Europeans and Americans to harm children, mainly from poor families and orphans. We also discuss Saudi Arabia using toddlers and small children as jockeys for camel racing, starving the child to control their weight and using hormonal injections to retard their growth to be competitive so the camel races faster with less weight from the child. It overloads my mental circuits to absorb so much foul treatment of children; it pisses me off that I can't do nothing, and I can't stop thinking about Ninah and other children suffering.

The next discussion is about slavery in our country—one student says slavery ended in the late 1800s. Mr. Borden says he is partially correct, but child slavery did not end in 1865. It is prevalent today with child abduction and people brought here illegally to work as indentured servants or outright held captive to work without rights or pay.

Ninah and Amber—Ninah is from central Africa, hidden by

the doctor, and Amber—where is she? Is she being held against her will? Was that guy her boyfriend or pimp?

The internet pumps out horror stories of girls exploited by guys who are real-life pimps. They look for girls in chat rooms under the cover of posing as possible boyfriend material and give them gifts and things to gain their confidence.

Amber was always fronting she had bank, her father was rich, and she did not have to study in school. The real truth was that she was broke, no money, and her parents were working-class people, a big difference from Molly, Sophie, and Gwynne.

Tiki and I later learned that Gwynne and Molly gave her lunch money; then suddenly, she was popping with a designer this, designer that, a thousand-dollar iPhone, money to buy her crew lunch, even though they, with the exception of Lauren, did not need it. She had money with no explanation.

Owen and I look over at Tiki, who is not paying attention to Mr. Borden, though he does not seem to notice or care. Her arms are supporting her head on the desk. I nudge her to wake up. She is rubbing her eyes, telling me she did not sleep well last night. Owen perks up to listen to her. She stops, drawing a scowl on her face just for him. I motion her to text me.

The landlord kicked my sister out. Matt got arrested. Dumbass broke the no-drug rule in the project. I'm so done! So tired of living like a homeless person.

Where did you sleep? I text back.

She pauses to palm-rub her eyes and responds, *In the car. Sasha got an appointment with the Housing Authority board this afternoon to plead her case. She got a Legal Aid lawyer to help her. If she don't take that idiot back, maybe we can move back in. So glad they didn't throw our shit out on the street, yet. You gotta show up at the housing board meeting; if you don't, they will chuck your stuff out and padlock the door. I've seen the housing guys do shit to people. They crying while tossing their stuff out with neighbors watching like it's a freak show. Oh, it gets better: guess what? Stupid took Speed back.*

Where are you staying tonight? Tiki responds before I can hit send. She has the fastest text fingers.

Legal Aid gave us vouchers to find a place for the night. She got us a room at the shit hole motel. I'd rather sleep on molten lava. The women in my family are fucking stupid. Can you buy me lunch? I'm so hungry.

CHAPTER FORTY-EIGHT

Ninah and I laying on a blanket, not doing a good job preventing the night grass dew from absorbing into our nightgowns. We both do not care. We're enjoying a night picnic, staring at the stars, counting, connecting dots, unable to keep count, doing it again, and being silly. Her eyes lit up upon seeing all the stuff I brought for our nightnic (instead of picnic). Surprisingly, Ninah said to hold off eating, she wanted to savor the beautiful warm night and, in her words, "the good company of a friend." She wanted to take in what it was to feel freedom if only for a little while.

She giggles in a mischievous, impish way of doing a bad deed and being unbothered by the consequences. "I fixed Madame doctor for the night."

"Tu es une mauvaise fille! You're a bad girl." The corners of Ninah's mouth upturn, leaving a flat line in the middle. I let go a small laugh and keep hold of some minuscule worry about what she'd done to the doctor.

Ninah waves that we should begin our feast. "She got more because she was crying again. I put her in bed, brushing her hair as she cried for her dead father, who loved only her. Then I sang a song her father sang to her when she was a small girl, so she be quiet and sleep."

A wave of sadness appears on her face like an unremovable stain. "Do you know how it feels to sing to a beast? Madame doctor told me I have a beautiful voice."

Reading the concern on my face, Ninah suddenly remembers to smile. "She will not interrupt our time. She will be okay for a long, long time for us."

"You didn't give too much... to... you know?"

Ninah laughs like the crickets speaking in the night. It's a laugh that had been suppressed for a long time. She tosses her spiral curls against the gentle wind, showing her white teeth, then splays her palms at me in a soothing stance. "No, I give her what she takes—I watch her sometimes take more than what she should. Her heart is sad, but her stomach is strong."

Ninah's laugh dissolves as quickly as it surfaced, and she gazes up at the fairy lights of stars against a black backdrop, trance-like. I lean close to her and whisper: "Is this the same sky you see at home?"

"Stars are the same everywhere. Night is peaceful."

"It's scary to me sometimes, especially when I watch horror movies."

"Horror?" She leans on her elbows, focused on me.

"Yeah, you know movies that scare you."

Her laughter returns. "Rubena, I know about cinemas. I just haven't been to any."

"Never?"

"Well, once, when we lived in London. Madame doctor, in a nice moment, let her driver take the boys and me."

"What movie did you see?"

"Peter Pan. I wanted to be like the fairy Tinker Bell, wave my magic wand, and make all the bad go away."

We finish the tuna sandwiches, apples, Kit Kat, then move on to brownies Marcus made for what he thought was for Tiki and me; we were short two because my sweet-tooth dad could not resist.

It made sense to me why Ninah identifies with Tinker Bell and her magical powers. If I possessed it, I would use it to make Ma better, ease Grandma's pain, and help Tiki. I would take away the pain of Amber's family, everyone in the world suffering. One tap, and it would be all good—no more mistreated children or animals.

If only Tinker Bell was real, I'd WhatsApp her for help.

CHAPTER FORTY-NINE

Tiki has unfollowed and blocked me. I'm shocked her phone has not been disconnected. She left several unanswered messages and texts that I did not bother to respond to and came to a conclusion about our friendship.

Her life is a mess, nothing but drama, but she acts like she's the only person suffering. Ninah's suffering, but she don't bitch like Tiki. I needed a break from that. She gets on my nerves with her whining and people who have done her wrong, and I am sick of being an ear to her screwed-up family, so I took a pause from her like parents sending kids to summer camp.

Now, in class, she only talks to Owen, and I only talk to Owen, which makes him feel something he has never felt before—popular. We ignore each other and become silent when Owen talks to the other. I refuse to turn around to look at her, and she stares straight ahead at the front of the classroom like a horse with blinders on.

We had a fight two days ago. I am sorry about it today, but I'll never admit it to her. She was all in her feelings, saying I was abandoning her for Ninah after I told her we were getting to know each other and becoming friends.

I said, "You need to get a life—it's not my problem you can't make friends like I do. *It's not my fault nobody likes you.*"

She clenched her fists, shrieking: "Nobody likes you neither!"

"That's because I'm around you!"

She pushed me, screaming, "I trusted you!"

I caught my balance and charged at her. "You better keep your paws off me before you get an ass-whupping your mama forgot to give you!"

She fell on her ass. Luckily, it was on my front lawn and not the sidewalk. "I trusted you. You the only person I ever trusted beside my Peggy: now I can't trust you!" she started hollering like a soiled-diaper baby. "You bitch."

I attempted to diffuse the situation, joking, "Dumbass."

"You think you better than me?"

I grimaced at her for not making sense, for being pissed off because I neglected to tell her about Ninah. She knew I was trying to make contact for a long time. "Now you're really acting like a dumbass."

Her face turned fire-red. She started hyperventilating and, in a low growling voice, said, "I'm not a dumbass. Stop calling me that. I'm sick of people calling me that."

"We always call each other names. It's a joke we have with each other, remember, duh?"

She slowly got up, dusting her behind, not looking at me. "Lorna called me that when I was little. She stopped when I got big enough to call her names that hurt her more. I'm not a dumbass. I'm working hard in school to get away from all this shit and people who always fuck me." She calmed down, moving closer, and said, "I thought we were good. I can't trust anyone. I fucking hate people, man."

She pushed my arm off like a mad hornet and walked away, ignoring me as I called her.

The commotion surfaced the doctor to her front door like the swamp monster coming out of the lagoon, smiling at me.

A crocodile could not smile any better.

CHAPTER FIFTY

Two large Louis Vuitton suitcases parked at the front door must belong to Marcus as they are far too extravagant for Dad's frugal tastes. Surprise was not my reaction upon seeing them near the door, but a gut punch of realized expectations. It had only been a matter of when, not if, Marcus tired of Dad's fiscal chokehold, the overwhelming suffocation of him being inflexible.

I'm startled to see Dad home earlier than usual and more surprised that he is sitting in the dining room, elbows on the table, hands clasped, staring out the window, and not aware I am standing at the entrance. The sound of heavy footsteps on the stairs, sadness in the air—I'm about to choke. Unable to move, my eyes jump from Dad in the dining room to Marcus trudging, wrapped in a jacket, shoulder weighed down by a knapsack. I'm lightheaded, chanting inside to keep my head and ears clear, though they want to shut down like Dad.

Marcus kneels before me as I tower above him. "Beenie, this is not easy. Your father and I decided to separate for a while."

"Those suitcases say it gonna be more than a while."

He looks over at Dad, who is looking stone-faced at the window without acknowledging Marcus. "I'll be close by. I'll give you my number."

"Why?" I ignore him, directing the question at my father.

"It's for the best right now," Marcus answers for him.

I close my eyes to focus on breathing and keep my feet planted so I don't collapse.

"Dad, say something!"

He unclasps his hands, inhaling every molecule in the house, selfishly leaving Marcus and me with nothing. "Princess, it's complicated."

"You don't like pushback, *that's complicated*," I return fire. "How are people supposed to love you when you cut them off when it's complicated?" I mock him. Dad looks at Marcus then back at me.

I will not cry in front of him. We're so alike and I hate it. We bury our feelings deep where no one can find them. "Ma was right about you. You just shut down everybody, problem solved, move on."

Marcus rubs my arm. "You're my daughter, always will be. I'm here anytime you need me." He lifts himself up, wrapping his sinewy arms around me tight, then with a hand on the door, Marcus gives Dad a long hard look, hesitant, and after a moment, knowing what would not happen, closes the door.

I jerk at the sound of the deadbolt and run over to the dining room window, watching Marcus load his suitcases and then get in his SUV. "If you love him, you would stop him."

"I do love him. That's why I have to let him go."

"You think he's a boomerang? So sure he'll be back?" I spin around, my face heated from the blood rush, looking at him. "That makes no sense. If I leave, will you let me go too?"

His face long, touching the floor, eyes forbidden to shed a tear before an audience, not even himself.

I will not comfort the broken heart *he is responsible* for.

As I leave him alone, I fire straight at his broken heart. "You've ruined everything."

CHAPTER FIFTY-ONE

I'm so over adults in my life.

All they do is fuck up.

I no longer know where home is, if it ever existed—with my mother, my grandma, and now my father. The home I missed has gone with Miss Lulu Bell. She always made me feel better, no matter how hard it was.

There is no home for me, only the one in my head where people cannot disappoint me, cannot hurt me if they can't reach me.

Everything is temporary until it is time to leave.

There is no such thing as home.

And for Miss Lulu Bell Davis, no one retrieves her remains, no immediate family or distant relatives come to claim her. She is held longer than administrative protocol. The hospital tries in earnest to find anyone to take charge of her remains; a former in-law of her father and a distant cousin by marriage on her mother's side who were contacted did not want the bother—or they were estranged because of her authentic self and falsely claimed poverty at the expense of her arrangement.

Something finally touched Grandma's heart and made her realize Lulu Bell was a true friend, a person who loved her. She finally accepted the responsibility. Miss Lulu Bell left the instructions years ago for Grandma, her sister in Christ, her one and only true friend, to handle her affairs. Grandma accepted my offer to help her, and I was glad to get away from Upstate from my father, Tiki, and their drama.

In Reverend Wright's office, he does not receive us with his usual jolly self. A smile abandoned his face long before Grandma called him for a meeting. He sits in his big leather chair in his tiny office, hands clasped tightly, ready not for prayer but for a prepared answer for Grandma.

He dictates to Grandma that Miss Lulu Bell's homegoing will be done by his birth name. *Richard Bell Davis, Jr.* can have service in his church but not *Miss Lulu Bell Davis*. He supports his decision with scriptures about man being a man and woman being a woman.

Grandma is torn; I can see it by the anguish on her face between her religious upbringing, her conviction, and her dear friend of decades. "Reverend Wright, she's been a faithful servant to God. I'll testify for her. She loved the Lord more than anybody in this congregation, been a blessing to the church and the people, been tithing as long too. Lulu—"

"Richard," Reverend Wright cuts off as he unclasps his hands, flat palms his desk, "can have his homegoing."

He is a man of short stature with a fading hairline and a beauty mark on his chin. When performing Sunday sermons, he jumps up and down like he riding a pogo stick, mouth wide open with the worst teeth on display, jagged like a dragon.

His tongue is firm, but his eyes are gentle, mindful that Grandma is his elder. He tries to appease Grandma. "The military is sending staff to stand by his coffin in honor of his valiant service in Vietnam. He was a fine man—"

I cannot sit on my hands anymore when I jump up. "She was a fine lady too!"

"Hush Beenie!" Grandma yanks me back to my seat.

I ignore her. "She may have been a fine man, but she was a great woman."

* * *

Hypocrites—all of them. Grandma too.

Grandma and I are waiting for a cab to take us to church for the service. Several of the neighbors, the ones whose lives were improved by Miss Lulu Bell, are not dressed for her funeral, don't plan on coming. Grandma does not judge them for their stupid reasons for not paying respect to Miss Lulu Bell.

Miss Gracie Lawson in a tacky housedress and raggedy slippers, holding garbage weighing more than she does. She looks down at her feet and squeaks good morning at us. I ignore her. Grandma does not chastise me for it. She knows what Miss Lulu Bell done for Miss Gracie. It was Miss Lulu Bell who accompanied Miss Gracie to the clinic for her chemotherapy, cleaned her house, and cooked her meals when the chemo made her too weak to feed herself.

Miss Bette Mitchell closes her blinds when I look up at her window, staring at her. Maybe her dementia is more severe than her husband's. She seems to have forgotten that Miss Lulu Bell loaned her money to buy Mr. Horace medication when her good-for-nothing crackhead son stole money from them.

Mr. Cicero Bird's cancer has returned like a dreadful enemy, and he cannot make it. He said his nephew Louis Jordan will play the saxophone in his place at the funeral. A fine man, Mr. Bird is, Grandma said.

I don't want to go, but I must say goodbye to Miss Lulu Bell. I am no longer pissed at Grandma for denying me that right at the hospital, but I will never forgive her for not standing up to Rev. Wright. She was the one who told me to stand up for right even when everyone else was wrong.

I close my eyes while riding in the cab. Grandma thinks I am napping, but I am remembering Miss Lulu Bell, her outrageous home, her big hats, big personality, her perfume choking me when I sat behind her in church. Her clapping louder, playing the tambourine in the choir, wearing beautiful robes she made and did not charge the church for.

Her peach cobbler and sweet potato pie, rallying the seniors fighting for housing rights with a bull horn and big voice that awakens the dead, visits and prayers for the sick and dying. Her drinking and spilling tea, the children in the neighborhood projects she helped raise. The Queen of senior housing, that's the Miss Lulu Bell that I love and will always remember, not some soldier with badges of honors.

I'm standing before her on display, flanked by two marines with faces of stone, and there is not a trace of Miss Lulu Bell's authentic self. Her golden skin buried under thick mortuary makeup, not a trace of her perfectly coifed hair, defined and perfectly arched eyebrows, and full lips—she is gone completely.

Where are her pretty dresses, her gorgeous hats? Who put this uniform on her? I hate what they've done. I hate Grandma for being a spineless wuss.

The men Miss Lulu Bell served with in Vietnam speak about how she helped them as newbies to the bush. She comforted a boy she pulled out of enemy fire who lost his legs and moments later his life. Another man spoke about when he was walking point how Sergeant Richard Bell Davis spotted a booby trap from a distance and detonated it, saving the lives of the men in the platoon. He never ran away from helping. He was a man's man, another one said.

Among the few church members that attend is Miss Delores Baker. She sings one of Miss Lulu's favorite songs, "Victory is Mine." That would get Miss Lulu Bell up and shouting, jumping in her high heels. I was always afraid she would fall and hurt her ankle.

The last one to speak is Grandma. She gets up, standing before the microphone with Miss Lulu Bell's coffin behind her. She looks at Richard, a stranger to her in his Marines uniform, white gloves, and cap, then over at Rev. Wright, who eggs her on with a nod, smiling, the first on his face since he denied Grandma to provide Miss Lulu Bell her proper service.

"This man you speak of sounds mighty fine. A God-fearing man who done well in his life." She takes a deep breath and looks again at Richard. "But I don't know no Richard Bell Davis. Let me tell you about a great friend of mine, Miss Lulu Bell Davis. I loved her like a sister. She was more kin to me than my own.

"If a mother needed diapers, she brought them. If a person was sick, Lulu Bell took care of them. If someone needed a piece of bread, Lulu gave them the whole loaf. She followed the steps of Jesus, comforted the sick, fed the hungry, and clothed the naked. She was a God-fearing woman; I will testify before my God about her. A mighty *fine woman.*

"If ever a person gonna sit on the right hand of Jesus and our God, Miss Lulu Bell Davis will be first in line before any of us."

My jaw hits the floor as my eyes pop out of their sockets. The entire congregation, including Rev. Wright, is paralyzed into silence. You could hear a feather drop.

Grandma gently touches Miss Lulu Bell's hand. "Forgive me, Lulu Bell. I didn't do right by you." She removes her bright pink hat Miss Lulu Bell made for her, placing it atop her military-gloved hands. She straightens up, motioning me to follow her. As we walk the long red church carpet, the exit door seems miles away. I squeeze her hand—she squeezes back. I was wrong. Grandma is a true Christian soldier. "I guess you have to find another church, Grandma."

"The Lord will steer me to the right one."

CHAPTER FIFTY-TWO

Lately, Dad drinks more than he eats. There is a big hole in his heart, unable to heal. He looks at the food on his plate, waiting for it to feed him without effort, pushing it around like a child not wanting it.

The good fortune of home-prepared delivery food services prevented us from starving; the instructions made it possible for Dad and me to be good cooks with food that was surprisingly edible. We prepared, cooked, and followed the menu in silence with an occasional inquiry from him about me, school, or anything except the subject that hurts. We worked in silence, no music blaring in the kitchen, no covered pot on simmer while dancing. A morgue was more alive than our home.

"I'm meeting Marcus at the food bank Saturday," I announce as we are clearing the table.

Dad perks up, releasing a wistful smile upon hearing Marcus's name, the first in weeks since he left us. "Do you need a ride?" There is pleading in his voice that he wants to.

"No. He's gonna pick me up."

Dad solemnly nods as he haphazardly places dishes in the washer.

I place my hand before the dish rack. "Marcus says to rinse before placing in the dishwasher, so food waste doesn't clog it."

He pauses. An afterthought landsides against his head like granite stones. "He always took care of the kitchen; I was forbidden here."

"'Cause you're careless," I playfully tag him.

His lips purse, his brows connect tightly as lines form deep in his brown skin, and he says quietly, "I don't know much, do I?"

"You got a lot to learn, Dad. People have feelings."

Suddenly, like a hit on the head, Dad looks hard at me as if he has difficulty understanding English. The dish in his hand suspends; he unable to release it, holding it like an answer. I wait a second, then take the dish from him, placing it in the rack.

After dinner, I take to my room, Dad to the living room, brandy in hand in front of CNN with Anderson Cooper, History Channel, the local news, and then bed. The chair opposite him empty.

I return to the living room, where he is planted firmly, and hug him.

"It feels weird giving one night hug instead of two."

"I know."

* * *

Marcus and I are on our way to work at the only food bank in Upstate this morning. He said this was something he wanted to do for a long time since moving here. He did help at the food bank in the city. He told me I needed something to take my mind off all the drama that never seemed to stop.

"How's Dad?" he inquires at the stop light.

"We miss you."

"I miss you too."

"What about Dad?"

"Beenie, you never stop loving your husband even when you don't agree."

The heartbreak on his face prompts him to focus on my life, and I tell him about Tiki and I not speaking.

"You and Tiki will get it together." Marcus flips the bird to a driver's mad honk. "Let her cool off. If that don't work, there's nothing like a hot bath and chocolate chip cookies of mine she loves so much to make ya'll friends again. She can't stay mad after that." His attempt to make me laugh falls short, but I muster up a half-smile in gratitude for his effort.

It is early. Normally the Food Bank is closed, but recently it extended the hours of operation because of the need to help the underprivileged of Upstate. American citizens, refugees from Sudan, Central America, Iraq stand in line, waiting. So many people outside already before we got there, the manager says that is the norm. I'm amazed at the number of people lined up. Homelessness, poverty, poor people are even here in Upstate, one of the most affluent villages in New York.

Mrs. Buck, a sweet grandma lady with gray hair and blue veins, waddles over to greet Marcus and I with her caffeinated breath. Her clasped hands show she's happy to have more helpers. She assigns me to disburse the bags at the front receiving area when people enter while marveling at Marcus's sinewy arms, perfect for off-loading. She gives him a job working in the back lifting, opening boxes, and stocking the shelf.

Manning the front desk alone, I scan the faces lined up, thinking how Miss Lulu Bell would be here, directing and delegating while singing, praying, and making everyone smile with laughter. I imagine Grandma beside her, not smiling and barking at everyone, complaining about folks with no manners getting on her nerves with Miss Lulu Bell saying, "C'mon Eudora, we serving

God serving these folks. Now you gotta slap a smile on your face like lipstick for a hot date."

Giggling escapes me, feeling the blessing of her eyes upon me as I carry a heavy, second stack of bags after the first stack disappears seconds after opening the door.

"Hi." Tiki is holding baby Madison on her hip as she takes a bag from me.

"Hey. You here alone? Where's Sasha?"

Tiki shifts the baby on her other hip, holding the bag. "She's trying to find a parking spot. This is the worse place for this building. We can never find a parking spot." She shifts her eyes, clearing her throat. "I'm following you again. My phone's working." Tiki releases a nervous laugh.

"Oh yeah? I haven't had a chance to check," I lie to make her squirm some more.

"You never know when I'm on, when the bill is paid." She shifts the baby again.

"The truck's bringing in a lot of new foods, crap you like." I offer this up as a sign of forgiveness.

"Oh good, hope they got frosted flakes. That runs out quick. So does the mac and cheese. I told Sasha we gotta get here early to be first in line so we can get what we want. She finally listened to me." An elderly woman taps her shoulder. Tiki spins around at her. "Waitaminute!"

Sasha breezes in, cutting in line to the annoyance of the elderly woman and others. She takes the bags from Tiki, moving the line to the woman's relief.

"You gotta help," Sasha says to Tiki as she drops a hello to me in a hurry, moving over to the first aisle where the cereal and mac and cheese are located. The old woman snarls like a toothless wolf. Tiki returns fire, growling, then steals a smile at her. Sasha calls her again.

"Can I come by the house to talk?"

Arms folded in thought, not because I'm unsure of letting her back into my orbit, but just to prolong the agony scrawled over her face like a baby desperate for a diaper change. I want to punish her for adding more drama than I needed, but her puppy eyes, refugee-orange face, and dry lips of hunger for a friend, tell me to stop being a bitch. So, I let my empath take over. "Okay."

* * *

I arrive home from a day at the Food Bank to see Tiki sitting on the sidewalk in front of my house like an eager puppy. My feet and body hurt from standing all day, dealing with irritating people, language barriers, moving, stacking as truck after truck kept coming with food, yet it still was not enough to feed the hungry in Upstate. Despite the headache, I was glad Marcus convinced me to do it, to see how the other half lives, to be reminded I was once the other half, and know all too well how they live.

I cannot disappoint Tiki and muster up the energy to reconcile. We talk a long time about what happened, realizing it was miscommunication and just dumb to be mad in the first place. I reassured her we are friends, and Ninah is a new friend she will meet soon.

I make myself clear: I cannot be her *only friend*; she must learn to share and accept that I will have friends other than her.

She inhales more air than needed to satisfy her lungs. "I'm a dumbass for spasming over nothing. My bad. I'm always losing someone important to me; scared you'd be next. You just want to be around that person so much, 'cause when they around, you feel like it's all good. Shit ain't as bad as it is when you got your friend. I get scared they'll be gone. So hard to trust people, ya know. They always disappointing me."

"Me too."

"I'm sorry."

"You're not a dumbass," I gently push her.

She instinctively, out of character, hugs me tight as she whispers in my ear. "You my ride or die friend. You're still a bitch though."

"I know—and you're a smart-ass."

Dad gave Tiki permission to spend the night. She stayed in the whirlpool tub so long Dad made me check on her again to make sure she did not drown or dry up to a prune. Marcus used to joke about the tub ring he will have to scrub clean. He teased Tiki being my little skunk.

Tiki, towel drying her hair, says, "I don't want to leave."

"What's the deal with your sister?"

"The housing advocate pleaded her case. They gonna let her back in as long as she don't bring Matt back to live with her. Sasha's so man-hungry, no telling what she'll do a few days without that loser shithead," Tiki pauses, detangling a hard hair knot. "I don't know how she missing having some random dude around: they never have a job, she's working like a slave, so she's never home, and I'm stuck with Madison. I don't mind at all, but I gotta look at some asshole-stray in the house with me while she's working twenty-four seven. Soooo like stupid Lorna. If she gets her brains back, it'll be so dope with only us three: me, her, and the baby. But knowing her, she'll sneak him in or go back to Tinder where she got him from. Thirsty bitch."

* * *

I awaken in the morning, hearing a voice that saturates me with joy as I leave Tiki in the bedroom. Marcus is in the kitchen having coffee with Dad. The smile on my face will strangle me if I don't stop. Dad's smile has asphyxiated him.

It is a school day, but Marcus prepares us a Sunday breakfast of pancakes, bacon, grits, and eggs. He does this for Tiki's sake, knowing there is rarely enough food in her home to make a meal.

The television is on with *Good Morning America*; Robin Roberts is not smiling, as she usually does, as Tiki scoops a seat.

The body of a young female was found in a suitcase floating in the Yellowstone River in Eastern Montana on Sunday. Police identified the victim as—

My eyes jump from the phone to the television, where they stick.

——Dawn Johnson, fourteen years old, of Greenhill, who has been missing for five years since being abducted from her home.

Now, Tiki looks up; Greenhill is next to her town. "What the fuck? Sorry, Dad, Marcus. Rubena, that's her. She's the one we saw Amber leaving with." She puts her phone down with one hand while stuffing pancakes in her mouth with the other.

Dawn's recent photo shows she no longer has brown, exposed roots. Her hair is platinum blond. We see CCTV footage of Dawn, a black man, and a busty young girl with brown wavy hair at the Yellowstone Inn in Montana.

Tiki's jaw drops. "That's Amber. What's she doing in Montana?"

Marcus sighs sadly, pouring milk for us. The granite gets most of it. "Oh God, please keep that child safe."

My eyes are not playing with me. It is Amber Mills with the man we saw when she got into his truck at school. The police are looking for her and the man in connection with Dawn Johnson's murder.

CHAPTER FIFTY-THREE

"I'm sorry about your grandmother. She special to you, non?"

Ninah's English is improving rapidly, like a sponge soaking up as much as possible, as if she is preparing something, for what I do not know. "Very special, but she was not my grandmother; she was a very special person, a good friend of mine and my grandma." I look up at the window on the second floor, knowing the doctor can turn on the light at any moment and catch us. "Is this safe for you?"

Ninah's smile reveals a naughty deed she cannot wait to confess. She places her hands against the side of her face to pantomime sleeping. "No worry, Madame has given the gift of night. I am worthy of it." Her laugh is like a scream from being hit, a strain for her small body, every fiber needed to create it. She nudges me to join in the laughter. "I gave her a sleeping pill."

"Aren't you afraid she might die from too much?"

Ninah clicks her tongue, then snarls, "The Devil does not want her!"

"You so bad, for real, on purpose?" My eyes are as large as the night, amazed at this cunning little girl.

"I always give it to her, remember?" Ninah laughing, gassing off my fear. "No, no. She is a—how you say it in English when one cannot sleep?"

"Insomniac?"

"Insomniac." She enunciates the word slowly, tasting it in her mouth and liking the flavor. "She ordered me to get her pill and bring a glass of wine. The doctor will sleep until the morning. If she is in bad mood, I will be greeted by her with this."

Her smile melts like snow near fire. She pulls her sleeve up, revealing bruises on her forearm, snaking to her shoulder blade. She then half turns her back to me, lifting her gown. The welts are raised on her back and buttocks. They crisscross like tic, tac, toe. Tic tac toe. I'm unable to hide the horror on my face. How could anybody endure a beating, a whipping, so hard the skin raises? There are welts that look like the marks of a belt.

"She hits me when the professor is away with his mistress. She is angry at him but beats me. She drinks every night until she is drunk. Passes out, a lot. Sometimes she is awake, attacking me. Her mother was the devil giving birth to her. The doctor very sly, like a fox. She convinced the professor to send the boys away to school so she could have him all to herself. It did not work." Ninah laughs maniacally. It sounds like a strangled cat, frightening me. I think she might choke. "He gave his free time to his mistress. When he is home, I hear him talking to her in his office behind locked doors. They are making plans that do not include her to be together forever. I place my ears against the door and hear him saying loving words to her. Her name is Clara. She American."

"Can't you go home?"

Ninah adjusts her nightgown, pulling the sleeves down to her wrists, ignoring me as though I asked a stupid question. She stares hard at me for a second, searching my face, then relaxes. "No."

I instinctively hug her, careful not to touch her back. "Tell me about your life back home. How'd you end up with this evil woman?"

Ninah looks up at the midnight sky, focusing on the moon, preparing to tell a story of her journey.

"I am from a village near the river Congo. There is little electricity or running water. Mother died after the birth of my youngest sister, leaving me with my father, four sisters, and one brother, who is the treasure in my family. My family is what you Americans say, piss poor." She laughs proudly, embracing American slang as an additional language.

"I was a good student, the best in my class. I want to be a doctor someday. When the professor and the doctor are at work, I read the books in the home in French, and now, any book I can get in English, I read it over and over. Father saw no need to further my education. He saw my future in marriage to the wealthy men in my town more important. At the age of nine, I was promised to Father's brother-in-law, a man of thirty years. This was four years ago. I brought shame to my family by refusal to marry him. Father beat me, but I did not yield to his wish.

"My brother, a boy of sixteen, said he will kill me with his bare hands; Father said he will feed me to the crocodiles in the Congo River. It was the love of my sister who begged her husband to help me escape my fate with the river of death. I was brought to a wealthy friend of his whose cousin is a doctor preparing to move to London who needed a servant. I was sold to his cousin, the doctor, who paid my father handsomely.

"They brought me to the doctor in the city at dusk. I thought I was in paradise: a warm bed, running water, electricity to read. I was so grateful, I thought surely divine providence intervened for me. Father saved face with gossip in the village, saying I committed suicide by drowning in the Congo River to preserve our family's honor.

"I can never go home. They would kill me as sure as I am looking at you, Rubena. I must not anger the doctor. She always tells me she will send me back to shame my family. My worry now is if the professor leaves her, the doctor will go back home, and I will never be free."

A knot sticks in my throat. I'm unable to swallow or push out the words to comfort her, to say that I'm here for her. How can a grown-ass woman beat a small girl like Ninah with little fat to protect her from the violence of a belt? Rubbing my eyes, unable to absorb her pain—it is too much for me right now. I need to sleep, think about things. It is quarter past two in the morning.

"Ninah, gotta get ready for school."

"I would love to go to school."

"Someday you will. Someday you will be free."

She hugs me, not wanting to let go, then takes a step back, penetrating me with her stare, wanting something I cannot decipher. I said the magic word *free,* and it seemed to light up her beautiful black face against the night.

Without permission from my brain, my mouth blurts, "You gotta get away, escape."

A glimmer of hope, the possibility of daring to think it could happen, the words she wanted to hear, the excitement of it shows in her eyes. Her smile is as wide as her face allows. "Is it possible? But how?"

I did not have an answer, but the desperation in her eyes told me I must do something. What, I didn't know—where to start, what to do. I wanted to take my words back, cheer her on that it would all work out somehow, without me involved, like the miracle stories in the Bible or Grandma retelling how Jesus healed the leopards and made the blind see.

I must do something, I thought. I could not take back what I said as she looked at me like a life jacket to her drowning. "I don't know, but it gotta happen."

The light in her eyes doubled in wattage against the night. "You are a good person, Rubena. Please let's meet again soon. It is so good to be in the kindness of people."

CHAPTER FIFTY-FOUR

Knowing she is an early riser, I call Grandma to check on her. Her voice is filled with sadness, the fire gone. She asks me how I am doing in Upstate and says that it is a blessing I am finally in a secure home with two wonderful fathers, that I have food and clothes and no worries. She is happy that I'm happy. For the first time ever, she acknowledges Marcus as my father, as a person important in my dad's and my life.

I tell her I am fine, but I am sad for her.

She tells me Penguin is moving out of his mother's apartment and she is grateful Jamal is going with him. "I just need Penguin to finally get it right, stay out of trouble, be a grown man, and take care for his son. Jamal needs him." Grandma's voice rings hollow.

And alone in her apartment where no one can see her, Grandma will cry for hours, never stop the ocean of tears that will drown her. I know this by her words.

"Grandma's tired, Beenie," she is talking to the air in her apartment not to me.

Grandma needs to be in the kindness of people right now.

CHAPTER FIFTY-FIVE

"They don't talk about her anymore." Molly Simpson takes a large bite of chiliburger, unable to catch the grease rolling down her forearm, chewing like an assault, a mutiny to her body for eating it. Sophie takes a bite after Molly passes it to her, who then tries to give it to Lauren, whose nose is scrunched, hands tucked under her legs, yelling at the group that she's now a vegetarian. Gwynne declines to take a bite, opting for her lunch of soup.

Sophie takes a century to chew and digest, then finally says, "I miss Amber."

"Where could she be?" Lauren asks, looking for anyone in the group to answer.

The mean girls have called a truce, hearts broken, sad Amber is not here, not knowing where or if she is alive.

A coup has taken place. Molly has been overthrown; the new leader is Gwynne, who relishes her crown of thorns with a smirk on her face like a stain that can't be removed. She says nothing and adds nothing to the missing Amber Mills discussion.

She is not news anymore. Amber now missing for months, replaced by war, mass shootings in schools across the country.

Dawn Johnson joined the obscurity of cold-case news along with Amber. No one cares for them.

"My mother took me to the precinct to tell them what I know, which was not much help," Sophie says. "We went together, me, Lauren, and Molly."

"Did you go, Gwynne?" I ask. She has remained silent, not contributing at all, preferring to look at her soup instead of us.

"No."

"Why not?" Tiki, now as curious as I am, asks.

"The cops came to your house, Gwynne, the day after Amber went missing," Sophie offers up.

Gwynne shoots a glare at Sophie, intimidating her into submission. "They were not at my house."

Lauren, incredulous, squints at Gwynne, gathering bravado. "Yes, they were. I saw them. I was with Sophie at her house. We were all going to the movies together, remember?"

"No."

"What the fuck is your problem, Gwynne?" Tiki has a short fuse with anyone playing dumb.

"I'm out." Gwynne grabs her phone, leaving her lunch and friends.

I follow her out of the cafeteria, out the door, down the steps, heading to the parking lot, yelling at her to wait. She stops short as I bump hard into her. "What!"

"What up with you? Amber is your friend—"

"The bitch ain't my friend. She's a user!" She sees Tiki coming toward her. "What does Stinky Tiki want?"

"Why you lying, Gwynne?" Tiki inquires between gasps for air. "I don't care for Amber either. We were beefing. But I don't want to see her dead or nothing—not anymore."

"You got heart now?" Gwynne folding her arms with a scowl on her face. "She used me to get to my cousin Dolby. You know she like niggas; lame-ass hoe. Once they got tight, she had no use for me."

"Is she with him?" I ask.

"How should I know? I don't know where Dolby is."

"What about Dawn Johnson?" Tiki asks.

"*I don't know no Dawn Johnson,*" Gwynne snarls and mimics Tiki. "Dolby has a lot of hoes. He's a rapper. That's how he gets with them."

I cannot locate an ounce of sorrow for Amber on Gwynne's face. She is not the quiet girl I first met with Amber my first day in school. "She's dead."

Gwynne looks at me, missing any drop of empathy. "Ok. I'm sorry she's dead."

Tiki, hands up, palms exposed, shaking her head, says, "You are one psycho bitch. Amber is missing—"

Gwynne erupts in laugher at Tiki. "Catching feelings for Amber? She fucking hated you. Later."

CHAPTER FIFTY-SIX

Ma was released from rehab before I arrived for the weekend at Grandma's. She has a therapist and attends weekly counseling. She looks healthy and calm, eyes bright, and her skin is clear. She puffs her chest and exhales deeply without the smoker's cough; no more cigarettes, no more wasting money, she laughs. "My lungs thanked me. It's the first step to get my fiscal groove back."

She says she has clarity now with therapy and medication. She tells me repeatedly she is good, ready to be a good mother again, a steward of God, and going on some interviews in a week to get her career popping back in finance.

Penguin echoes Ma's small feat, telling her for me to hear how proud he is of her. He was annoyed at Grandma's skepticism and her taking a wait and see if she screws up again stance.

"Eudora is a hard driver," Penguin sighs. "God gives everybody a second chance, even me; I don't see why she can't do it for her own daughter."

Ma, not surprised by Grandma's reaction, adds, "She'll never change, and I don't expect her to." She looks directly at me, mustering up a smile of a peace offering. "You believe in second chances, don't you, Beenie?"

"I do!" Jamal yelps, wrapping his arms tightly around Ma. She gently taps his head with hers, grateful for her perpetual cheerleader.

"How about you, Beenie?" Penguin asks as her advocate and then looks at Ma, aching to reveal a surprise.

"Yeah, I believe everybody deserves a second chance."

"Should I tell her or you?" Penguin's smile is about to strangle him.

They exchange looks, unable to stop smiling. "We found a place," she says. "It's really nice, a two-bedroom. It has a playground for Jamal. You'll have to share a room with Jamal until we qualify for a three-bedroom, which shouldn't take too long. The landlord will be the state instead of some slumlord foreigner who don't fix things."

"Where is it?"

They are like two kids, excited I'm asking about it. They see a glimmer of hope. "Cornwall Housing; one train ride from Grandma and Grandma Henderson, ten minutes from Jamal's school. We're near the trains, supermarket, and the parks. Imagine an elevator that works, air condition, girl, even a laundry room. No more walking in the cold or the heat to the laundromat," Ma says, laughing.

Penguin adds, "They real selective who gets to move in, but I know the super, an old friend who helped me. You're gonna love it, Beenie."

"Oh, I'll love it for you because I'm not leaving Upstate."

I could have shot them down with a feather. Ma too numb to react; Penguin thunderstruck. Jamal hits me hard on the forearm. "You ungrateful, Beenie."

I ignore him, looking at Ma and Penguin, stupid for presenting their plans to include me without asking. "You expect me to leave a two-thousand-square-foot home in a baller neighborhood *with my own room, my own bathroom,* looking out at a large oak tree and a yard for miles on, for low-income housing, sharing a room with my little brother?"

"Beenie, check yourself," Penguin snaps at me, the first time he has ever done that. He wants to be on Ma's side, show her he's down for her even when she ain't making no kind of sense.

Ma raises her hand at him to stop, the shock worn off, eyes shooting lasers of anger at me. "I can make you stay."

"No, you can't. Dad's got deeper pockets than you." Ma knows Dad is a formidable opponent who will win at any cost. She knows that.

Penguin jumps back in, upset by the hurt scribbled all over Ma's face. "You need to fall back, girl."

"You left the city, now you better than us?" She says it so low I can barely hear her, but I see the steam coming out of her ears.

With folded arms, defiant, I say, "I left the city to get a life I couldn't get with you."

"You're not going to forgive me for the mistakes I made."

"I forgive you. I just don't want to live with any more of your mistakes. I have stability now with Dad and Marcus."

"Selfish girl," Penguin mumbles.

"No, Penguin; *self-preservation.*"

Ma more hurt than angry, quivering, unable to counterpunch with words. "You are a stranger to me; that makes me sad. I don't know you, Beenie."

I will not cry in front of her. I'm more pissed than upset. The nerve of her wanting to put her happiness first, her need for support money more important than appreciating the care I get from Dad. Ma was the selfish one. Penguin's too much in love to see that.

She was never a stranger to me: I've known her nonsense all my life.

"You never did."

CHAPTER FIFTY-SEVEN

"Ninah, this is Tiki. She's my best friend. I trust her with my life—you can too."

Earlier, I texted Tiki to come to my house for something very important, top secret. Before I end the text, she hauls ass to my house. "What's up," she manages to ease out between shortness of breath. I tell her about my plans. She listens, blinking rapidly to focus hard.

"I'm gonna do it. We gotta do something, save her."

"How? We don't know squat about this." Tiki resting her arms on the window ledge, surveying nothing. Then she suddenly spins around, processing on delay what I said, slapping her cheeks, excited at the idea and scared. "Ya think we can rescue her in time for school in the fall?"

"I dunno. Mr. Greenly can help us."

"That old turd?" Tiki shakes her head. "He's a snitch. He'd turn her and *us* in."

"He's a lawyer. Mr. G follows the law. He'd help if he knows a crime is in the hood."

"How do you know it's really a crime?"

"Child abuse. I saw her scars. She's a prisoner. The doctor's been hiding her."

Our plans must be flawless, Tiki wants to discuss it in French for practice.

A moment of doubt seizes her. She pulling at her lips, thinking and re-thinking, then she fires, "But what if the doctor finds out? She may take her away. What if she calls the police on us if we hide her? Would your fathers get in trouble too?"

I do not have an answer like Tiki always expects me to have in school or advice on her life. "The beatings won't stop if she stays with the doctor. We might get in trouble, but we gotta do something. I need your help. We got to get her out of there," I fake-plead to make her feel she is an important player.

Tiki mulls over my request again, then eyes me evenly. "You trust me, right?"

"I was wrong about you. You're my friend." I cross my heart, then pinky hold with her. "I trust you with both my life and my father's life."

"I will help you."

Ninah narrows her eyes, questioning if I betrayed her. She says nothing. I cannot tell if it is shyness or something else as she stares at Tiki's orange skin blending with the midnight sky. She speaks to me in French. "Why did you bring her here?" Her voice has a bit of an attitude. I hope this is not a problem of old friends, new friends drama.

Tiki claps back in French. "I can understand you." The whites in Ninah's eyes appear cartoonish as she leans her head back. After seconds of absorbing Tiki, her shock morphs into giggling, watching Tiki's bright red face in the dark. Tiki says, "I speak better English than you. You're the one a slave, not me. We got something in common. Crappy families."

Ninah raises her hand in deference. "I have never seen a face as orange as the sun. No, please, do not be offended."

"The *sun is yellow, not orange*," Tiki corrects.

We share a meal of spice ham sandwiches with cheese, pickles, orange juice, and homemade brownies under the moon with the stars high above as lighting.

Ninah inspects the sandwich, lifting and smelling it, then takes a tiny bite, prompting Tiki, who is eating her sandwich like a fine meal, to laugh. "You don't got spice ham in Africa?" She shakes her head no. "It's mystery meat. You don't want to know the secret. Good, ain't it?"

Ninah enjoying warm company over the sandwich. "It feels good to be with caring people. I have not had that in a long, long time."

Mr. Greenly's flashlight interrupts our night picnic, inspecting us and the food spread on a blanket. "Evening ladies," he says, looking over the unfamiliar faces of Tiki and Ninah, who show no trace of fear in Mr. Greenly's presence.

"Hi, Mr. Greenly. My friends are spending the night, and I thought it would be great to have a picnic."

"At this time of the night?

"We're renaissance girls," Tiki offers, "like to do stuff out of the norm." Tiki stares at Mr. Greenly hard, jogging his memory. He raises an eyebrow, recognizing the past offender of his neighborhood, but says nothing. Tiki mumbles to me in French while locking eyes with him, a smile plastered on her face, "He's the turd that kicked me outta your hood."

Mr. Greenly hums, nodding as he turns off his flashlight. "Please, girls, just clean up after yourselves. We don't want to feed the vermin. Good night."

"Good night," Ninah says in an exaggerated French accent for our amusement.

We stay silent, watching Mr. Greenly wobble back to his home. When his lights are off, Ninah turns to me and says, "I trust you, and if you say she is a good friend, then I will make her my good friend too." She extends her hand to Tiki. "Nous sommes bons amis, oui?" *We are good friends, yes?*

"What?" Tiki snaps to the alarm of me and Ninah cracking up. "Just kidding. Oui, salope!" *Yes, bitch!*

If Tiki is proficient in any language, cursing is at the top.

CHAPTER FIFTY-EIGHT

I head to Miss Lulu Bell's apartment for my every other weekend visit to chat over tea and peach cobbler and stop mid-step—she is no longer here.

Mr. Cicero Bird not getting better. I'm so worried Grandma losing another friend. She still mourning the loss of her best friend, my true friend, Miss Lulu Bell Davis.

Her apartment is being emptied out. I failed to connect the moving van in front of her building. A Santa Claus-looking man carrying a table out of her apartment. I decide to wait until the super or Grandma return since she was not home.

After waiting a few minutes, I hear several voices; one is Grandma. Standing at the entrance to Miss Lulu Bell's apartment is a young white woman, slim with brown hair plaited. Next to her a black man wearing tortoiseshell glasses, a beard, small ears cascaded with earrings, and massive ink on his forearms. His weight held up by a cane; he in a foot cast. Grandma motions me in, smiling. "My granddaughter. Beenie, this is Lulu Bell's nephew, Gordon Davis, and his wife Cecelia. They from Italy."

"That's where you live? You weren't at the funeral," I say in a reprimanding tone not detected by Grandma.

"I was in the hospital in Rome," he says, seeking my forgiveness while he taps his cast with his cane. "I got this cast skateboarding. Sadly, I could not make it to Aunt Lulu Bell's homegoing. I take comfort knowing you and Miss Eudora stood in for the family—"

"Nobody showed up."

"We couldn't locate any kinfolks of Lulu," Grandma adds. "Lord knows we tried."

Gordon shifts his weight on his cane with his head down. "It's shameful the way our family treated Aunt Lulu Bell. She was special to me. I knew who she was before anyone in the family took the time. They would not understand anyway. She accepted me and my wife when the family wasn't cool to us."

He takes a sigh of regret. "She tried, but no surgeon would touch her. She failed so many medical clearances. Too risky, she was told—her heart." He taps his chest. "She suspected it was due to her time in Vietnam and exposure to Agent Orange. It prevented her from transitioning. You serve your country to come back home with health problems you never imagined. Despite this, Aunt Lulu Bell never regretted serving her country, and she was never bitter. An amazing woman."

The apartment quiets as if we are memorializing her again. Grandma dabs the corners of her eyes, forbidding them to cry; they disobey her for the first time as the tears flow.

"Miss Lulu Bell would clown us right now." I decide to remember anything funny she said. "She'd say who died, whatcha need for the repass, but don't let Miss Bette Mitchell make them tough old collards greens."

Her apartment flows with laughter. Even Grandma cracks up. "Beenie, that ain't respectful," she slips in, unable to stop chuckling.

Cecelia chimes in, "Aunt Lulu accepted me immediately as family. I loved her sweet potato pie."

"Me too—did you get to taste her peach cobbler?" I ask.

"Nothing better than Lulu's cooking," Grandma joins in.

"Cecelia is a better soul food cook than me, if you can believe that," Gordon adds.

"I have the recipes. She didn't want to give it to me at first, but she finally let this white girl have it." Cecelia smiles brightly. "We just moved back to the States. You must visit us in Brooklyn for Sunday dinner. I will do my best to honor her culinary-wise."

"There will never be another Aunt Lulu Bell," Gordon adds wistfully.

Grandma dabs the corner of her eyes again. "That is our loss."

CHAPTER FIFTY-NINE

A traitor. A snitch.

Jamal, my little brother, called me that. At the entrance of the courthouse, I stood with Dad and his attorney opposite Ma, Penguin, and Jamal, who hissed at me like a cobra ready to pounce. I did not think he possessed the capacity to think of those words with his learning disability, much worse to call me that. He said what Ma was thinking, not using words of traitor or snitch, but betrayal.

Ma's face was scribbled for me to see like a neon sign at midnight; the hurt a knife to her heart. Her eyes wandering about like a confused child, gripping Penguin's hand tight as if she did not want to be abandoned.

Dad, unbothered, bounces up the steps like he already has a win in a suit more expensive than his lawyer, who is wearing one just as expensive. Maybe it is a contest of who can dress better, who paid more for it. Ma and her legal aid lawyer are no match against them. They are as equally paired as a lamb against a lion.

I silently count the number of muffin tops the bailiffs and sheriffs in family court have. They stand all day, walking people to and from the courtroom.

Ma's attorney is a petite woman who looks like she just got out of high school. Her suit is similar to the ones I see at fast-fashion stores, and her white shirt missing an iron. Her thick glasses constantly slide down her nose. Between pushing her glasses up and looking for papers the judge asks for, she seems unorganized. Despite this, she gathers herself and stands tall, looking straight ahead, ready to battle Dad, his lawyer, and their expensive suits.

Dad's lawyer does all the talking, knowing, for the money my father paid, he'd better talk up a win. And he does, reciting every single offense Ma committed and that designates her as unfit. For added measure, he enlists people, "victims," in his words, that Ma swindled, including her former employer and the condo owner, Old Fart. He even presents unpaid bills from the grocer, Mr. Ali. At this moment, I want to yell at Dad, the lawyer to stop beating Ma into a puddle of nothing.

Ma will not look at me. Her eyes are on anyone except us. She does not blink. She would rather stare ahead at the oak panel that dwarfs the judge, an older woman who looks like a bunny without fur in a black robe.

Moments earlier, alone in her chamber, the judge motioned me to take a seat facing her while answering her question. The Judge had warm brown eyes like dollops of melting chocolate.

I tried to find a way to tell the truth without hurting Ma.

I breathed a sigh of relief, grateful Ma and Dad were not in the room with me and the judge. "With my mother, I never knew— with my dad, I know." The bunny in the robe tilted her head, pushing me to explain. "She tried, but living with Ma was always a question mark, like, when will we get kicked out, will there be food in the house, and where will we live? I don't have that with Dad and Marcus."

Eyes were all over me like a rash when I returned, except for Ma's.

Dad and his attorney smile broadly, anxious to fist pump when I enter the courtroom. They will have to await the family court judge's response, but they presume to know the outcome of her decision. Ma knows too. I wait for her to blink to keep them moist, not to cry. She will die before she lets us see that.

Penguin looks at me for a moment, letting go of a small smile while Ma is not looking. Jamal narrows his eyes, and his face twists in knots at me, tellin' me all I need to know. He will forgive me eventually. I will have to bribe him with soda and Doritos.

They will all forgive me, but the hurt has to go away first.

The judge's decision: my dad won, but we lost.

CHAPTER SIXTY

And then there were three...

Gwynne refused to talk. She had a breakdown, was all we heard. Her parents won't return her to school. We don't know why.

She is in the hospital, refusing to talk to anyone: her parents, her lawyer, the police. They are linking her cousin, the fake rapper-gangster-wannabee Travis "Dolby" Sanders, to the disappearance of Amber. He's a person of interest in the murder of Dawn Johnson and a convicted sex offender. Dolby and Gwynne are tight. The investigators and detective know she knows something. The rumor mill is on blast, saying Gwynne recruited Amber for Dolby and she got money for doing it. Rumors are spreading that Gwynne was finding girls on social media for him.

The drama at school and the whispers about Gwynne and her cousin were too much for her to handle. Maybe it was pressure from the detectives. Someone said the FBI came to her home and took her phone and laptop. She was not strong enough. Her mother found her in the tub with slashed wrists and an empty bottle of alcohol.

"I guess she couldn't make up her mind to drown or bleed out,"

Molly finally says after a long silence amongst us. No one around the lunch table adds to it or says any more.

Her parents refused any friend visitors.

Molly is the reluctant interim leader, though she does not relish it. She sad all the time, not smiling her malicious smile anymore. It's as if she does not want to be around this drama. She does not want to be a part of this madness.

"I just wish this would go away, be like the way it was," Sophie finally adds.

"Go back to being mean girls?" Tiki sardonically inquires.

Lauren yells at Tiki. "Don't start drama. Sophie didn't mean it that way."

Tiki slumps back in her chair, biting her lower lip, thinking. She then says something totally out of character, "My bad. Sorry."

We huddle together to watch on Sophie's tablet as Dawn Johnson and Amber Mills are discussed on the ID channel by Paula Zahn. She talks to Dawn's parents with a gentle voice of concern. During a second segment, Paula talks to Amber's father and stepmother, who, as expected, hogs the airtime. Amber was on point about Pam Mills—she really is thirsty.

Her mother appears with skin paper-thin. Cancer has feasted on her body, her eyes are larger than her head, and her hair is wispy without direction.

We were never interviewed as witnesses. The reenactment shows two girls on the school steps supposed to be me and Tiki. My character has a tacky lace-front wig even a blind man can see is fake; Tiki's character's red wig is way worse than mine. The only character they got right was Dawn Johnson, who had exposed blond roots, was tall and slim, and had a belly ring.

I guess it was ID channel and Paula Zahn's way of paying their respects to the dead.

* * *

Tiki and I decide we wanna be stars on YouTube. I want to rep stuff kids care about that adults don't get right. Dad and Marcus gifted my birthday in advance with a vlogging camera that has a built-in mic. The price shock prompted Marcus to whisper, "I got Ruben to open his wallet and had to jump out of the way when the dust bunnies hopped out," he laughed.

We decide that Ninah will be our first guest once she's free.

Tiki can't shut up about the idea of being famous. "Man, I'm hyped. We gonna be bomb on YouTube and have a lot of followers. We gonna be stars," she says. "Think we gonna make paper too?"

"I think we can make coins, but first, we get Ninah away from the witch," I remind her.

We finally figure out how to operate the damn camera, playing around, taking turns filming, recording each other, the hallway, and the bedroom ceiling, laughing so hard that Dad yells from his bedroom, "Lights out!"

Tiki hogs the comforter like she is the only one sleeping in my bed. The pings against my window awaken me confused. It is still not yet dawn from what my sleepy eyes tell me, but it gets louder, each tap against my window forcing me finally to toss what little comforter was left. I get up and go over to my window, squinting to remove the dream state. It is Ninah, looking around then up to my window.

"What's wrong?"

"Please come, important."

I gently steal out of the room, down the stairs, and out the door. Ninah's hands are shaking. Sweat beads down her frightened face. "I sorry, Rubena."

She's been crying. Her eyes release large droplets of tears down her face. "The doctor, professor big fight. He told her Clara his lover, gonna get a divorce. He left with big, big bags of stuff to the city." Ninah's arms flail repeatedly to emphasize how much luggage the professor took with him.

"She screaming. Crazy doctor pulling her hair, hits the professor, he cannot leave, hands on his face, cursing her. Go back to Africa, he tells her." Ninah pauses to catch her breath, wiping her tears away again. "I cannot go back home, Rubena." She is gripping my hands, stock still, her eyes laser lock as a command to me. "I cannot go home."

Rubbing my face hard as to what to do, I say, "We gonna do something now."

Tiki appears, rubbing her eyes. "What the hell's going on?"

"I'll tell you later." I grab Ninah's hands to reassure her. "We gotta do it now. Go back to the house. I will send you a sign."

Our hearts are beating so hard and loud that the world can hear us. I'm scared Tiki's hyperactivity will alert people we don't want to wake up. She's excited by the idea of being a super girl, red cape ready to rescue. Our plan must work. Most importantly, Ninah must be brave and not let the doctor's bullying change her mind. She knows what she has with the doctor, but what's to come will be a brighter future for her.

I recall Mr. Greenly telling me the type of work he did to help people in trouble with Legal Aid. She is a victim of domestic servitude, a person in bondage against her will. No doubt he will help us. If a person will be persecuted when they return home, political asylum works too. We promised Ninah we'll protest like rabid dogs if they send her back. We will get petitions, anything, make the news, to prevent her from deportation. I told her she must be willing to take the risk. She agreed, but I felt the fear in her heart.

Vlogging camera in hand, Tiki is confident she can record events as they unfold. She stands guard at the window, watching, waiting for Ninah to bring the recycle bins. If she is alone, she can make a run for it. I will hide her from the doctor in my bedroom. I'm praying she slipped enough pills to keep the doctor asleep but not enough to be fatal.

"She's coming out," Tiki whispers excitedly upon seeing Ninah. "So far, no signs of the witch doctor."

I stand beside Tiki as we see Ninah alone, separating glass and paper, looking every second at the doctor's bedroom window. We wait for a few minutes. "I don't think she's coming out. Let's go," I say, waving for Tiki to follow me.

We are assisted with warm air. The sounds of the night rise above the sound of my heart about to jump out of my chest. It's the same fear as when I ran back into the apartment to warn the neighbors about the fire in the slumlord crib in the city. Dad will allow me to miss school for this. The courts will be open for business, and we can keep her with us until then.

I told Ninah to bring clothes to the recycle bin so that when she makes her escape, she can do it quicker with just the clothes on her back.

The planned date for escape is now because the professor leaving the doctor. Tiki and I wait outside in the dark near the brush, carefully concealed, watching for Ninah, mindful of the doctor, hopeful. Nosy Mr. Greenly nowhere in sight.

Ninah greets us with a wide smile of pending freedom. Her teeth white against her coal face. Her English has improved where we can talk. "My heart is breaking from happiness."

"Where are your clothes?" I ask, my eyes looking up at the window.

"Did you give her something to sleep?" Tiki inquires.

Ninah's face twists as second thoughts nag her. "I want to give her more tea so she will sleep longer for my escape."

"Hey, where you going?" Tiki whispers.

"I'll be back."

She returns with a bundle in a garbage bag, showing us a necklace made of shells and stones. "I cannot leave without this. My sister made it for me. Someday, I will see her again when I am free and educated."

"Oh shit!" Tiki yelps.

The bedroom lights are on. The doctor throwing on a robe. Tiki and I run quickly to the house. I look back for Ninah, who is frozen in the middle of the street, legs cemented visibly by the light that revealed her to the doctor. I run back to her and stop yelling at her in English—she seems to not understand. I start screaming in French.

"Ninah, tu dois courir. C'est tu chance pour la liberté."

Ninah, you must run. This is your chance for freedom.

She snaps out of her daze, but before she can lift a foot, the firm hand of the doctor's talons swoop in like a bird of prey. Grabbing, cursing, yelling, hitting her with a belt, screaming in French, "How dare you try to kill me, you ungrateful beast! You try to end me with sleeping pills! I will send you back to Africa, you stupid little bitch!"

Ninah, disabled in pain, falls to the ground. I run to her, yanking on the doctor's robe in the back, pulling it off, revealing a satin slip with sagging breasts. She tries to swat me away like a fly, cursing at me in French.

Ninah, something in her resolved, forces herself up, wincing in pain, pulling against the nightgown collar in the doctor's fist, fighting as I yell to keep resisting the doctor. The doctor's hand, aimed at Ninah, hits me. I bite her as hard as I can without breaking my teeth, freeing Ninah. Tiki grabs her, pushing Ninah behind her with one hand, firmly holding the vlogging camera with the other. She instructs Ninah to run to my home, screaming as loud as possible to wake up the neighborhood, Grandma in the city, Miss Lulu Bell in the ground, and the rest of the dead. Ninah is safely deposited at my front door, crying, in a praying stance. Tiki runs back towards me, camera now secure in her hands, recording the doctor and yelling. We are wild dogs dodging the claws and the bite of a captured bear.

"Watch out, Rubena!" Tiki screams, dodging the doctor's kicks.

Somehow, Tiki manages to avoid the doctor's foot and gives her the middle finger.

We are circling the doctor, running, yelling, and cursing. The doctor keeps missing her aim to hit me. I am adept at ducking her blows. As she raises her hand for a good aim, her arm is yanked out of its socket, forcing her to scream in agony.

It was the firm hand of my father with a look on his face that even frightened me.

My hero.

I always thought he was clueless about my life, me, but I was wrong. He has always been there for me for as long as I can remember, from the first day of school to my rescue from the wicked witch. I never realized how blessed I am to have my dad.

I do now.

Mr. Greenly has his spotlight on us.

I tilt in the direction of Ninah, who is stunned and wrapped in Tiki's arms, and then I tilt over to Mr. Greenly.

I want him to know, *yes, I was feeding raccoons.*

But most importantly, *I was feeding a human.*

CHAPTER SIXTY-ONE

Tiki finally got her wish: a house with no men. Her sister got rid of Matt for good. Their home is a house of women: Tiki, her sister, and the baby. She is so pumped about it.

"I can finally enjoy a nice hot bath without the hassle," she tells me at school. "I hope she don't take him back. She says she is ready for a new life without him. Fingers crossed." Sasha qualified for subsidized housing to help her with rent. "Oh my god, it has helped so much. We're rarely behind now," Tiki beams.

Gwynne was admitted to the psych ward in the hospital. She keeps trying to kill herself and will not talk to anyone. Her parents allowed Molly, Sophie, and Lauren to finally visit her, hoping she would be her old self again. Gwynne was not known to be a sociable girl, always the quiet one of the group, withdrawn. She is now in a completely silent prison, an island no one can get to and that she cannot escape.

Lauren is the de facto leader, though they are no longer the hottest mean girls. They are no longer popping, no more counting calories, or communal yogurt and bananas—I don't think they care to be. They are the sad girls. A group of newer mean girls evolving in my school: that will never change as long as there are insecure girls.

The trial for the doctor and the professor is coming up. They face multiple charges of child endangerment, physical abuse, and abduction. Ninah, who is the bomb in English now, wants to testify against the doctor but not the professor. She may not be able to save the professor since he was also charged.

Mr. Greenly agreed to be a working lawyer again, representing Ninah as her immigration lawyer. "Rubena, he is such a kind, warm man," Ninah remarked.

She is enrolled in a state-funded program, taking ESL and remedial classes; she will not be there much longer. She is assisting the teacher, helping immigrant students in her class. Her host family is so nice, and she loves them to pieces. We often have dinner with our parents at one another's home. Ninah loves Marcus; I think she has a crush on him. She misses her family and dreams of seeing her country one day as a doctor.

"They will be so proud of you, including your father and brother. They will forgive you for running away from marriage."

Ninah smiles. "Rubena, they are not so forgiving. It is my hope to bring my sister's daughter to America for a future."

Amber's mother died of cancer. I'm sure it was a broken heart.

I pray for her.

One thing I know for sure is Miss Lulu Bell is greeting her with a big honey child hug and peach cobbler.

I pray for Amber Mills, asking God to protect her from harm and bring her back home safely to her father and little brother.

"God, like Grandma says, as only you can."

* * *

The universe decided to give Ma a warm spring day for a wedding, and no one is more grateful than her. I'm vlogging the event as wedding gift for Ma.

I look out the window down at the backyard, watching Marcus directing and delegating where to place chairs for the ceremony and tables for guests to eat. His decoration skills are the bomb and Instagram-pretty.

I film Jamal through the window. He unable to stay still and wrestling with a guest's rescued mutt. Dad, intervening, dusts Jamal off and reminds him to stay clean long enough for the vows, then he can play with the dog.

Ma says to make sure I capture the decorations in the yard that Marcus designed. She is scared she will be seen, and that will be bad luck. Back in my room, I give her a preview of the filming so far for her approval and then upload it to her new Instagram account, NewDoll100. She is going crazy at Marcus's skills; we will probably overdose on selfies today. Her followers from both Dollfam and MzDoll100 (minus the pics and dirty old men) followed her over to her new account. Together we read comments while the hairstylist and makeup man work on her.

Our yard in Upstate is a massive bed of cartoon-green, so pretty Dad may have to hire the landscaper once the guests leave. He was honored to offer our home for Ma's wedding and is the one giving her away to Penguin. It is their peace offer to each other.

I see Uncle March, who is next to Grandma, and on her left is Mr. Cicero Bird with his saxophone. I watch Grandma allow Mr. Bird to place his hand atop hers, but he quickly pulls away then slips her a smile and a wink. Grandma swore he was invited to play at Ma's request, but Ma says she offered up his services without his permission, saying fresh Upstate air be good for Mr. Bird's cancer. I can't stop giggling at the unremovable smile on her face. She is acting like a VIP, a hand to Marcus's kneeling before her, both laughing. I'm happy to see the light in her face again. Miss Lulu

Bell Davis's spirit is here, pushing "Old Eudora to wipe that sour puss away."

No one in the family is surprised Aunt Nelle declined the invite, citing migraine as her go-to excuse.

I am honored, too, to have Ma use my room to get ready. It is the first time she has been to our home in Upstate. She marvels at the size of my room, the view, and the massive oak tree that feels like we're in a treehouse. "No wonder you didn't want to live with us," she is laughing.

Ma is so beautiful. Her natural hair is intertwining with baby's breath and a single white rose. Looking in the mirror, not believing she is the person staring back at her and at peace. "It feels good to feel good," she finally says, now staring at the mirror again but looking at me.

"What?" I ask as I close the clasp on the pearls Grandma loaned her.

The glam squads excuse themselves at Ma's request. We are alone.

Ma looks down at her hands in her lap, bites her lip, and pushes, "If you're happy in Upstate, I'm happy too."

"I am. The food's better."

Ma shakes her head so hard a flower falls to the floor. "Smart-ass."

"I got it from you."

"Beenie, please put the camera down for a moment." Her smile melts, grabbing my hand, holding it close to her face. "I know I gave you reasons to hate me—please, let me finish. I want you to know how sorry I am. I want you to be happy even if it means you're not living with me. Your father gave you something I failed to do—a home, stability. But I'm hopeful, Beenie—I'm hopeful about us. It's the best I can give without lying to you."

I'm going to allow myself to trust her again. I want it more for her than for myself. "Ma, just let people help you be well again. That's what I want."

Ma is rubbing my hand as if it is a lamp. She hoping the genie jump out so her wish can be granted. "I want to get to know you, Beenie—as a person. I want you to know you can talk to me. Maybe when Penguin and me get back from the Poconos, we can start by having date time, just you and me—how about it?"

I place my chin on Ma's neck as we both look in the mirror. "I think you're ready for the 'gram."

Ma spins around and shoots up, giving me a bear hug while wrinkling her linen bridal gown. "I'm ready for us to be a family again."

"We are. Always."

ACKNOWLEDGMENTS

There are many wonderful individuals responsible for the birth of this novel. First, my creator, for instilling faith to continue despite rejections, setbacks, Phyliss Mathis, my creative writing high school teacher who saw talent long before I knew it existed, my sisters, Christine, Princes Mae, Thelma, and Patricia egging me on with humor and ridicule, Janet Olivier Charles, the first reader whose keen eyes saw the story despite my typos, Nadia Giordano, editor of WINK and Mississippi Crow, and Jim Reed, editor of Birmingham Arts Journal, the first publishers who accepted my work, the motivation needed to push on which lead to more published works in Delmarva Review, The Avenue, The Wax Paper, Danielle Ofri, editor of Bellevue Literary Review, who validated me a writer paying for my work. My gratitude to Lisa Kastner, editor/founder of Running Wild for acceptance and lastly RIZE editor, Cody Sisco, whom I am forever grateful for helping me navigate the terrains of editing, storytelling and revisions.

RIZE publishes great stories and great writing across genres written by People of Color and other underrepresented groups.

Our team consists of:

Lisa Diane Kastner, Founder and Executive Editor
Joelle Mitchell, Licensing and Strategy Lead
Cody Sisco, Acquisition Editor, RIZE
Benjamin White, Acquisition Editor, Running Wild
Peter A. Wright, Acquisition Editor, Running Wild
Resa Alboher, Editor
Angela Andrews, Editor
Sandra Bush, Editor
Ashley Crantas, Editor
Rebecca Dimyan, Editor
Abigail Efird, Editor
Aimee Hardy, Editor
Henry L. Herz, Editor
Cecilia Kennedy, Editor
Barbara Lockwood, Editor
AE Williams, Editor
Scott Schultz, Editor
Rod Gilley, Editor
Kelly Ottiano, Editor
Carolyn Banks, Editor

Evangeline Estropia, Product Manager
Kimberly Ligutan, Product Manager
Pulp Art Studios, Cover Design
Standout Books, Interior Design
Polgarus Studios, Interior Design

Learn more about us and our stories at www. runningwildpublishing.com

www.runningwildpublishing.com, www.facebook.com/ runningwildpress, on Twitter @lisadkastner @RunWildBooks @RizeRwp